CENTRAL DIVISIONAL LIBRARIES

SKELMERSDALE

FICTION RESERVE STOCK LL60

AUTHOR	CLASS
MULISCH, H.	A F A

TITLE   The procedure

Lancashire
County Council
LANCASHIRE
COUNTY LIBRARY
Bowran Street
PRESTON PR1 2UX

100% RECYCLED PAPER

LL1

Lancashire County Library

30118084880289

D0267688

THE
PROCEDURE

ALSO BY HARRY MULISCH

The Assault
Last Call
The Discovery of Heaven

THE
PROCEDURE

HARRY MULISCH

Translated by Paul Vincent

VIKING
an imprint of
PENGUIN BOOKS

1084830289 23/8/01

VIKING

Published by the Penguin Group
Penguin Books Ltd, 80 Strand, London WC2R ORL, England
Penguin Putnam Inc., 375 Hudson Street, New York, New York 10014, USA
Penguin Books Australia Ltd, Ringwood, Victoria, Australia
Penguin Books Canada Ltd, 10 Alcorn Avenue, Toronto, Ontario, Canada M4V 3B2
Penguin Books India (P) Ltd, 11 Community Centre,
Panchsheel Park, New Delhi – 110 017, India
Penguin Books (NZ) Ltd, Cnr Rosedale and Airborne Roads,
Albany, Auckland, New Zealand
Penguin Books (South Africa) (Pty) Ltd, 5 Watkins Street,
Denver Ext 4, Johannesburg 2094, South Africa

Penguin Books Ltd, Registered Offices: 80 Strand, London WC2R ORL, England

www.penguin.com

Originally published in Dutch as *De Procedure* by Uitgeverij De Bezige Bij, Amsterdam, 1998
This translation first published in the United States of America by Viking 2001
First published in Great Britain 2001

1

Copyright © Harry Mulisch, 1998
Translation copyright © Paul Vincent, 2001

PUBLISHER'S NOTE
This is a work of fiction. Names, characters, places, and incidents either are
the product of the author's imagination or are used fictitiously, and any resemblance
to actual persons, living or dead, business establishments, events, or locales
is entirely coincidental.

The moral right of the author has been asserted

All rights reserved.
Without limiting the rights under copyright
reserved above, no part of this publication may be
reproduced, stored in or introduced into a retrieval system,
or transmitted, in any form or by any means (electronic, mechanical,
photocopying, recording or otherwise), without the prior
written permission of both the copyright owner and
the above publisher of this book

Printed in Great Britain by Clays Ltd, St Ives plc

A CIP catalogue record for this book is available from the British Library

ISBN 0-670-88929-6

DEED A

SPEAKING

So cleverly did his art conceal its art

P. Ovidius Naso,
Metamorphoses, X. 252

CPP	CLN
CBA	CLO
CFU	CMI 8/01
CIN	CPE 3/02
CKI	CRI
CLE	CSA
CLH	CSH 10/02
CLHH	

MAN

YES, OF COURSE I can come straight to the point and start with a sentence like: *The telephone rang.* Who's ringing whom? Why? It must be something important, otherwise the file wouldn't open with it. Suspense! Action! But I can't do it that way this time. On the contrary. Before anything can come to life here, we must both prepare ourselves through introspection and prayer. Anyone who wants to be swept along immediately, in order to kill time, would do better to close this book at once, put the television on, and sink back on the settee as one does in a hot foam bath. So before writing and reading any further we're going to fast for a day, and then bathe in cool, pure water, after which we will shroud ourselves in robes of the finest white linen.

I've switched the telephone and the front doorbell off and turned the clock on my desk away from me; everything in my study is waiting for the events to come. The first luminous words have appeared in the ultramarine of the computer screen, while outside the dazzling, setting autumn sun shines over the square. From the blazing western sky tram rails stream like molten gold from a blast furnace; between the black trees cars appear from the chaos, disappear into it, people walk at the tips of shadows that are yards long. From the position of the sun in my room I can see what time it is: the light is falling diagonally, it's six o'clock, rush hour, for most people the day's work is over.

The origin of man was a complicated affair. Much of it is still obscure, not only in biological, but also in theological circles. In the Bible, indeed, this creature is actually created twice, and to a certain extent three times. Genesis 1:27 tells us that on the sixth and last day of creation the following happened: "So God created man in his own image, in the image of God created he him; male and female created he them." So there were two of them; immediately afterward God says: "Be fruitful, and multiply." So the man was Adam, but the woman wasn't Eve, because the primeval mother of us all saw the light of day only later, when the week of creation was long since over; she wasn't created separately, but came forth from a rib of Adam's. The latter was very pleased about this, because in Genesis 2:23 he declares: "This is now bone of my bones, and flesh of my flesh." At last! This also shows that Eve was his second wife. But what about the first? Who was she? Fortunately experts have been able to ascertain this: Lilith.

Very self-assured, because created just as independently as Adam, she did not wish to subordinate herself to him. Consequently the rift between them centered on the manner of "reproduction": she was reluctant to be the party underneath. Another element in their conflict over sexual technicalities may have been the fact that Adam was already carrying Eve and so at that stage must have been a rather effeminate type. The row flared up in any case and Lilith finally did something terrible: she cursed. That is, she spoke the ineffable, seventy-two-letter name of JHVH, instantly turned into a demon and flew off. Immediately JHVH sent the angels SNVJ, SNSNVJ, and SMNGLPH in pursuit, who intercepted her over the Red Sea. But they couldn't eliminate her. Ever since, she has preyed on single men and strangled children in childbirth. In brief, in every respect Lilith is the opposite of the later Eve, the primeval mother, who through her creation finally made a real man of Adam.

But by that time—after the week of creation, that is—this Adam had been created for the second time. Anyone who still owns a Bible (otherwise he should just look in a bedside table at the nearest hotel), can read in Genesis 2:7: "And the Lord God formed man of the dust of the ground, and breathed into his nostrils the breath of life; and man became a living soul." The difference between this and the first time is that we are now given some concrete details, but too little to be able to make use of it for ourselves. Fortunately there are other sources besides the Bible. Over the centuries, without distinction between the first and second creation of Adam, a number of scholars have reconstructed the course of events on the sixth and last day of creation from hour to hour, but the timetables they have presented differ. According to one of them Adam appeared in JHVH's thoughts in the first hour. In the second hour JHVH discussed his brainwave with the cabinet of archangels. Some of them thought it a good idea, others were opposed; but while the angels were still debating and squabbling, in the third hour JHVH began collecting red, black, white, and brown earth. This was, of course, not just any old dust, but the finest dust from all corners of the earth, and particularly from the spot where subsequently the Temple of Solomon was to arise. In the fourth hour, using the purest water, he kneaded it into clay. In the fifth hour he formed Adam's body. In the sixth hour he made a golem of him, an "earth germ": an entity that was no longer inorganic, but was not yet a human being either. In the seventh hour, on the same Temple Mount where so many memorable events were later to take place, he breathed a soul into the embryonic creature, after which in the eighth hour he finally set Adam ("Earth") in Paradise, where the latter showed himself capable of speech by giving names to the animals: "chimpanzee," "orangutan . . ."

In heaven the archangels were meanwhile still quarreling

about the desirability of man, but JHVH said, "Why are you still talking? He has already been created." He seems to have had other problems with his ministers for that matter, because according to some sources Adam was initially as large as the whole universe, which they saw as a threat. Thereupon God reduced him to more moderate, although still gigantic proportions. Only after the fall did he and his Eve acquire the dimensions still customary today.

In this way we learn more and more. I myself am—professionally—curious to know further details about that mysterious sixth hour. What did JHVH actually get up to in it? Intermediate stages, origins, decay, twilights, metamorphoses, are always more interesting than what's already there, is not yet there, or is no longer there. The transition in the seventh hour from organic matter to man through the divine breath of life is less essential than the transition from dead to living matter in the sixth hour. The difference between an amoeba and a human being is less than that between a crystal and an amoeba, because in the latter case the difference is almost 100 percent. (Almost? Not 100 percent? What then? 99.999 . . . percent? Patience!) So that during that transition, in the sixth hour, something really fundamental happened. What exactly?

I have great news. In the virtually endless twists and turns of Scripture there is a piece of writing that tells us something about this: *Sefer Yetsirah, The Book of Creation.* It was written in Hebrew, presumably in about the third century in Palestine, by an anonymous Jewish neo-Pythagorean, and is the complete antithesis of what is regarded at the end of the twentieth century as a readable text. I doubt whether at this moment more than a hundred people in the entire world are poring over that mysterious book; it's rather like a secret, metaphysical royal chamber in the pyramid of the written word. For that matter, "book" is too grand a word; it consists of six short chapters, divided into eighty-one sections, all in all less than two thousand words, that is, scarcely five A4 sheets. I must confess that this fills me with immeasurable jealousy: five A4 sheets! Since quantity is also quality, every writer wants to write a book of a thousand pages—but a treatise of five pages, which has been studied for century after century, has been followed by innumerable commentaries, and has still not yielded up its secret, that goes a step further.

The text concludes with the statement that Abraham also studied the book and understood it, thereby becoming in creative terms virtually the equal of God; the rest of humankind could not make even a mosquito among them. In the Middle Ages people who should know added that initially he devoted himself to study in solitude, but then suddenly he heard the voice of JHVH—the real author—and was told that no one could understand *Sefer Yetsirah* by himself, there must be two of you. For this purpose Abraham chose his teacher Shem, the son of Noah. This rule, that there should be two, still applies to the present day, so that suits us well because there are two of us too, you and I.

Listen. Of course you know that the world and Adam were created by the word—but how that worked technically can only be read in the mysterious manual that JHVH himself used and therefore dates from before creation. In it linguistic creation is not taken figuratively, as usually happens, but—with the inexorable consistency of Judaic mysticism—literally.

Because words consist of letters, as molecules consist of atoms, we must focus attention on the elementary components' building blocks: the twenty-one letters of the Hebrew alphabet, called "othioth." Because don't forget that the world was created in Hebrew; it wouldn't have been possible in any other language, least of all Dutch, whose spelling will not be settled until heaven and earth pass away. To make a distinction I call that exalted othioth the "alephbeth": Aleph [א], Beth [ב], Gimel [ג], Daleth [ד], He [ה], Waw [ו], Zayin [ז], Heth [ח], Teth [ט], Yod [י], Kaph

[כ], Lamed [ל], Mem [מ], Nun [נ], Samekh [ס], 'Ayin [ע], Pe [פ], Sadhe [צ], Qoph [ק], Resh [ר], Shin [ש], Taw [ת]. It consists exclusively of consonants. The aleph and the 'ayin are also consonants. For example the aleph is not the sound "a" but a hard click in the throat, as one makes when one suddenly cuts or burns oneself, the so-called glottal stop, for which, according to philologists, one should imagine having a fish hook thrown into one's throat which is immediately jerked back. Those consonants form the visible body of the words—the vowels are their soul and hence invisible. Or rather: TH VWLS R THR SL ND HNC NVSBL.

The first chapter concerns the "thirty-two hidden paths of wisdom": the mysterious, "infinite numbers without anything" from 1 to 10 plus the 22 letters. JHVH himself is 1, the 22 letters he derived "with mud and clay," from 2 and 3; only 4 gives birth to the heavens and the angels. Then he took the three most important letters (A, M, SH: the "three mothers"), which under the dominance of the numbers 5 to 10 as height, depth, east, west, north, and south he sealed with permutations of his ineffable name JHV, JVH, HJV, HVJ, VJH, and VHJ. There is no more talk of numbers, only of letters.

To give you an impression, I will now show you in confidence the second chapter of JHVH's instruction manual:

1. Twenty-two letters: three mothers, seven double, and twelve simple. Three mothers A, M, SH, their foundation: the scale of merit and the scale of guilt, and the tongue is a moving hand between those two. Three mothers A, M, SH: M is mute, SH sibilant, and A brings the two into equilibrium.

2. Twenty-two letters, he designed them, carved them out, weighed them, combined and transposed them, each with all; with them shaped the whole of creation and everything that remained to be created.

3. Twenty-two letters: three mothers, seven double, and twelve simple; they have been designed in the voice, shaped in the air, and put in five places into the mouth. The letters A, H, CH, AJ in the throat, G, J, K, Q, on the palate, D, L, N, T on the tongue, Z, S, TS, R, SH, on the teeth, B, V, M, PHe on the lips.

4. Twenty-two letters, they are put into a circle like a wall with two hundred and thirty-one gates. The circle can turn forward or backward, and its sign is this: nothing surpasses AJ N G (= "contentment"), in goodness and nothing surpasses N G AJ (= "disaster") in evil.

5. How did he combine, weigh, and transpose them? A with all others and all others with A, B with all others and all others with B, G with all others and all others with G, and they all return in a circular form to the exit through two hundred and thirty-one gates, and so it is that the whole of creation and all language arises from one name.

6. He created something from nothing and made the non-being into a being; and he fashioned great columns from intangible air. This is the sign: he beheld, spoke, and produced the whole of creation and all things from one name, the sign of which is twenty-two things in one body.

That one name, from which everything originates, is therefore the ineffable name of God: the tetragrammaton JHVH. In the four remaining chapters everything is given birth to in space and time through obscure combinations and permutations by the "three mothers," the "seven double," and "twelve simple," with countless correspondences among nature, the human body, and the year.

The Book of Creation is the loftiest ode to writing ever written.

SECOND DOCUMENT

THE CHARACTER

YOU SEE, our intention succeeded. We are alone. Your impure
fellow readers have fled head over heels from all those ghostly
letters. "This looks like nothing on earth!" I heard them cry.
You said the same, but differently: "This is incomparable." Only
you are still there. I can't see you, I don't know your name, it's
as if I've dialed an arbitrary telephone number as lonely lunatics
are wont to do.

   After years of meditation on this file, experiment, failure,
sometimes to the edge of exhaustion, I realized that I needed
help, like Abraham. But where could I find it? You weren't there
yet. Even to be able to begin this story—which, meanwhile, has
begun, though up to now even you don't think it looks much
like a story, but that'll come right—I decided to go higher up
and turn to my transcendent colleague himself. Because his creation too—the world, man—is linguistic in nature, ultimately a
question of spelling, just like the world and the people that I in
turn wish to conjure up. They too appear through nothing except letters and numbers. If I look at my keyboard, all I see are
the alphabet and the numbers from 0 to 9, which appear as con-

figurations of light on the screen; the remaining signs are incidental. Moreover, in the alephbeth the letters are also the numbers—and if one can therefore read words at the same time as numbers, if recounting is at the same time counting, that of course opens up undreamed of possibilities.

So as I now prepare myself for an *imitatio dei,* as JHVH's shadow, my name too must be the shadow of his ineffable name. The signs are favorable. Since the "three mothers" A, M, SH, which JHVH added to his name, are the initials of my very own Jewish mother, it must therefore come from there, just as I myself also come from there. It is therefore preordained. Now I need involve only my Bohemian father, whose parents were married in Prague—and lo and behold: *Victor Werker!*

First there follow three additional considerations.

First additional consideration. Poets are word writers and hence untranslatable, because in the process of translation their words disappear. Every word has a sound, which in another language changes into a different sound, which the poet didn't have in mind. It's as though a sonata of Beethoven would be performed in the Netherlands with the first note a third higher, the second a fifth lower, et cetera: and in France with a fourth lower and a seventh higher, et cetera. Novelists, in their turn, can be divided into sentence writers and book writers. Nabokov wrote unforgettable sentences, Dostoyevsky unforgettable books. At this point opinions differ as to what constitutes a "good writer." Nabokov is a good writer, Dostoyevsky is a great writer. Little is left of a sentence writer in a bad translation; with a great writer it doesn't make much difference. The language must disappear completely, only the narrative must remain. When prose casts envious glances at poetry and calls attention to itself, like a dandy in front of a mirror, then the same thing happens as with someone who knows that he is beautiful: it makes him, and particularly her, ugly. Only children and animals can be perfectly beautiful.

And in my case—if I may make so bold—it's even worse. When at a certain moment in my life I write a certain letter, for example three words ago the letter "i" in the word "write," then I'm not simply writing that letter, that iota with that dot but when I wrote that "i" I wrote the "i" of the word "write"; and when I wrote the "i" of the word "write," I didn't just write that word "write," but this whole sentence, and the one before, and the one after too, all these sentences, this whole chapter, all this whole book, all 72,654 words of it—indeed, everything that I've ever written and have yet to write. I'm not a word writer, or even a sentence writer, but a writer of an oeuvre. I wouldn't have been able to write that one "i" if everything did not in some way already exist. But where? Not in this world, because even for me it only appears in it by being written. So there is another world—that's proven.

Since this is how the land lies, I must set to work cautiously. That boils down to writing an average of one sentence an hour. You in your turn read that sentence on average in ten seconds. This disproportion is eliminated if that one sentence is read by $6 \times 60 = 360$ readers, that is the edition size of a hermetic volume of poetry. My reward begins with the 361st reader. The first edition of this book consists of 50,000 copies. If it remains at that and each copy is read by no more than one reader, then 500,000 seconds will be spent on each sentence—that's almost a week!

Second additional consideration. For a hundred years a story was not supposed to look like a story, but only like so-called reality; for that century, therefore, the narrator had to be just as invisible and anonymous as the listener. That rule derived from Flaubert's overcoat. (A strange expression? Dostoyevsky once said, "We all derive from *The Overcoat* by Gogol.") When the narrator said "I" he mustn't mean himself, "I" had to be someone else: "the narrator," a narrating character. That was called "realism," but it was the exact opposite. This constraint is now behind us because a story, as narrators discovered, once they'd calmed down, ultimately had no other existence than as the narrative of a narrator. I myself have never paid any heed to that Flaubertian camouflage. Simultaneously with the death of the narrator Nietzsche proclaimed the death of God—but from the very beginning I was convinced that a story could only appear to give a picture of a world in which free will and chance reign, because in a story even the smallest detail has been foreseen and is predestined by the omniscient, omnipotent, all-preordaining narrator, even what is apparently free and incidental. Every story, I thought, even that of an inveterate atheist, of necessity depicted a created world in which an ultraorthodox God reigned. Literature, in short, was essentially theological in nature, and in my view it must therefore relinquish the illusion that it could give a faithful image of existing reality.

But with hindsight the matter turns out to be not so simple. I overlooked something, which nevertheless had been clearly visible all those years. The narrator of a story is at the same time *not* the narrator. The story itself is the actual narrator, it tells itself; from the first sentence onward the narrative is a surprise to the narrator too, as all narrators know. The real adventure is the *narrating* of the adventure. It isn't that the Flaubert narrator exists but is not allowed to exist and must hide; actually he doesn't exist, while at the same time he of course does exist and tells the story. And in that sense, through its predictable/unpredictable manner of creation, through its free will, a story does after all give a faithful image of the world—just as physical reality itself is only determined to a certain extent by cause and effect, but in the last instant is subject to fundamental uncertainties, probabilities, chance.

Therefore: a writer who says that his inspiration has dried up because he's "got nothing more to say," was never a real writer. He said what he had to say, but a real writer precisely never had anything to say: only his stories have anything to say, first and foremost to himself—and that remains so until his death on the literary field of honor.

I'm in good company with my mistake, though. JHVH was also wrong: he thought initially that his creation was "good," but that turned out not to be the case; afterward a flood and subsequently a Messiah were necessary to put things in order. Looking back, even those draconian measures were not sufficient—he will have to think up a third event. Time is pressing.

Third additional consideration. A narrator who exists and doesn't exist—what can such a logical impossibility be compared to? Answer: to a creating God, and an aloof patriarch, reigning with a clear consciousness in an abstract, hygienic realm of numbers, letters, and words. But also to a woman giving birth: for months she's made her child without knowing how she did it—although she did it, it was not *she* who did it; nor does she know whom she's giving birth to. That only becomes apparent at the birth in blood, shit, screams, pain, or actually only months, years later.

"In the beginning were blood, shit, screams, pain; and the blood, the shit, the screams, the pain were with Goddess; and the blood, the shit, the screams, the pain were Goddess."

Since the procedure of the patriarch and that of the matriarch, the word and the blood both apply, the two must be joined in matrimony. If a masterpiece is to be created, then the *imitatio dei* must go hand in hand with an *imitatio deae*.

In fact, something else could have put me onto this track. Whenever I've been writing fruitfully for some time, I can never remember afterward how I did it—just as I don't know during the day what it's like to dream, although I have no problem at night. When I have the wind in my sails as a writer, I can't imagine what it's like *not* to write, but if things flag, I can't imagine how I'm supposed to do it, write. No, really, no idea, even if I've written thousands of pages. The image of a sailing ship of yore then appears to me, at the equator, bobbing helplessly in the becalmed ocean. Naturally the captain, patriarchlike, can give the order to row, but that's nothing compared with what happens when suddenly the matriarchal wind gets up again, when the limp sails begin to flap and are later filled with wind.

How is a story created? Think of the film of a factory being blown up. You see the explosions, the crashing of the walls, the tall chimney collapsing in a zigzag, until there's nothing to be seen but a pile of rubble and a huge rising cloud of dust, which is dispersed by the wind. Then forget that film. You see the last image, and then suddenly the film is slowly wound back. In the sky a miraculous cloud of dust forms that moves downward into the rubble, which is subsequently transformed into a building, a chimney climbs up in a zigzag, walls rise into the air, until there is a factory standing there. That's what it's like. The question then poses itself: how is that possible, if it's not a reverse process but the process itself? So did that building then exist in some way before it existed? Perhaps. Where? I don't know.

Why does a person actually do it, again and again? Because he wants to live in two worlds. This one is not enough for him. The problematical story that, counter to the second law of thermodynamics, is again unfolding before my eyes and that I'm about to narrate, is not my invention but uses me to exist, as the child does its mother. "I," who is narrating this, am narrating it not only for you, but mainly because *I* want to know what story "I" is telling. I can't repeat it often enough. If I already knew, why should I bother to narrate it? All that effort! All those calculations! All those birth pains! It isn't simply a process from me to the screen, but to an even greater extent from the screen to me. It's an interaction, a dialogue in which not I but the story has the last word in order to have its way.

I hang on my own lips, all ears, and you can listen in while I listen to my story that is not my story—that didn't actually happen, but is actually happening: here and now.

Once upon a time, in a very distant country . . . no, not like that. There is now, in this country, a man called Werker. I'm sure of that. Victor Werker. Don't ask me how I know, because I don't know. Doesn't it matter what his name is? Does the creature simply have to have a name? Could Adolf Hitler also have been called Bubi Mauskopf? *What's in a name?* asked Shakespeare. Everything—JHVH is my witness. In the New Testament it says that an angel appeared to Joseph in his dream and said that his wife was pregnant by the Holy Ghost and would give birth to the Messiah, who was to be called Jesus. Imagine that Joseph had ignored that instruction and called the child Maurice—what would have become of Christianity? Nothing. *That's in a name!* For his arrogant remark Shakespeare has been punished from time immemorial with theories maintaining that he himself never existed, but that his name was Francis Bacon or Edward de Vere.

It's already growing dark, it's autumn, October, it's raining. Turned sideways, Victor Werker sits on the sofa in his study and looks at the photo in the large album lying next to him. In a long dress, as white as the peplos that women wore three thousand years ago, flanked by tall green bushes, she is sitting with her feet apart in the shadow of a boulder that seems to have rolled down from Olympus and come to rest right next to her. Behind her the dark entrance to a cave is visible. She is blond and broad-shouldered, like a swimmer; in her hand she has an apple from which a bite has been taken. The foreground is covered with thistles and dried grass; that afternoon the light and the heat lay over the deserted ruins of the Athenian Agora like boiling water, but none of that violence can be read from her. She looks at him with an unfathomable smile, which only now does he think he understands. From the speakers of his hi-fi system Mahler's Fourth conducted by Bernstein booms out.

He gets up with the album like a broken tray in his hands and walks over to his desk. Now two things strike us: how tall and slim he is, and his hands. "Leptosome" is what Kretschmer called such a build in a book that no one has read for ages, but that he studied in his youth—like the even older works in the same genre, by Lavater, Gall, Carus, which are still on a bottom shelf in his bookcase. A good-looking man in the prime of life, that's how I would have described him in the physiognomic days of Lavater: high forehead, gentle eyes tending toward a smile, powerful nose, broad, delicate mouth, wavy dark blond hair, a little too long perhaps, but with a distinguished tinge of gray at the temples. He is wearing an elegant dark gray suit with a black polo-neck sweater. But his slim, hairy hands look as if they were once burned, or attacked by acids; on a few occasions that very nearly happened, but it's vitiligo, which in fact mars his whole appearance. His fingers and most of the back of his hands are deathly pale, even the hairs there are white; the transition toward normal skin is formed by an arbitrary coastline, like that of Greece, with here and there a few pigment-free islands. The small discolorations he had even as a child but in the past few years they've suddenly spread. It's as though he once plunged his hands up to the wrists in death.

He sits down, puts the mobile phone aside, switches on the desk lamp, and with a magnifying glass studies her face. He knows that the earth is large, also that at the moment there are six billion human beings, most of them with faces. But it's as if this one face of the woman there in the shadow of that boulder is of a different order from the other three billion women's faces. And of course it is, and that applies to all those other faces too—but for him it applies only to hers. It's large and a little lopsided, making it look as if she's always smiling a little; the lid of her right eye is also a little lower than that of her left eye, which gives her a look at once sleepy and ecstatic. She looks at him with an unfathomable gaze.

Of course she's not looking at him. This moment she may be looking at someone entirely different: Dietrich Jäger-Jena, her cheerful, acclaimed baritone, in one of the baroque, red-plush dining rooms of the Hotel Sacher in Vienna, with between them two fragrant plates of *Tafelspitz* and a bottle of Blauburgunder; or via the mirror in his dressing room in the Staatsoper, where with the tips of his middle fingers he is sticking on an impertinent mustache and transforming into Don Giovanni. Nevertheless, she is now looking at him—although he is neither in Greece nor in Austria. So in what impossible place is he? Because he sees *her*, not her photograph, which he himself took last year, not the result of routine chemical process that has no secrets from him—no, not a latent image that has been made visible, involving the use of silver, but herself: Clara.

There's no doubt that she's called Clara. Clara Veith. She's getting on for forty but looks ten years younger. Something in her strong features reminds him of the face of his father. The unfathomable quality of her gaze, he suddenly realizes, maybe resides in the aura of aloofness that surrounds her as she looks at him, and that distance between them is death, although at that moment it hadn't yet taken place.

Suddenly he starts to sob.

THE GOLEM

HOLD ON TIGHT! Subterranean rumbling, creaking, the world shakes, suddenly a menacing dark shadow falls across this report. What's this? What have I brought upon myself? Something has suddenly begun moving and colliding, like shifting continental plates. I must immediately interrupt the fable of Victor Werker again, just when he's finally taken shape. From the cosmogonic chaos rises a colossal, eruptive formation. All those towers and bridges? That castle there on the hill? Isn't that Prague? The Hradschin? And that labyrinth of alleyways and hovels on this side of the river, where it makes an almost right-angled bend—isn't that the ghetto? But surely that has long since ceased to exist! What year is it there?

It is 3 Adar of the year 5352 after the creation of heaven and earth, and the rabbi walks across the threshold in tall black boots onto the hard-packed snow.

"You can't go to see the emperor like that, Jehudah!" says his wife in the doorway of their small, lop-sided house. She holds her scarf over her head with one hand and points to the egg yolk on the lapel of his caftan.

He glances at it and shrugs his shoulders.

"He takes me as I am. I do the same with him."

"That's just as well. You'd best be a little careful with those people up there."

"He's always been good to us up to now, Perl."

The words come out of their mouths like steam. Although it's still early afternoon, it's as though night has already fallen in the ghetto. There's a thick fog, the sky is as dark as a coal bunker and the only light seems to come out of the earth, from the frozen snow, in which footprints and cart tracks have been preserved like fossils. The bustle and shouting in the caverns is the same as that in the preceding and coming centuries, as is the stench of sewers and the smell of onions; the smoke from the chimneys descends, and through it fires flicker here and there. Semi-subterranean junk shops are crammed full with rags, broken household utensils, rusty scrap iron, and things whose provenance cannot be traced; the decrepit wooden hovels above them, with their rotten walls and their vague, subsided outbuildings and stairs move forward and backward to the lewd singing of whores in the brothels and the psalm singing of the Orthodox, which blends into a marvelous cantata that can be heard nowhere else. Inside, one can sometimes see how cramped rooms have been divided into apartments with chalk lines, in turn full of merchandise, dove cages, pots and pans; there are sacks of straw with sleeping children on them, the sick, the dying. The taverns with their smoky oil lamps are full; female fortune-tellers, palmists, card readers screech for attention; cripples covered with ulcers and spots and dwarves cling on to passing legs and call for alms before they are kicked away.

Only those who live here know the way through the labyrinth of twisting alleys, courtyards, and passageways. Among all those poor people, who often wear not shoes but swaddling bands of rags, the appearance of the rabbi is almost that of a rich man. Between his great hat with its fur edge and his long, almost white beard two bright blue eyes survey all those oriental scenes of scattered Israel in wintry Prague. Everyone knows the venerable scholar, founder, and rector of the Talmudic college, people make way for him with bows, as they do not for the grubby rabbis from one of the scores of synagogues that the ghetto possesses, and who are at the same time still butchers or tinsmiths. On the little square near the Altneuschul, the oldest synagogue in the Jewish quarter, a group of people are standing, looking up in amazement. The building is detached, which means that since the Middle Ages it has been spared the fires that periodically sweep through the district. Above the gray, flaking walls rises the huge Gothic stepped gable, behind which are the attics where no one ever ventures. The steps of the gable are each crowned by brick spires—and there an astonishing manifestation is going on. In the mist, seven or eight little flames the size of a hand are leaping up and down the steps, tumbling over one another, turning pirouettes, merging and then diverging again.

"What's that, Rabbi?" asks a young woman with startled eyes. "Shouldn't we put it out?"

But a smile has appeared on the rabbi's face.

"That's not a fire, Miriam. It's an angel's dance." He raises his arms and starts singing, leaping from one leg to the other.

That is infectious, and a little later everyone is leaping and turning and singing to the rhythm of the dancing flames; quickly it is transmitted through the alleyways, even where the flames are not visible, and half a minute later the exuberance has taken hold of the whole ghetto. Far beyond its walls, in the rest of the town, the din of the thousands can be heard. "The Jews have gone crazy again," the Christians there say to one another, pointing to their foreheads. But then, as if a higher power has blown at the gable, the flames are suddenly extinguished. The rabbi, who has been dancing around with Miriam, lets go of her hands and gets his breath back, panting and sweating. Around him, too, calm also returns.

"And how are you faring generally, my child?" he says, putting a hand on her head.

Miriam takes his hand and presses a kiss on it. A few months ago she gave birth to an animal, a dog, which ran three times through the room, scratched behind its ear and died.

"Time heals all wounds," she says as her great, dark eyes grow moist.

Time! The rabbi looks at the clock of the Jewish town hall, on the corner opposite the synagogue; since Hebrew is written from right to left, the hands turn anticlockwise. It's two o'clock, he must hurry. Through the throng and the stench he walks past the hovels and the caves of the rabble in the direction of the river, past the cemetery, where the thousands of tombstones stand as crooked as the rotten teeth of an antediluvian monster, with a few enameled remnants of snow on the cutting edges. Watched suspiciously by the two Christian sentries, he passes through the gate in the city wall near the bridge of the Moldau. There it's suddenly quiet; only on the muddy bank, near the saltpeter pits, is there some activity. As he hears the ice floes bumping against the wooden piers below, he leaves—as if it were a religious dateline—3 Adar 5352 and enters February 16, 1592.

On the other side he is welcomed by churches and pathetic images of saints, which disgust him, because one shouldn't make a graven image or any figure of what is above in heaven or below on earth, nor what is in the waters under the earth. All bastards of the Golden Calf, all the work of his overinflated colleague, the false Messiah, who has degenerated into the Savior of the anti-Semites. Although . . . did not JHVH, praised be his name, trespass against his commandment when he created Adam in his own image? What is man but a living image? The rabbi has the feeling that this is the germ of a small tract, because JHVH, praised be his name, must of course be absolved of all blame.

The castle up there is still invisible in the fog; groaning, he starts climbing the rising path, again and again slipping on the ice. He has no idea what the emperor wants of him. The invita-

tion had arrived while he was teaching at the college: an imperial courier on a white horse had appeared in the ghetto and had
handed Perl the dispatch without dismounting. He'd talked
about it with his friend Mordechai Maisel, the court Jew and fin-
ancier of the emperor, and also patron of the Jewish quarter, but
he was equally ignorant. Perhaps Tycho was behind it, the Dan-
ish astronomer and imperial mathematician, whom he has met
a few times and with whom he got on well.

It's as though he can see himself from a great distance, a
small, slithering black figure on the white slope. Behind him,
down below, the town and the river disappear farther and farther into the cloud which has covered the earth, from which
only church towers still protrude and in which a few flickering
fires can be seen here and there, but above him it becomes
lighter at every step. On the narrow steps up to the castle, the
last section to the summit, he stops and pants now and then in
the icy wind, puts a hand against a tree trunk, and bends over
coughing. These are not the kind of walks for a man of sixty-
eight. Under a blue sky the palaces and the cathedral of the castle lie in the thin winter sunlight. He feels lonely, but that
disappears when he has shown the court's invitation at a barrier
and has had to endure the suspicious look of the lancer: what
business has a Jew in the castle?

He walks through the sulfurous fumes of Golden Street.
There, in a long, winding row of dollhouses, built into the wall
of the fortress, and so small that the gutters scarcely rise above
his hat, the emperor has housed his second-rank alchemists.
With the reflection of the fire on their faces the practitioners of
the hermetic art sit at their arthanors, their tiny accommodation
crammed to the farthest corner with alembics, cucurbits, and
other instruments. A few are kneeling with their hands folded
in prayer, looking at the distillation process of sulfur and mercury in order to conduct it into the right channels during the
phases of the Great Work, from the *materia prima* to the *lapis
philosophorum*, the *coniunctio* of the Red and the White, of sun

and moon, the chemical union of Rex and Regina, from which eternal life is born, the appearance of the homunculus in the retort. A couple of lancers patrol up and down to ensure that the adepts do not leave their ovens for a moment.

The rabbi has seen it all before and can't stand it. The world is irrational and full of wonders, just as, recently, the boy who was born with a gold tooth, and those miracles must of course have their place in doctrine; but one should not seek to perform them oneself; human magic tricks, whether it be alchemy or something else, are all nonsense. All that has any point are the things to which he himself has dedicated his life: the Torah, morality, and mathematics, on which he has written fifteen books. He wants to avert his eyes, but then, at a window at number 22, he suddenly sees a quite different scene. There a man of about thirty sits hunched over a table writing feverishly, legs apart and extended, scarcely taking the time to dip his quill. When he looks up for a moment, the rabbi is struck by the shining, melancholy look in the dark eyes: eyes like dark puddles in a park, left there after a downpour. Through the middle of his thick black hair runs a sharp parting, showing white scalp, as if a meticulous executioner has made room for the ax that is to cleave his skull. How had he wound up here among the alchemists? The rabbi would have liked to ask him who he is, but there's no time for that now.

Suddenly he is struck in the back of the neck by a snowball.

"Jew! Jew!" cry a couple of exuberant boys when he turns around and they go on pelting him with snowballs while the soldiers watch and laugh.

By the time he reaches the busy courtyard with the Saint Vitus Cathedral in it, where demolition and building is in progress on all sides, he has shaken them off. He goes toward the terrace of the palace, through the throng of beggars and rooting pigs and chickens. An elegant officer with a large hat, thigh-length boots, and a sword is waiting for him, flanked by two musketeers—and then he finds himself inside the well-oiled machine of monarchy. He stamps the snow off his boots and follows the officer inside, along the soft carpets, across a hall, up a marble staircase, and then through a series of corridors and chambers, each lavishly furnished with paintings, tapestries and gold-colored furniture, on which no one is sitting. He has never been here; what strikes him is the deathly silence at the center of power. Despite himself he feels uncertain and nervous, and that annoys him. At a double door, framed with marble eagles, lions, and other aggressive fauna, he is received by a second officer, who salutes, turns on his heel, knocks on the door, and without waiting for an answer, opens it.

In the middle of a large room, on both sides of which two huge fires are burning, twelve or fourteen men sit eating at a fully laden table, served by as many lackeys in red, gold-embroidered livery. There are great terrestrial and celestial globes, the walls are covered with paintings, maps, and bookcases. The rabbi stops; the officer closes the door behind him. All faces have turned in his direction. At the head of the long table he has immediately recognized Rudolf II, with the protruding Hapsburg lower lip in his puffy face, lord of Austria, king of Bohemia and Hungary, emperor of the Holy Roman Empire. Behind him stand a couple of court dignitaries; to the side, at a small table, a secretary is sitting, writing.

The rabbi takes his hat off, bows, and says:

"Your Royal and Imperial Apostolic Majesty."

The emperor nods. He's about forty years old, but is already balding and thickset. Chewing, with a joint of steaming meat in his left hand, a glass of red wine in his right, he surveys the new guest from top to toe for a while, with a melancholy look in his deep-set eyes.

"Well," he finally says. "So there he is in person, our famous Maharal, Jehudah Löw Ben Bezalel. Like all rabbis, you look like all rabbis. Why is that?"

"That's because there's really only one rabbi." Löw immediately realizes that a dangerous question about the identity of that one rabbi may follow, but obviously the emperor has decided to spare him.

"All well with the chosen people in Prague?"

There is a titter of laughter at the table.

"They have the feeling that they needn't worry under your regime, Your Majesty."

The emperor nods again, but doesn't pursue the subject. He wipes the fat off his chin with his sleeve.

"Would the Chief Rabbi perhaps like to eat at my table?"

Löw doesn't really like the tone of that question; although the smell of the roast venison is making his mouth water, he refuses politely. Obviously the rule here is: whoever isn't going to eat does not sit, because no chair is offered him either, although he's obviously the oldest person in the company.

At table, the interest in him begins to wane, the faces turn away, and the conversations are resumed. He doesn't know what to do with himself, but he realizes that he must stand where he is and wait until he is addressed again. He himself has sometimes put a pupil in a corner like this; he resolves never to do it again. One by one he surveys the men at the table. They have not got the smooth visages of courtiers, but each of them has a characteristic head, some of them look decidedly wild and down at heel. His eyes meet those of Tycho Brahe, a stocky man of nearly fifty, with a gold artificial nose; he is the only person the rabbi knows here. The astronomer looks questioningly at Rudolf, who gives him a short nod; he gets up and comes over to the rabbi.

"In the vicinity of princes a man must always be prepared for humiliations," he whispers.

"To say nothing of a Jew, but we are used to that. Did you set up this meeting?"

"I forget," says Brahe, looking him straight in the eye.

"I understand." Löw nods. "The Secret of the Castle. Who are those men?"

"The flower of Europe, supplemented with a bunch of inter-

national confidence tricksters and other rabble, but hopefully
that will stay *entre nous*." He scans the two rows at the long end
of the table and quickly tells Löw who is who. "That monk on
the emperor's right is Giordano Bruno, an interesting writer
and philosopher. According to him the universe is infinite, with
its circumference nowhere and its center everywhere."

"So here too," says Löw.

"Here too. Here particularly, perhaps. That fellow next to him
is of much less stature, Sendivogius, a Polish adventurer and alchemist, but the emperor is infatuated with him. You've no idea
the kind of charlatans and frauds who manage to force their way
in here, all because the emperor is filled with the fear of death, if
you ask me. Then there's Cornelis Drebbel, that blond young
man over there. He comes from Haarlem, he seems to have invented a submarine; I expect they need something like that in
Holland, since it rains all the time there. Apart from that he's
not without merit as an engraver, and naturally, he's also an alchemist. Next to him there's another cheese-head, Adriaan de
Vries, a competent architect and sculptor, who's been raised to
the nobility by the emperor. Then there are two Englishmen.
The man with that pointed goatee beard is John Dee, a favorite
of Queen Elizabeth's, a magician, alchemist, astrologer, mathematician, geographer, and God knows what else. He maintains
that he can speak the language of Adam."

"Lunatic," said Löw.

"Nevertheless, he seems to be not entirely without significance. In any case that chap next to him, with the hooked nose,
and those ears that have been cut off, is a thoroughgoing
swindler and hysteric. A certain Edward Kelley, some sort of
medium; on his own testimony he converses with the angels.
Yes, Rabbi, sometimes I think I've found my way into a mad-
house, the emperor has turned his court into a mirror image of
his poor, confused spirit. And this is just his human collection, a
small part of it, that is; you should see his other collections.
There's nothing like it anywhere else in the world; the whole

palace is a collection of curiosities, the treasures are indescribable. His agents comb the whole of Europe to buy everything that's going, from the most precious Cranachs and Dürers down to the most appalling kitsch such as muzzles and painted coconuts. To the left of him sits his favorite painter, Arcimboldo, who has risen to Count Palatinate here. There are some portraits of his."

With his shiny golden nose, Brahe points to the wall. Shaking his head, Löw looks at the fantastic faces, now composed of fish, then fruit, then kitchen utensils, or all kinds of animals. The things the goyim dream up, instead of immersing themselves in JHVH's law.

"That young man next to him," continues Brahe, "with those burning eyes, who from the look of it is arguing with Sendivogius, we're going to hear a lot about him. He is my Copernican colleague, Johannes Kepler, who uses my observation results for a whole new theory about the orbits of the planets, which I don't like at all. But just try holding young people back when they're as brimful of ideas as he is. At the moment he is in some difficulty, his mother has been indicted for witchcraft. Next to him sits Michael Maier, the emperor's personal physician, an iatrochemical follower of Paracelsus; I read a nice book of his, *Atalanta fugiens,* he's perhaps the most interesting of all the occultists here. We've almost finished. That over there is Roelant Savery, a South Netherlandish painter, and finally there's some Italian black magician or other, Angelo Ripellino, I think he's called. Yes, Maharal, and now you're here too then, you seem to fit into this weird company."

Löw raises his arms.

"But how?"

"That will become apparent shortly. Come on, I think that's enough. We'll just go and sit down; if the emperor doesn't like it, we're bound to hear."

He takes Löw by an elbow and points him to the empty chair at the end of the table, right opposite Rudolf. Their arrival is scarcely noticed. The mood among the guests has got better and better; the lackeys in their worn livery, generally too small or too large, pour wine uninterruptedly, their left hand neatly on their back, and everywhere there is ringing laughter and loud conversations are being conducted. The emperor himself doesn't join in. Sunk in saturnine melancholy he sits in his great chair, his head slightly bent, his eyes half closed. That's obviously what he wants, thinks Löw, to be there and not to be there. He also sees that the emperor puts his hand on Giordano Bruno's for a moment, as if as a sign of affection, which is jealously observed by Sendivogius. Arcimboldo, no longer as young as he was, has fallen asleep, with his head on the table in the middle of the gold cutlery. Kelley is drunk. He knocks his glass over, which is immediately refilled, gets up unsteadily, so that his chair falls over, and obviously wants to propose a toast to the emperor, which Dee is able to prevent him from doing by tugging him back down again by his sleeve. Löw is also given a glass of wine, which he brings to his lips but which he does not drink. When he raises his eyes, he's looking directly into those of Rudolf—and it is as if that moment is felt by everyone at the table. In the silence that suddenly falls, the emperor asks:

"What is a golem, Rabbi?"

So that's it. Löw realizes immediately where things are headed, but he decides to play dumb for as long as possible. He shifts the black skullcap on his crown and says:

"That's a Hebrew word that occurs in Psalm 139, verse 16. It means something like 'imperfect substance.'"

"Is it just a word?"

"Just a word . . ." repeats Löw. "What is more important than the word, Your Majesty?"

"Yes, yes, stop that," says the emperor wearily. "I know a bit about your views. The word 'table' is just a word, just like the word 'God,' but there are also tables, and God exists too."

"And do basilisks exist because the word 'basilisk' exists, Your Majesty?" asks Kepler.

The emperor looks at Maier.

"Of course," says the latter. "Otherwise the word wouldn't exist."

Löw nods.

"So that means that everything exists."

"That's right."

"Come, come," says Kepler. "So if I now invent a new word, for example, 'kraldor,' then according to you there is such a thing as a kraldor in the world?"

Maier thinks for a moment.

"Yes."

"But half a minute ago, when I hadn't yet made up that word, was there a kraldor too?"

Maier starts shifting backward and forward in his chair. He looks at the emperor for a moment and says:

"I shall have to think about that."

"If not, then I've just created it. But I actually thought that the creation of living beings is the privilege of God."

"And what about the homunculus?" asks Dee indignantly. "Does that not exist either then?"

"You will have to prove that."

"Paracelsus made one!"

"So he claims. Have you repeated his experiment?"

"Not yet."

"Until that's happened, and as long as other people have never yet seen a homunculus, it's just a word. It's as the Maharal says, otherwise there will be an infinite number of things, as many as you can make words." A crooked smile appears on his face. "Whoever would have thought that I would agree with a rabbi!"

"Calm down Johannes," says Brahe. "Know your place."

"Perhaps," suggests the emperor, "God created the world in such a way that everything is possible." There is a sound in his voice from which one can conclude that he now regards this topic as having been dealt with. "People have told me that a golem is also a kind of homunculus, an artificial human being, the ideal servant."

Löw sighs deeply.

"Those are just legends. The Jews have always been good at making up tall stories."

"So is it just a story?"

"Now that's the same thing again . . . just a story . . ."

"Listen, Löw," says the emperor and sits up a little in his chair. "I understand that you as a Talmudist have a difficult relationship with tall stories, but I advise you quite quickly to become somewhat more concrete." Out of the corner of his eye Löw sees a look from Brahe, which means that he must watch his step a little.

"Have you ever seen a golem?"

"No, Your Majesty."

"Do you know anyone who has ever seen a golem?"

"Not that I'm aware of."

"Do you know of anyone who has ever seen a golem?"

"It's said that Abraham and Jeremiah did."

Drebbel bursts out laughing.

"That's a long time ago."

"According to the Talmud it happened a few more times about thirteen hundred years ago."

"And in our age?" asks Savery helpfully.

"Of course I don't know all the things that are happening in Jewry, in the Rhineland and in France and Spain and Italy, and all what those magicians are getting up to, but I heard a rumor that in Poland Rabbi Eliyahu Ba'al Shemu from Chelm is supposed to have made one."

The emperor turns aside a little and raises a weary hand to the dignitary obliquely behind him, who quickly leans forward. "Get that chap to come here," he says without looking at him.

"Unfortunately that will be impossible, Your Majesty," says Löw. "He died ten years ago."

The emperor's patience is suddenly exhausted. With a quick

movement, which one wouldn't have thought possible in his languid body, he gets up and beckons Löw with a crooked forefinger, as a schoolmaster does a pupil. Löw gets up and follows him, while the company remains behind, somewhat dismayed. Rudolf is wearing a long brocade dressing gown, down to his gold-embroidered slippers and with a determined tread he walks toward a side door, which is open by a bowing lackey. They enter a small chamber, hung round with large colorful paintings, covered with fantastic scenes. Löw has no time to take them all in, the only thing that remains with him is a cross-bearing Christ figure with closed eyes, surrounded by indescribably repulsive faces, which are undoubtedly intended to be Jews. In the middle stands a large table, laden with alchemical instruments; but unlike on Golden Street everything here is made of silver and crystal. Obviously he himself experiments here.

The door is closed behind them and the emperor turns toward him.

"Let's not beat about the bush, Rabbi. I want a golem. Can you make one for me?"

Arms waving, Löw turns away and then back toward him.

"You must understand, Your Majesty, that the creation of a golem is a mystical ritual, in which the creation of Adam is repeated. Once it lives, it's immediately undone, otherwise it's probably sacrilege. The sole object is to prove the power of the sacred letters."

The emperor glances at the egg yolk on the rabbi's lapel.

"And your Polish colleague, did he also leave it at that?"

"No, I believe he let it live and used it. But that's only an idea of the most recent times."

"And what if you did it too?"

Löw shakes his head.

"My problem, Your Majesty, is that I'm not a Cabalist. I'm just a simple bookworm, who tries to initiate his pupils into the exalted secrets of the Torah. I've got my hands full with that."

"Your modesty becomes you, but maybe you've heard my

question anyway. Naturally there would be something in return."

Löw quickly reflects. It was, of course, not a question, it was
an order. If he didn't obey, the consequences would be dire.
What could be set against possible sacrilege? Nobility? Estates?
Or simply money? They weren't well off, Perl and he, but if he'd
wanted to be rich he would have chosen a career like that of
Mordechai Maisel. He wonders if he's on the point of ruining
his life—but suddenly he knows how he can perhaps appease
Elohim.

"Your will is law, Your Majesty, but I can't promise you anything. I've never occupied myself with those kinds of practices,
but of course I will try, although it is not impossible that the
magic sources are nowadays blocked."

"That wouldn't surprise me." The emperor nods in displeas-
ure. Obviously he's heard that argument before. "And what do
you want if you succeed?"

Löw stretches his back a little.

"The promise that my people will have nothing to fear even
in the long term here in Prague."

The emperor continues to look at him.

"The long term is a long time, Löw."

With his hat in his hand, Löw makes a gesture of resignation.

"I know that the humiliation of Israel will be greater than it
has ever been just before its liberation. And it's precisely from
that that it will emerge."

"That doesn't tally with what you've asked me. But very
well, I'll do what I can, Maharal, although some things are not
even in my power. Even I can't rule beyond the grave."

Löw is sorry that no one witnesses the promise—but on the
other hand, the emperor wouldn't worry at all about a witness.
If necessary he'd throw him in a dungeon, or even more deci-
sively have his head chopped off.

"I don't like it," says Perl.

"Neither do I," says Löw, lighting a candle. "But what can I do?"

"And if you don't succeed?"

"Then we've got a problem. If we do succeed as well, for that matter."

"Oh that's always the way with those kinds of people, they always get other people into trouble. The emperor's got everything already, why does he want a golem as well? Why, for goodness' sake?"

"Because," says Löw, "when you've got everything you really haven't got anything. All you've got are your desires."

"An ordinary person is happy with a new ladle."

"Oh, the emperor would like nothing better than to be happy with a ladle. But in a little while when he's got a golem, he won't be happy with that either. Then he'll have set his heart on something else."

"Poor man," says Perl, shaking her head as she dishes up the onion soup. "Let's hope you succeed. But we can rely on you."

After his visit to the castle hill Löw has to get used to his poky accommodation, of which ten would fit into a medium-sized chamber in the palace. But that comment of his wife gives him more strength than anything he's derived from all those great minds up there. Of course he'll succeed although it's inconvenient for him, not only religiously but also practically. He's writing a commentary on the Targum and the Midrash, which he will now have to interrupt in order to immerse himself, perhaps for months, in all those strange writings that are so unappealing to him by nature—to begin with *Sefer Yetsirah*.

Helped by his ex-pupil, follower, and assistant Rabbi Jacob Sason ha-Levi, a cheerful, fidgety man, who is the only one who knows his way through the libraries of the Talmud college and the Altneu synagogue, he spends the next few weeks searching out and reconnoitering those scurrilous treatises, while outside in the alleyways there is the hubbub of the people, for whom only the here and now exists. Day after day, sighing and bent over the scrolls, which are so many leaves of the Tree of Knowledge, he reflects that he, on an imperial order, must in his old age become a sorcerer too. He had counted on entering history as a prominent Jewish scholar of the sixteenth century, or perhaps more than that, but now it looks as though he'll be remembered in a completely different way—at least if he succeeds in making that stupid golem, which JHVH permit. But obviously that's how life is; there's no point in trying to fight it.

According to all the sources both Abraham and Jeremiah had heard from JHVH that they as mortals were not capable of penetrating on their own JHVH's creative manual *Sefer Yetsirah;* thereupon Abraham had turned to the son of Noah, Shem, and Jeremiah had turned to his son Ben Sira. In his own circle Löw finds only his own son-in-law, Rabbi Isaac ha-Kohen, the father of his grandsons, triplets. To begin with the latter is not at all interested, but when he hears in confidence about the agreement that his father-in-law has struck with the emperor, he is prepared to help him, although he is a skeptical rationalist from the school of Maimonides, and although in his opinion he's got better things to do as a baker. He regards all that Cabalistic mumbo jumbo even more than Löw as a pernicious, an impure reversion to the mystical prehistory of rabbinical orthodoxy. What else is a golem but a graven, or at least a kneaded image? But obviously this is how JHVH wants it to be this time. He raises this with his father-in-law, to which the latter reacts with irritation and says that it's all much more complicated than that and that he will write a study about it when this affair is over. Isaac's hair and beard are red as a blazing fire, which seems to point to an ecstatic character, but the opposite is the case. Esther, Löw's daughter, also found that out too late; but that's nothing out of the ordinary, since virtually everyone marries the wrong person.

"Whyever is it, my boy," Löw asks him, "that you never really get enthusiastic about anything? You don't have to teach me anything about the problematic nature of the Cabala, but as things are, we've got to make a golem, whether we like it or not and that can't be done in the same way that you bake a loaf. Rabbi Nathan wrote three hundred years ago that a perfect golem can only be made by a perfect human being, who is in a state of complete unity with Adonai, praised be his name."

"Go on," says Isaac. "You're a brave one."

"And so must you be brave. You're not doing this for yourself but for your people. What will you say if we don't succeed and a pogrom breaks out and the emperor doesn't intervene?" And when Isaac is silent: "For that matter, I recently had a terrible vision. In Rabbi Menachem Ziyyon's commentary on the Torah I happened to read that our twenty-two holy letters are written on Adonai's arm. And then I saw a flash of a man who was called 'Manquake,' just as you have an earthquake—and even a moment later I saw Israel going toward death in endless rows, with letters on their arms that had to be read as figures."

Nodding, Isaac continues to look at him for a moment.

"Perhaps you should start being a bit careful, Father. You're not as young as you were."

"I'll leave being careful to you, I've never spared myself. But of course you're right. In the evenings, when I'm lying in bed next to Perl, with my eyes closed, I sometimes find myself still reading. I see clear letters, as though there's a scroll open in front of my eyes."

"But there's nothing there, so that's impossible."

"And yet I can read it. I read things that I've never read before."

"And that no one has written."

Löw sighs.

"That's right. We live in an incomprehensible world, Isaac."

After a month—the ice has disappeared from the ghetto, and occasionally a smell of spring comes wafting from the hills—everything is in readiness for their real study. They know that Abraham and Jeremiah took three years to understand *Sefer Yetsirah*, but hope that they will be finished in a couple of months with the dozens of commentaries to hand. But as they read and read and discuss the *Book of Creation* it imperceptibly becomes summer, autumn, and in the cemetery the yellowing leaves are again falling on the tombstones. By then they not only know the impenetrable text by heart, it's as though it has penetrated into their intestines and bones, although they still don't understand the book. But they're closer than they had come with their understanding; it's as though they've changed into it, have themselves become it: they think of nothing else and at night they dream about it.

Isaac too. Suddenly some barrier has burst in his legalistic mind as a result of the endless combinations and permutations, the twenty-two letters, the three mothers, the two hundred and thirty-one gates, the seven double, the twelve simple. . . . Esther, who has always been irritated by her husband's dullness, now longs for it to return, since his enthusiasm is even more intolerable than his surliness. Not only does he scarcely talk to her these days, for months he hasn't even slept with her. Despite her beautiful round breasts and broad hips, sexuality had never been his strongest point anyway. . . . By siring triplets in one go, he seemed to want to save himself the trouble twice over. What she'd most like would be to gather together her belongings and her sons and leave him. For Perl on the other hand it is nothing new. Her Jehudah is always like that when he's properly at work. She doesn't begrudge him it, although the look in her eyes has grown darker from year to year.

At the end of the Christian year 1592—Löw is sixty-nine by now—the emperor's courier, surrounded by little boys, again appears in the ghetto, towering above the crowd on his horse. His Apostolic Majesty, says the dispatch, wishes to know what's happening about the golem. Obviously he's growing impatient, but he's not forgotten, which is a good sign with a view to his promise. In his reply, which he has to give the messenger to take back, Löw writes that he is working on the commission day and night, except for the Sabbath, but that this fundamental experi-

ment is just like the transmutation of silver into gold: excessive
haste produces only lead. But because the golem will protect the
Jewish people against persecution, His Apostolic Majesty can
rest assured that the great work will be completed not a day
later than is necessary. He has even thought of a name for it:
Jossile Golem.

Nevertheless, they return to their studies with redoubled
zeal. The first and most important commentary on *Sefer Yetsirah* that they have Sason put on the table is that by Rabbi
Eleazar Ben Judah of Worms. Written in about the year 5000,
that is in the thirteenth century of the Christians, it contains
extensive practical indications for the necessary thousands of
computations and recitations of letters, arranged at the end
of the book in long tables. These latter tables, highly secret of
course, are missing from most manuals, but not from the copy
of the Altneuschul. This manuscript is almost as great a classic
as the *Sefer Yetsirah* itself and the innumerable later commentators base themselves on it without exception.

Aware of the imminent danger of death, in which, according
to Rabbi Gershom from Berlin every creator of a great work
finds himself, they spend the following months learning by
heart and repeating the complicated procedure. They quickly
observe that sitting at the table doesn't work very well; thereupon Löw finds Sason prepared to play the part of the Jossile-to-
be. Because there are many busybodies wandering around the
Talmudic college, and because whispers are already circulating
in the ghetto that the Maharal and Rabbi ha-Kohen are engaged
in mysterious practices, they move their working place to the
cold, dark attic of the Altneuschul a few alleys farther on. Foundation stones of the mysterious building were long ago brought
by angels directly to Prague from the devastated temple in Jerusalem, on condition that if the temple were ever rebuilt they
would be returned, and Rabbi ha-Levi does not feel completely
comfortable as he lies on the creaking, dusty floor and allows
the rituals to pass over him. Still, he's happy that he can make

himself more useful than by simply digging out classical manuscripts from the alcoves and delivering them. Sometimes he falls asleep for a moment, whereupon he is immediately visited by grotesque dreams full of creatures that look like the paintings of Arcimboldo, about which Löw has told him, but which are not composed of fruit or pots and pans but of strange apparatuses and machines, which can fly. When he wakes with a start and sees the two men fluttering around him like bats in the light of the flickering candles, with huge shadows against the sloping roof, intoning magic sounds, the feeling comes over him that they are involved with things which are far beyond their power.

When the winter is over again and they know the sequence of their actions as well as the map of the ghetto, Löw decides to spend a few more months on the study of later commentators. In the summer they must finally do it. Anyway, he will be seventy by then; his birthday, II Tammuz, seems a suitable day to him.

"Not to me," says Perl. "You should be at home on your birthday."

"By making a golem I'll be at home in a higher sense."

"Yes, as long as it's higher, it's always all right with you."

"That's true. But you don't understand, because you're a woman."

"You should be glad of that."

"And so I am."

"And what does Isaac think about it?"

"He'd sooner get started straightaway."

"He'd do better to get started with Esther straightaway. The poor child is becoming desperately unhappy."

"You still don't go short on that score, even if I'm a man who's about to turn seventy and is always thinking of higher things."

Not wanting to let him see her smile, Perl turns around quickly and starts peeling onions.

Rabbi Abraham Abulafia, Rabbi Reuveni Sarfaty, Rabbi Isaac Ben Samuel of Acre, Rabbi Judah ben Moses Albotini, Rabbi

Joseph Ben Shalom Ashkenazi, and naturally the famous Rabbi Isaac Luria and many others, such as the modern rabbi Abraham ben Shem Bibago and Rabbi Jochanan Ben Isaac Alemanno—in the commentaries of all these authorities he finds additional technical information for the formation, which they benefit from. In the work of the youngest generation of Christian Cabalists, such as Johannes Reuchlin and Agrippa von Nettesheim, they find only vague, general Cabalistic reflections, with which every pupil of the Talmudic college is familiar at the age of sixteen and which is of no technical use to them. The only discordant note is struck by the views of Rabbi Moses ben Jacob Cordovero. While Rabbi Isaac of Acre was convinced that using *Sefer Yetsirah* a complete human being could be created, according to Cordovero it was only possible to produce a very inferior, soulless creature, scarcely higher than an animal, although extremely vital. A person killing a golem is not breaking any commandment. The other views were somewhere in between: the golem was an undeniably animate but soulless being, hence dumb. He who is made through speaking, who *is* nothing but speaking, cannot himself speak, since otherwise the Cabalist would be like a god, which in view of original sin is not possible.

"A golem," says Löw pensively to his son-in-law, "is a human being without language. So you could see him as the antipode to a figure from a play, as the latter consists of language without a human form. That is only supplied by an actor."

Meanwhile, things are not going well with Rabbi Jacob, who is playing the golem. In the spring he starts coughing and he looks worse day by day; he complains of exhaustion and a few weeks later there's nothing left of his cheerful nature. He's as pale as a hard-boiled egg, he's rapidly losing weight, and worrying black patches the size of coins start appearing on his neck and arms, as if the Devil has spat on him. According to the doctors it's not the plague, thank God, but some unknown disease for which there is no cure. By the time summer comes, he's too weak to get out of bed, he can no longer speak, and shortly afterward he dies. At Jacob's funeral, under the umpteenth stone in the cemetery, Löw and Isaac notice that people are casting sideways glances and avoiding them.

During the singing of the Kaddish, with their faces turned toward Jerusalem, Perl whispers:

"You must quickly put an end to this, Jehudah. There's something brewing in the ghetto."

"Do you think I can't see that? As if I were doing it for myself. This is all for their own good, except that I can't tell them. If I break the Secret of the Castle, there will be disasters."

But there has already *been* a disaster, Jacob's death, and what he thinks about that he won't even tell Perl. Perhaps he's made a terrible mistake. Perhaps the Cabalistic mechanism works in such a way that the same rituals which turn clay into life kill a living person. He's never read anything about that, probably because no one has ever come up with that wretched idea before. In that case he has Jacob's death on his conscience, and that can only be compensated to some extent by the creation of a golem.

And a few weeks later the second disaster happens: Esther has disappeared with her triplets. When Isaac comes home in the evening, he finds only silence, a house turned upside down, and a letter. She's finally had enough, she writes, he must look after things for himself alone from now on, he obviously doesn't need her, except to cook and wash his clothes. He'll miss his sons, but that's the price he has to pay, they won't go short of anything. There's no need for him to look for them, because he won't find them, she's made sure of that. She wishes him well, much joy with the golem, and may she never see him again.

He looks in bewilderment at the epistle in his hands, but even at that moment his mind is not entirely on it but on a mystical passage that he's read in a Cabalistic text of three centuries earlier "JHVH lives in the depths of nothingness." So did he also create himself out of nothingness? Or does he simply not exist? He starts trembling, he doesn't know what has affected him more deeply: the disappearance of his wife and children or the shadow that has now suddenly been cast over JHVH. But then he comes to himself, utters a loud cry, and struggles through the throng in the alleyways toward his parents-in-law.

"Oh God, oh God, oh God," wails Perl and starts tearing at her clothes, but Löw silences her with a short movement of his hand and says:

"She'll turn up again. Where has she to go to? These are the whims women have."

"I'm going to the police!"

But although the Jewish police also involved the imperial police, no trace of Esther was found. Looking for her in the ghetto is a hopeless task, but if she were there it wouldn't stay secret for an hour; and on the exit roads from Prague a woman weighed down with packages and bags with three identical boys would certainly be quickly found.

"All the fault of that damned golem of yours!" cries Perl. "When will there be an end to those satanic arts?"

"Next week will be my seventieth birthday," says Löw in a tone as though he were just deciding it.

The day before his birthday is devoted to fasting and prayers. After sunset Perl gives him a kiss on the threshold of their house, her eyes filling with tears. As a sign of reassurance he shakes his head with his eyes closed for a moment.

"You go off to bed."

"Do you think I can sleep now?"

He walks silently through the crowd, who have no inkling of what is about to happen that night for their sake. In the synagogue Isaac is waiting for him; Abraham, the old shammes, has already lit candles. They descend into the *mikvah*, take a ritual bath in pure rainwater, shroud themselves in gowns of white linen, with hoods over their heads, and recite Psalm 119—a fairly uninspired, legalistic text, divided into twenty-two eight-line stanzas, each bearing as a title a letter of the alephbeth, which is also the initial letter of each line. Jerking their upper bodies back and forth the monotonous verses of the longest of all psalms cross their lips, while the narrow windows grow darker and darker.

Once they are outside with a bundle of servants' clothes for the golem, Isaac looks up at the town hall clock on the other side. By the light of the full moon, high in the sky, the hands are clearly visible: It is midnight.

"It's your birthday, Father. Many happy returns!"

Löw strokes his beard reflectively.

"At this moment it could also be an ordinary clock."

It has grown silent in the ghetto, only here and there is there still light; from a dark hovel comes the squalling of a baby. The town gate is open, there is no war yet, but two sentries bar their way with their lances. By the light of a smoking torch they survey the two white figures from top to toe.

"And where do we think we're going?" asks one.

"Down here." Löw points to the wooden steps which lead to the riverbank.

"To do what?"

"To make a golem."

"To make a what?"

"A golem. It's too complicated to explain, gentlemen, but you're quite welcome to watch, we've nothing to hide."

"Nothing's going to be made here now, Jew. It's the middle of the night."

"That's the best time."

"Hold your impudent tongue, you stinking Yid! About-face and on your way right now!"

Now Löw plays his trump card. He produces the dispatch, in which the emperor insists on haste.

"Are you sure that you want to defy an order from His Apostolic Majesty?"

Of course they can't read it, but at the mere sight of the imperial seal they shrink back.

Down below on the shore, with his boots in the clay, Löw looks around. In the still, sultry night the river shines like flowing moonlight, as pale as the face of Jacob on his deathbed. The bridge is empty and on the castle hill in the distance everything is dark. Is the emperor asleep? Is he dreaming that his throat is being cut by the sultan? Or is he still at work in his laboratory, surrounded by fumes of sulfur and mercury, which will make him crazier and crazier? The stars in the cloudless sky are almost outshone by the moon—only the brightly glowing light of two planets, close together in the constellation of Leo, refuses to be ousted.

Löw spreads his arms wide, and helped by Isaac he begins reciting the second chapter of *Sefer Yetsirah*, with the feeling that the whole of creation is listening to him. Then he kneels down at the edge of the river and gets to work. Because a golem can only be made of virgin, uncultivated earth, by flowing water, this is the ideal spot; certainly nothing has ever been cultivated here. While Isaac, now bowing and swaying, reads appropriate texts from the Midrash in a singsong voice, Löw kneads from the rich river clay the crude form of a lying figure, with outspread arms and legs. He was dreading this, he was frightened of creating a monster, but to his own astonishment he manages quite well, the proportions are immediately correct. He claps his hands in elation—and looking at Isaac now and again he begins to model the face, while he feels himself becoming more and more excited. The closed eyes, the nose, the mouth, appear almost by themselves, he sniffs, groans, hisses, jumps up, stands at a distance, kneels down again, casts a glance at Isaac's ears and forms the labyrinthine shells, which he puts in the right place with a thumb, the upper edge at the height of the as-yet-invisible pupils. Löw feels as if there is a direct connection between his eyes and hands, bypassing his brain. After forming the nipples, their mutual distance equaling that from the chin to the hairline, he indicates the navel with the tip of his little finger, but then he hesitates. Should the golem have a navel? Of course not, it has no mother, just like Adam, who hence also had no navel. He takes a little clay from the lump in his left hand and with his right thumb closes the navel again. When the hands have finally acquired fingers and the feet toes, there is only one thing left. The penis. He can't see Isaac's and he doesn't want to—even Esther seldom got to see it—so he'll have to work from the memory of his own. Standing, he models a circumcised sexual organ, not too small and not too large, with the left testicle slightly lower than the right. He carefully plants it at the fork in the trunk.

Only the back of his robe is still white. Breathing deeply, with his head askew, he surveys his work. Will that gray, beardless face really come to life in a moment? He has had to be careful that it didn't turn into a portrait of Isaac, but the Jossile-to-be is better looking and younger, about twenty-two. His baldness suits him. He lies motionless in the silent moonlight at the edge of the water.

Isaac, who has stopped his recitations, looks at him open-mouthed.

"How can it be," he says, "that you have so much talent for an activity that Adonai has strictly forbidden? You—the Chief Rabbi!"

Löw shrugs his shoulders and shows the smeared palms of his hands.

"I'm amazed myself."

"So that gift cannot derive from Adonai, praised be his name, only from Satan, who already has the cult of the Golden Calf on his conscience."

"Odd to hear something like that from your son-in-law. Anyway, in the Talmud there is the story of Rabbis Hanina and Oshaiah, who years ago once made a calf golem."

"I know. Which they then slaughtered and ate."

"Obviously there's something strange going on with calves." Löw smiles. "In the future lots more strange things will happen with them."

"How can you stay so calm? If I were you I'd be seriously worried about such a diabolical gift."

"But you are not me, my dear Isaac, and you're not very likely to become me. Don't be so logical all the time, think more deeply. What if you were to look at it this way, that Adonai, praised be his name, has involved even Beelzebub tonight for the preservation of his people in Prague. What would you say to that? Anyway, if everything goes well with this image, this image will not remain an image for very long."

Now, after a year and a half of study and practice, the moment has come to erect the circular wall with the two hundred and thirty-one letter gates.

Löw positions himself at the head, Isaac at the feet—and after looking into each other's eyes, like a singer and his accompanist, they start walking slowly around the image, in the opposite direction to the Christian clock, while the thousands of combinations according to the rules of Rabbi Elazar come softly and rapidly from their mouths, three per second, all the vocalizations, each time linked to a letter of the tetragrammaton—the first of the twenty-one series always beginning with the glottal stop of the aleph:

" 'aBaJ, 'eBaJ, 'iBaJ, 'oBaJ, 'uBaJ, 'aBeJ, 'eBeJ, 'iBeJ, 'oBeJ, 'uBeJ, 'aBiJ, 'eBiJ, 'iBiJ, 'oBiJ, 'uBiJ, 'aBoJ, 'eBoJ, 'iBoJ, 'oBoJ, 'uBoJ, 'aBuJ, 'eBuJ, 'iBuJ, 'oBuJ, 'uBuJ, 'aBaH, 'eBaH, 'iBaH, 'oBaH, 'uBaH, 'aBeH, 'eBeH, 'iBeH, 'oBeH, 'uBeH, 'aBiH, 'eBiH, 'iBiH, 'oBiH, 'uBiH, 'aBoH, 'eBoH, 'iBoH, 'oBoH, 'uBoH, 'aBuH, 'eBuH, 'iBuH, 'oBuH, 'uBuH, 'aBaV . . ."—and all the other combinations of the A and the B with the V of JHVH, followed by the second gate: all aspects of the A and the G, the third letter of the alephbeth, again with the letters of the tetragrammaton and then all of A with the H, the third gate . . . as they mutter they turn their circles, their eyes constantly focused on the figure, while their feet form a gradually deepening channel around it.

But after five minutes something unexpected happens. When they have reached the eleventh gate, Isaac suddenly sinks up to his waist into the clay. He tries to raise himself by pushing, but cannot. He looks helplessly up at his father-in-law, who has also stopped reciting and observes him, shaking his head.

"What was the last thing you said?" he asks sternly.

Isaac bows his head in embarrassment.

" 'aLaJ," he whispers.

"Just as I thought, you idiot. First you give me a lecture on my talent, and then you do the most stupid thing of all. Surely you know as well as I do that if a letter is missed out when copying the Torah it can mean the end of the world! What kind of a rabbi are you? 'aL—or 'eL as we say nowadays—is the oldest name of God, and you can't conjugate God with God, how many times have we talked about that? So you must immediately continue with 'aMaMaj of the twelfth gate.' "

"I was getting a bit sleepy."

"Already! We've just begun! Anyway, I'd better quickly cancel it out."

Löw takes a couple of Christian clockwise steps, saying in reverse order:

" 'aLaJ, 'uKuH, 'oKuH . . ."

Immediately Isaac rises vertically out of the earth, which closes under his feet. His white mantle is not soiled.

After this incident they take up the thread again and continue the strict pattern without further mistakes. Gradually the uninterrupted speaking and turning puts them into a trance, which means that they no longer feel their exhaustion—and as they approach the end they perform strange ecstatic little leaps with increasing frequency. An hour and a half after they had begun they complete the supernatural program with the conclusion of the two hundred and thirty-first gate:

". . . SHiTuV, SHoTuV, SHuTuV."

Suddenly exhausted and giddy they sink to the ground.

When Löw comes back to his senses after a minute, he feels as if he's been in a dreamless sleep for hours. At the end of his strength he looks up. Nothing has changed. The clay figure lies motionless on the bank. It's become cooler, the moon and the two planets are on their way to the western horizon. He sighs deeply and makes a dismissive gesture with his hand. In fact he'd never really believed in it. That crazy Cabalistic combination of extreme precision and extreme phantasmagoria is wonderful, but that's all you can say about it, because apart from that it's nonsense, attributed by gullible people to mystical miracle-working rabbis. So fortunately the death of Jacob doesn't have anything to do with the ritual either. It remains strange, of course, that Isaac should suddenly have sunk into the mud just now and then risen from it again, but that was obviously an incident; apart from that they are all delusions. Tomorrow he'll go to the emperor and explain to him that it's now been proven, and that Christianity therefore has no need to harbor irrational aggressive fears of Jewry because of its supposed magical links with the Devil.

Isaac squats down and puts the back of his hand against the cheek of the sculpture.

"It's getting warm," he says.

Löw tenses. For a moment, a minute, two minutes, he looks at the statue, but nothing changes. Then he stretches out his arm and in turn feels the cheek—with a cry he pulls back his hand and puts his fingers in his mouth: he's burned himself. From then on everything goes faster and faster. The shape starts glowing gently, the glow becomes dark red, bright red, passes into white, so that they can feel the heat on their faces and have to take a step backward. A little later, as if the process is extinguishing itself, clouds of steam with the smell of fresh bread and old blood begin to escape all up and down it. The steam climbs vertically upward, forming a white column, higher than the bridge, where the two sentries are leaning over the balustrade thinking that they're dreaming. Gradually the column becomes thinner, more transparent—and suddenly the steam has disappeared.

Then for a number of seconds the only movement is a falling star.

"I can't believe my eyes," murmurs Löw into his beard.

A living being is lying there. The clay has become flesh, the chest goes up and down breathing calmly, like that of a person asleep. On the forehead three letters have appeared, which he didn't put there: A M T—the first and last letter of the aleph-beth, with the capital M between them.

" 'eMeT,' " he reads. "Truth."

"We've done it!" rejoices Isaac. "We've done it!"

But with an imperious movement of his hand Löw silences him and bends forward a little. Something's not right. Something's gone wrong. The creature has unmistakable female breasts, not large but with a clear curvature. He quickly looks a little lower: the penis has not turned into flesh, but has become baked clay. He carefully takes hold of the organ and lifts it up. It immediately comes free. He looks at Isaac reproachfully.

"Schlemiel!" With a sweep of his hand he hurls the terra-cotta penis into the Moldau. "Now I understand. After your stupid mistake with 'eL came 'aM, that is 'mother.' That obviously caused a short circuit. So we haven't imitated the creation of Adam, but that of Lilith."

"I . . ." Isaac starts to say, but Löw immediately interrupts him:

"Leave it. We could reverse the procedure and start again, but I'm too exhausted. Perhaps it's even better like that. The emperor is crazy about curiosities, perhaps he'll appreciate a female golem even more."

His thoughts are racing. He knows that the word of princes is not worth much, but the promise of the emperor that nothing will happen to the Jews of Prague for the time being if he is given a golem may perhaps hold good. As far as he is concerned, he's now certain that his scores of learned treatises will now pale beside what he has achieved tonight like the light of the stars beside that of the moon. So be it. Obviously thought cannot compete with action.

"Right," he says and thinks for a moment. "So this is not Jossile, but . . . Mensjele Golem." He stretches his back, focuses his eyes on the sleeping face, and says, raising his voice, "Mensjele!"

A shudder goes through the body with no navel, she swallows, her Adam's apple goes up and down for a moment, then she opens her eyes. Löw has never seen such a look. It's as though he's looking into a pitch-black cellar. Isaac can't take his eyes off the slim, boyish body, which was modeled after his own.

"Get up!" says Löw in an imperious tone.

The bald young woman gets up and continues staring at him. He points to the bundle of clothes.

"Get dressed!"

She obviously doesn't need to learn how to do it. A little later a synagogue servant in a long black coat with black stockings is standing there; the black cap covering the three letters on her forehead.

"Come with us!"

They climb the wooden steps and in the sentry box Löw sees the two soldiers, kneeling, their hands folded, looking up at a crucifix and mumbling by the light of a candle.

The moon, having grown ever larger and redder, has set and has returned the black sky to the stars. As they walk through the sleeping ghetto, with Mensjele between her two fathers, they do not speak; it's as though the speechlessness of the golem has infected them. Groaning, Löw struggles on. He may have reached the age of the very strong today, but never before has he felt so tired. When they reach his house, the dawn begins coloring the eastern sky.

"What a sight you two look!" cries Perl in the doorway. "Who is that servant with no beard?"

"This is Mensjele Golem, Perl. We did it. Shortly I'm going to present her at the castle, it's too early for the moment. Make something to drink for us, and we'll wait here until about nine o'clock."

"She's not coming into my house! No golem in my house! Go and wait somewhere else with that monster."

Perl will not be appeased. Löw suggests going to the *schul*, but stuttering a little and rather nervously Isaac says:

"She can come with me, can't she? I've got an empty nursery. And you can sleep for a couple of hours, you need it."

"Good idea," says Löw and to Mensjele: "Obey Isaac until I come and fetch you!"

She nods and continues to look at him with her dark, frightening eyes. It suddenly strikes him that she doesn't blink.

Löw dreams that he's in an iron wagon which is rolling down a hill, but then he sees that he's riding by the side of the river, although there is no horse hitched to the cart . . .

"Jehudah! Jehudah!"

He looks up in alarm and is looking into the bewildered face of Perl.

"What's wrong?"

"Get up right away! Something terrible seems to have happened! To Isaac!"

He slips his boots on in a hurry and runs outside. The whole ghetto is in turmoil. The morning sunlight is shining in the alleyways, hundreds of people are running in the direction of Isaac's house. There he has to force his way through the screaming throng to get to the door. A policeman stops him.

"What's going on?"

"Rabbi ha-Kohen has been murdered by a crazed servant. He's still inside."

"Let me through!"

"Are you sure you want to see it, Maharal?"

"Let me through, I say!"

"But for heaven's sake be careful."

In the bakery and the small living room there is turmoil and screaming too. In a couple of strides he has reached the door of the nursery, where he halts on the threshold. Isaac has been slaughtered. In an impossible, twisted attitude, as if his legs were attached to his trunk back to front, his almost naked corpse is lying half on the bed, half among the toys on the ground, covered with large black flies. Pieces have been cut or torn from his body everywhere, blood is smeared on the walls, even on the low ceiling. In a corner stands Mensjele, a long pointed knife in her hands; her face, her coat, everything splattered with blood. Kept at a distance by the look in her eyes, no one dares to approach her. Then Löw hears someone cocking a pistol next to him. He pushes the barrel downwards and says:

"Mensjele! Give me that knife!"

Openmouthed and with bated breath everyone watches as she slowly walks toward him. Still looking at him, she hands him the bloody knife.

"Take your cap off!" When her bald skull becomes visible, with the letters A M T on the forehead, a sigh goes through the rooms:

"'eMeT . . ."

Löw puts the tip of the knife on the aleph and looks deep into the night of her eyes. It's as though he remembers something from long, long ago, from before his birth . . . A sob escapes from his breast, and with a rapid movement he flips the aleph away, so that the word "truth" changes to "death" . . . *MeT.* At the same instant her eyes grow dull, her face begins to crumble, the skull too becomes grainy, the cap falls from her hands, and a little while later the whole body collapses with a rustle, leaving nothing except a pile of clothes and dried mud at Löw's feet.

He throws the knife onto the heap and turns around.

"Get someone to fetch a flour sack from the bakery."

No one else can say a word. The buzzing of the flies is all that is heard. When he has been given the sack, he kneels down and scoops everything into it with his hands. The crumbled clay, the stockings, the underwear, everything is still warm. He takes the sack over his shoulder and goes outside, where the news has already spread. Silently the crowd makes way for him as he approaches, bent under his load.

As he walks sweating through the deathly silent, sun-drenched ghetto to the Altneuschul, he wonders what could have happened. Did Isaac make a pass at the golem? She underneath, he on top? Or had he himself made his second cardinal error by modeling her body after that of Isaac? Couldn't she accept that because as a result she'd become a sort of second Eve rather than a second Lilith? No one will ever know. And imagine if Mensjele had been completed a couple of hours later and he'd delivered her immediately to the emperor, whereupon she had perhaps murdered the emperor—what would have happened then? Then all the Jews in the Holy Roman Empire and even beyond would have been exterminated down to the last woman and the last child. No, he must go straight to the emperor in a little while and tell him that a Jew died in his place, two in fact, and that he, Löw himself, saved his life by canceling out the golem. Perhaps that awareness will motivate him even more to keep his promise to the Jews of Prague.

Together with Abraham he lugs the sack up the narrow attic steps of the Altneuschul. The servant opens a small garret, where old chairs and cushions are stored. After he's cleared it, Löw places the sack in the middle of the wooden floor. He locks the door, puts the key in his pocket, and says, "Not a living soul must ever come up to this attic again. The staircase must be demolished."

VICTOR WERKER

THE VISION SINKS from view, it disappears like an iceberg that has broken free of the polar ice cap and drifts south, melting as it goes. The white ice in the blue ocean (my blue screen, the white letters on it), the monster as large as an alp, of which finally only a tiny lump remains, no greater than a mammoth's tooth. Perhaps a small pale girl looks at it over the railing of the ship taking her to Southampton, in June 1912. What she can no longer see is the last, transparent sliver of freshwater ice, as small as a nail clipping—until that also has disappeared, until nothing is left of the glacier that two months earlier tore open the *Titanic*. Where was I? Someone was startled by the bell: Victor Werker.

Victor Werker was fathered at the end of November 1951, on a stormy Saturday evening in Amsterdam by a major on a portrait painter. Since the father-to-be had himself come into the world in 1917, he had been fathered in his turn during the Battle of Verdun; perhaps that explains why, coming from a family of stockbrokers, he became a professional soldier. During the five-day war in May 1940 he fought the Germans as a second lieutenant, in the occupation joined a right-wing, monarchist resistance group, found his way into a series of concentration camps, rejoined the army after the war, worked for the military government as a first lieutenant, after which, from 1947 to 1949, he took part as a captain in the punitive colonial expeditions in Indonesia. After returning from—yet another—lost war, missing an eye, the tall, slim, muchly decorated Major Ferdinand Werker attended the Military Staff College, his hair always combed sideways above his stern face in a parting as immaculate as the path of a cannonball. In 1950 he married Gretta Rector, ten years his junior, and a few days after their wedding the war in Korea broke out, for which, believe it or not, he had volunteered; his wife announced that if he went she would immediately seek a divorce. The fact that he had not chosen someone from his own milieu but a confident young woman from left-wing circles, the daughter of the Trotskyist picture-frame maker by whom he'd been nursed in the typhus barrack in Dachau, had led to some raising of eyebrows among his colleagues. Undoubtedly he was general material, only thirty-three years old and already so much experience—but that marriage indicated that he couldn't be entirely identified with the war horse that he represented, and moreover, the picture-framer was a security risk; altogether it didn't augur well for his future military career. Of course he knew that himself perfectly well, but it left him cold. They must simply take him as he was. What had attracted Ferdinand and Gretta in each other was precisely the fact that they had nothing in common—although that was therefore what they had in common.

But in an erotic sense too they had little in common. Sex didn't mean much more to Werker than eating or drinking, he only felt really at home in a man's world, which included not only the army or resistance groups, but even concentration camps.

Once a week was enough for him, but Gretta preferred once a day. That occasionally led to the embarrassing scenes that everyone is familiar with and that I therefore need not describe—but those kinds of scenes, which touch the core of life, contain a critical dose of fissionable material and they can lead to the complete destruction of the relationship, even to murder and mayhem. Attempts to seduce him were without result; it only happened when he himself felt like it, in the middle of the night, for example, before she was properly awake. After breakfast, when he'd gone to work, Gretta would then crawl into the still-warm bed and satisfy herself—but after just a few months those satisfactions no longer satisfied her, and she couldn't resign herself to the prospect of this continuing for the rest of her life. Because she realized that the conflict was insoluble, and nevertheless didn't want to lose her Ferdinand, and didn't want to take a lover, she decided that she must therefore have a child. That would change the whole situation. She didn't know if Ferdinand wanted a child, they'd never talked about it, and it seemed most sensible to leave it like that. If he'd once said that he didn't feel like it at all, at least not for the present, then the topic would be dismissed. Before he came, he was in the habit of always asking whether he had to be careful: that in itself, of course, implied a negative judgment.

From then onward she always said no whenever he asked if he should be careful, even if he ought to be careful; but the frequency of four times a month was obviously too low for a quick accidental bull's-eye. After six months, in which to her disappointment she'd repeatedly had her period, she went to the office of the Malthusian Federation. In a small consulting room, with a display of books and brochures, two cups of tea on the table, and a dish of biscuits, a skinny lady with a gray bun and an obviously home-knitted sweater explained the Ogiono-Knaus calendar method. To start with she must note down very carefully for a year the first day of her period. That wasn't a problem, because Gretta did that anyway; the calendars at the front of her diaries showed the vertical row of crosses every month. Fine, her cycle could be derived from that, fluctuating , for example, between twenty-five and thirty days. In view of the fact that ovulation always took place between the sixteenth and the eleventh day before the following menstruation, and because an egg remained fertile for at most eight hours, and because spermatozoa remained fertile for at most three days, it could be precisely calculated when a woman was fertile and when she must therefore refrain from sexual intercourse. The first infertile period consisted of the shortest cycle minus nineteen days, then followed the conception time, which consisted of nine days plus one day for each day's difference between the shortest and the longest cycle, and the second infertile period consisted of the first ten days of the longest cycle. In brief, said the Malthus lady, if this information were applied the chance of pregnancy was virtually nil.

"But getting pregnant is exactly what I want," said Gretta.

"Oh, then I misunderstood you, that changes things. Or really not at all. But perhaps the temperature method might be more suitable for you."

On Saturday, November 10 Gretta started her period. When it had finished on Friday, November 16, in accordance with the instructions of Mrs. Malthus, she began taking her temperature each morning before she got up; because there was no need for Ferdinand to notice, she hid the thermometer under the mattress. When he'd been to the toilet and was putting on water for coffee in the kitchen, she quickly inserted it in her backside. On the last page of her diary she noted the results:

Sat 11-17	36.6°
Sun 11-18	36.7°
Mon 11-19	36.7°
Tue 11-20	36.6°
Wed 11-21	36.7°
Thu 11-22	36.6°
Fri 11-23	36.4°

The drop on that Friday, entirely according to predictions, was the "fall" in her core temperature. The following day ovulation should now start, the *release of the egg* as Mrs. Malthus had called it.

"Nice term."

"That's simply what it's called, you mustn't read anything more into it."

Sat 11-24   37.1°

It was right! She was there! The moment that she twisted the hair-fine, almost invisible column of mercury and made it jump into a silver ribbon that pointed above 37° it was as if she could feel the ejected egg her in her Fallopian tube. What next? Right away? But Werker had already got up and was reading the morning paper in the bay window; she wouldn't be able to persuade him to come back to bed. So it must happen this evening at all costs. If it was too late by then, then she would make sure she fixed it on the day of the fall next time. She decided to bring up the heavy artillery in order to subdue her major.

The storm blew directly against the windows of their grand upstairs flat in the city center that evening, the curtains were hanging diagonally into the room, as they do in a quickly climbing aircraft; behind them the rain clattered against the windows. While Major Werker sat reading the evening paper under a table lamp after dinner (in Korea the negotiators had agreed the demarcation line), Gretta put on a record of Georges Brassens. She took a bottle of wine from the rack and went over to her husband with it.

"Those eternal papers of yours the whole time," she said and with a flourish pulled the paper from his hands. "This evening let's let the world go hang for once."

"Hey, I say!" he said, his hands suddenly empty and helpless in the air. He looked at her in irritation, while the gaze of his glass right eye brushed past her and all the while seemed to be absorbed in reflections on the mystical visions of St. Teresa of Avila. But when he saw the open, impudent smile on her strong, somewhat asymmetrical face, the look in his own eyes changed and he didn't grab the paper back. She had obviously put up her thick dark blond hair with a couple of cursory movements; here and there it had come loose.

> *Partir, c'est mourir un peu*
> *À la guerre!*
> *À la guerre!*

She gave him the wine and a corkscrew, held the paper up, and asked:

"Did you know that you can easily tear a vertical strip from a paper from top to bottom, but that you can't do it from left to right?"

There was her technical tic again. With the bottle between his knees, the corkscrew in the cork, he watched her demonstration. And you, you look meanwhile to see what our officer looks like at home: blazer, checked shirt with a tight collar, regimental tie, cord trousers the color of wet sand, Bordeaux red brogues, most items still from before the war—but with her there's no sign of the Anglophile civilian uniform of the better-off circles. No silk scarf, no pearl necklace, no pleated skirt, but a homemade wide dress of bleached linen, which came down to her ankles and which just like the curtains at present, billowed out a little in front—which in this instance was caused by her large breasts, which always evoked the word "bosom" in him.

When the cork flew out of the bottle with a pop, she knelt down and folded the strip of newspaper lengthways a couple of times, pulled open the curtains, and began filling the chinks in the windows.

"This will save us a hundred guilders on oil," she said.

Valpollicella 1947. He poured two glasses, took off his blazer, and sat down next to her on the floor, where according to her instructions he tore new strips from the newspaper and handed them to her. She had got onto a chair, so that he could see her thin legs through the long split in her skirt. Those legs didn't match her breasts, but that was precisely what titillated him. Perhaps precisely because he wasn't a woman's man a woman had to have something physically illogical about her for him. Models and Venuses of Willendorf, whose breasts and legs were in complete harmony, might be exceptional people; as far as he was concerned, sexually they left him cold. And as for aesthetics—not too thin, not too fat, everything beautiful and perfect—his erotic preferences had even less to do with that than with logic.

Before he closed the curtains, he looked outside for a moment. Beneath the black sky the rain rushed across the light of the lamps, which was reflected on the wet cobbles; in the small, irregular square a couple of people were fighting with their umbrellas and disappeared jumping backward and forward in the winding streets. The houses on the other side were lower, so that in the distance, across the roofs and past the dome of the Basilica, he could see the garland of the bridge over the Amstel. They would probably have to be careful there now, to avoid being blown into the water. With a feeling of satisfaction he closed the curtains and turned round.

Gretta had nestled in a corner of the sofa with her knees raised and was looking at him from below, warming her glass of wine with both hands. Her skirt had been pulled up, the split had opened from behind—because she wasn't wearing panties, he was looking straight into the shadowy cave of her crotch. His left eye widened for a moment. Was it an accident? Design? He felt he shouldn't say anything about it—excitement swept over him like a dike bursting, more intense than he had ever known.

That woman there in the quiet, protected world of the room, his wife, he alone with her . . .

Je vous salue, Marie

With trembling hands he began loosening his tie, that dark blue regimental tie with the oblique stripes and a motif of coat-of-arms, he slowly went over to her, with a stiffness in his gait that was now no longer military in nature. When he sat down next to her, she placed a large strong hand on his thigh, the tip of her little finger not quite, or just, touching his erection; he put her glass on the ground, pressed his mouth to hers, laid a hand on her breast, and without his having made a deliberate decision his other hand wandered in the dark wood between her legs, which opened like the gates of a sluice. This suddenly turned out to contain a tropical swamp, such as he had seen in Sumatra and into which he now first of all sank with his consciousness; his good eye rolled upward and at that moment she took full hold of his penis, as one grabs a hammer. While her fingers sought the tip of his penis, he closed his eyes with a groan, while her smile did not fade—not yet. But suddenly it did fade after all, she shook his organ vigorously for a moment, and her face changed from one instant to the next into that of someone in unbearable pain; she pushed him away, pulled her skirt up to her waist, lay back full length, and with her middle finger began playing with herself. That sight was too much for Major Werker. He stood up shaking, kicking over her glass of wine, but whereas on other occasions he was ready to have an argument about an unemptied ashtray, now he didn't give a damn. With trembling fingers he tried to prize open his shoes, but couldn't: Because the shoelaces were old and too smooth he made a double knot in them, which was difficult to disentangle; completely out of character he put the tip of one shoe against the heel of the other and kicked them off. Shirt off, trousers off, pants off, and naked—that is, with only his socks on—he sat down opposite her on the arm of the sofa like a cat, his eyes focused on the things that she was doing with herself, yanking his penis as he once had in his boy's bed. How marvelous! But then something else new happened. She opened her eyes, stopped what she was doing and looked at him. Then she raised her right hand and she beckoned him with her forefinger, like a schoolteacher beckoning a little boy to come up to the blackboard. His place was to obey—but as an officer Werker had as little problem with that as with giving orders. He came forward and in the same movement she guided him into her, bringing her legs together and rubbing herself with redoubled fury. In order to give her room for this, he put his hands next to her on the sofa and pushed his sweaty upper body upward a little. Her face now really had the expression of an ecstatic saint; her breathing had almost stopped. In extreme effort her eyes had squeezed tight shut, her shoulders hunched, her face turned to the side, and a high, faint sound began to escape, like a white thread, from her pouting lips. Saliva from his own mouth dripped onto her cheek, and he needed all his strength not to come himself; he wanted to see it through to the end. Without moving any more, with his arm muscles trembling, with the long, crisscross scars on his back as souvenirs from Germany, he saw how she was swirled away into an orgiastic chaos, from which she began screaming louder and louder; one wave after another swept over her, one sometimes less intense than the previous one, then more intense, three times, seven times, twelve times . . . then it was suddenly over and the noise died away. But she hadn't forgotten him. She turned her head to the side, a little later put a hand on his bottom, with the other grasped his scrotum and began kneading it rhythmically, whereupon Werker collapsed onto his elbows, onto her soft bosom, and after a few seconds was in turn caught up in the surf.

"Must I be careful?" he groaned.

"No, go ahead."

With a feeling as if his soul were being milked, he suddenly thumped the cushion with all his force, shot up, gave a loud cry with his head thrown back, and began to roar words in a language from another world:

"Jachin! Joach! Schetja! Omfa!"

His hands began fluttering, it was as if he were flying vertically into the heavens like a lark, stayed there, flapping its wings for a moment, and then fell back like a stone into her. True, he hadn't had twelve, but he had had three or four orgasms one after the other—exhausted, muttering incomprehensible sounds he sank down next to her on the sofa and remained lying where he'd landed.

"It's never been like that before," he gasped.

She laughed.

"Well, let's make a habit of it."

He took her hand in his and for a few moments they lay next to each other with their eyes closed. The lines of the palms of her hands were gray with clay, which couldn't be removed even by brushing. When the telephone rang she got up.

"Be careful," said Werker. "There are slivers of glass."

With one long stride she stepped over them, took the receiver off the hook, and immediately put it down again.

"What are you doing now?" he asked in amazement, twisted his legs off the sofa and sitting up.

"You can see." At that moment Gretta realized that the seed might be dripping out of her now, whereupon she immediately lay flat on the ground.

"There may be something up!" The major had again returned into Ferdinand Werker—or vice versa.

"I'm sure it is, but here *we* are up. You've been mobilized here."

"What a funny way you're lying."

"I suddenly felt faint."

His eye fell on his crotch, where suddenly there was a large lump.

"Look at this," he said in alarm.

She crawled over to him, felt between his legs, and looked up at him.

"Your sack is empty, Ferdinand."

With a feeling of incipient panic he rubbed the lump, whereupon the sack filled again.

"There we are." She laughed.

And a month later:

"Ferdinand? I have a surprise for you. I'm pregnant."

Although it was a fairly obvious possibility, it had never occurred to him that he might one day have a child; he couldn't imagine it. For him babies were like worms in passing prams, which looked as identical as their prams. Children were, as far as boys were concerned, potential conscripts, while the task of girls was to bear children. But now it had happened to him anyway; she'd obviously set out to do it that evening and he was reconciled to it. He'd seen so many people die, and also caused so many people to die, that he might as well add someone to the existing stock. He left the rest of the logistics to Gretta, the fitting out of the nursery, the choice of pram; after all, she was having a child in a higher sense than he was. In return he demanded the right to determine the name of the child, but she didn't grant him that right. Month after month, as her belly became fatter and fatter, they returned to the subject.

"I've got it," he said. "If it's a boy, we'll call him Willem-Alexander."

"What kind of pretentious nonsense is that? It sounds like the name of a crown prince."

"Well, he is one, isn't he?"

"And if it's a girl, I suppose she'll have to be called Beatrix."

"Yes, why not?"

"Rubbish. If it's a boy we'll call him Tano, and if it's a girl she'll be Trophima."

"Over my dead body!"

"You must pay attention to the rhythm and the sound of the

whole name," said Gretta. "If you ask me most people forget that. *Willem-Alexander Werker*—what a mess that is, no one can get that out. That *r* and that *w* after each other, horrible. *Beatrix Werker*—*x w*, I ask you. If the surname begins with a consonant it's nicest if the first name ends in a vowel, and vice versa of course. Pablo Picasso. Albert Einstein. Two vowels in succession isn't nice either."

"Winston Churchill. Anthony Eden."

"They sound awful."

"Wait a moment," he said. "Since Werker starts with a consonant and since in polite Dutch most boys' names simply end in a consonant and most girls' names with a vowel, then according to you it would be better if it turns out to be a girl."

"It won't turn out to be something, it is already something, I can feel it kicking in my tummy, but I don't know yet if it's a boy or a girl."

The lists that Gretta kept on squared paper grew longer and longer, the names of all their friends and acquaintances appeared on it, as well as those of well-known characters, even names from death notices. As the birth approached it was reduced to two lists of ten names from which the choice must definitely be made. These final lists showed the unbridgeable gap between his authoritarian tendencies and her exotic tastes:

BOY

F	*G*
Lodewijk	Wibo
Frederik	Enzio
Reinout	Oebe
Matthijs	Edo
Willem-Alexander	Tano
Rudolf	Beike
Hendrik	Rode

Caspar	Menzo
Pieter	Melle
Diederik	Archibald

GIRL

Elisabeth	Milena
Catharina	Sjoerdje
Marijke	Cissy
Francisca	Anuschka
Beatrix	Trophima
Charlotte	Ludewei
Henriëtte	Naomi
Marjolein	Wanda
Astrid	Astra
Adelheid	Felice

"You know, don't you," asked Werker, "what the pygmies on New Guinea call their children?"

"How am I supposed to know that?"

"Philishave. Ford V8. Isn't that something for your list?"

When they'd still not agreed by the eighth month, he suggested a compromise: If it were a boy, then he would be able to decide the name. If it were a girl, she would.

"And why not the other way around?"

So that also failed—and so did all kinds of complicated exchange systems with a second and third name. But in the ninth month, when the crib had already been prepared and the diapers were lying there ready, Gretta came up with a new proposal:

"We're not going to decide like this. You know what we'll do? We won't make up any name at all."

"Brilliant idea. We'll ask the baby what its name is, it'll probably know best itself."

"If it's a girl, we'll call it after your mother, and if it's a boy, after my father."

He sighed deeply and said:

"That's it." So the baby would be called Marlene or Victor, after the man who had saved his life in the sick bay in Dachau. "Marlene Werker. Victor Werker. Sounds good. True, it'll be a boy with two consonants, *r w*, but, at any rate it's a kind of alliteration—even slightly nicer than mine."

He put out his hand and struck the palm of hers against it, like farmers at a cattle market. Because for a couple of weeks she'd been too tired to work in her studio, for the first time since he'd known her, her hands were completely clean.

Despite his dubious marriage with the daughter of a Trotskyist, Ferdinand Werker had meanwhile been promoted to colonel and even appointed as a garrison commander. His orders were gradually being obeyed everywhere, except at home. When the appointed day approached, Gretta announced that she didn't want to give birth in a hospital, and against his will she had had her way. Irritated by this insubordination, the senior officer had stretched his back and looked at her sternly with his good eye.

"And what if something goes wrong? In the hospital they've got everything to hand right away."

"Nothing will go wrong. Having a child isn't an illness— quite the opposite, I'd say."

Halfway through August, ten lunar months after their exuberant party, during a heatwave, Victor Werker decided that it was time to move out. The whole night long the baby had been restless in Gretta's tummy; she felt as if she were about to have a period. In the morning a certain regularity began to appear in the contractions, during which it was if she were being torn open by two horses with ropes.

"Ferdinand!" she cried in panic to her husband, who was downstairs at breakfast. "It's begun! You've got to help me!"

A few minutes later he appeared in the bedroom, in khaki uniform, with three rows of ribbons on his chest, the morning paper in his hand, which he was reading.

"Just listen to this," he said, not looking up from the newspaper. "That Sukarno has demanded Western New Guinea, on the celebration of the seventh anniversary of his so-called Republic of Indonesia. The scoundrel won't get away with that."

"Ferdinand, please . . ."

Legs wide apart, her awesome breasts resting on her belly, she sat on the edge of the bed, with the sheet around her shoulders; it was as if the white balloon of her belly would soon slowly rise up and take her with it, tilting and rocking her, and then come to a halt gently bobbing against the ceiling. Her face had opened in a strange, defenseless way, as if it had never been bare before. Some bloody slime dripped from her vagina. It was hot again; the windows were open and from the courtyard came the sacred smell of freshly baked bread, mixed with sweet gusts from the coffee roaster's one street away. During each contraction her upper body moved forward and backward, groaning, as in an Oriental prayer.

This was serious. He sat down next to her, and for half an hour he noted the contractions in the margin of the paper:

7:15:40	⟶	7:16:30
7:19:20	⟶	7:20:20
7:22:45	⟶	7:23:40
7:26:40	⟶	7:27:40
7:33:55	⟶	7:34:42
7:36:44	⟶	7:37:09
7:38:30	⟶	7:39:11
7:42:38	⟶	7:43:40
7:46:08	⟶	7:47:08

"This is it," he said and got up. "About every three minutes a contraction of one minute. I'll call the midwife. What's her name again?"

"Mrs. Bloch."

After Mrs. Bloch had listened to him, she said the child would be arriving today, but not for a while yet; first she was going to have a nice leisurely breakfast, because she'd had a bit of a late night yesterday. Then he called his office; the garrison would simply have to do without him today. The sergeant major, who was on the point of collecting him in the Jeep, saw that the national interest would obviously have to take second place in this case, the Russians probably wouldn't come today.

Werker had not met Mrs. Bloch before; when she appeared at about nine-thirty, he got the shock of his life. A colossal figure, despite the high summer weather, dressed completely in black, almost obscured the light in the doorway, deep black hair, a bright white lock by her left temple, large, strong-willed face, on her upper lip a shadow of a mustache—a woman like a man, who was definitely never intending to become pregnant herself. He wondered in alarm what kind of activities had kept her up so late yesterday. She in turn had also surveyed him quickly from head to toe.

"Well, well," she said. "The father-to-be has dressed for the occasion."

Immediately she filled the whole house with her presence. She washed her hands, listened to the child's heartbeat with a stethoscope, put her fingers into Gretta's vagina without further ado, noted a dilation of an inch and a quarter and a little later had disappeared again, on her way to another birth, not far away. For the first time Werker realized that everywhere in the city children were constantly being born, to replace those who were dying—an unnameable process hidden behind walls, a flywheel with the capacity of the earth orbiting the sun. With louder and louder groans the contractions were now coming every minute, leaving Gretta exhausted each time, like a bundle of dripping seaweed fished up from the sea. If only there were a woman in the house! He dabbed her face with a wet flannel and cooled her with the hair dryer set to cold. Where had Mrs. Bloch got to? Gretta saw his helplessness, but she couldn't do anything to help him. It was as if she consisted of two floors: on the top floor she observed everything that happened around her, on the bottom floor she was solely concerned with regulating and managing the waves of pain which swept over her. Perhaps there was also a cellar floor, where she was present with her child, but she didn't know that.

After a half hour Mrs. Bloch called and inquired how things were going. She wasn't very impressed by Werker's report; the best thing, she said, would be for Mrs. Werker to sit under a lukewarm shower. Werker took off the jacket of his uniform, put a wooden kitchen chair in the shower cubicle, rolled up his sleeves, adjusted the taps, and supported Gretta's colossal figure on its way to the water that was splashing onto the chair. The sight of it reminded her for a moment of a Dadaist "ready made," by Marcel Duchamp, or by Man Ray, with a silly title like *The Hermit Holds Back Niagara, Too*. As another contraction came, she sat astride it, with her arms folded on the back.

"Too hot!" she said, making a warding-off motion toward the showerhead.

He opened the cold-water tap a little more, and held his hand under the water.

"All right like that?"

"Yes."

She put her forehead on her arms. "Now leave me for a bit."

Downstairs was his interrupted breakfast with the half-eaten egg. He took a crunching bite on a slice of toast which had gone cold and hard, went over to the open window, loosened his tie, and lit up a cigarette. The heat was again quivering over the city. In the distance the river had turned into a ribbon of dazzling silver paper; it was as if the city itself were what created the immense blue dome. Gretta's cries, now further amplified by the tiles in the bathroom, reminded him of the torture sessions that he had attended. His whole life might more or less be dominated by death, but he could scarcely endure the pain that she was suffering— even though, in a manner of speaking, it was not negative but positive pain, in the service of life. That was the world of women, and as a man he had no experience of it, although thirty-five years ago he had been his own mother's torturer.

"Ferdinand!"

He leaped up the stairs three steps at a time. Screaming with pain, Gretta was trying to get off the chair.

"What's wrong?"

"The geyser's gone out!"

He quickly turned off the taps, wrapped a bathrobe around her shoulders, and helped her up: her skin was cold, her hair seemed to be wetter than when she came out of the sea in the summer. Back on the edge of the bed she waited for the following contraction, but it didn't come. The process had been disturbed. That gave her a feeling of relief, now she could rest for a bit, but it couldn't stay like that of course: the child had to come out.

"My feet are so cold."

He fetched two bright red woollen socks from the wardrobe, knelt down, and put them on her. Only half an hour later was there another contraction.

"It can't go on like this," said Werker. "If only we could reach Mrs. Bloch. Wouldn't it be better if I called the doctor?"

"Don't make a mountain out of a molehill. It'll all be all right."

The following contraction also half an hour in coming. At a quarter to one Mrs. Bloch finally rang, heard about the cold shower, said, "Fine mess," and a quarter of an hour later she'd again taken possession of the house.

"I could break the waters," she said in an ominous tone, "but I only do that as a last resort. Let's see how things go. I'll be back at about three o'clock. First I've got to help a pair of twins into the world."

Gretta saw that Ferdinand was beginning to get used the groaning and wailing. The contractions now came with a hypnotic regularity, so that she lost the sense of time; as the pain ebbed away after each wave, exhausted and sweating, she looked at him on the edge of the bed, with an exalted look in her eyes. She also saw that half an hour later he had to control himself so as not to laugh when a following contraction appeared; it was so predictable and mechanical, as if she'd turned into a clock.

"If you ask me you're starting to get bored," she said. "Go and do something, you can't help me anyway."

He didn't need telling twice. Obviously he went and worked on a report, because a little later she heard the rattle of his type-writer, interrupted by the harsh bell at the end of a line and the grating jerk with which he pushed back the carriage—but those familiar sounds were suddenly unbearable—like knives scraping across a plate.

"Stop it! Stop it for God's sake!"

After an hour she began getting spasms in her back, which were even more painful. She asked him to push down firmly with both hands in the area of her kidneys; because he couldn't exert any force he took off his shoes and socks, sat behind her with his back to the wall, put his feet against her waist, and pushed as hard as he could. She had to brace herself not to be pushed to the ground, but it helped. In the intervals, when the groaning subsided for a few minutes, she saw him sitting in his new role in the mirror of the wardrobe, as if on a bobsled, dressed in the remnants of his uniform.

"I'm sorry to do this to you, Ferdinand, but you've done even more to me."

"Women have children." He nodded. "Men don't."

She was reminded of an incident from her early childhood, when she was about five, in 1932, and she was going to tell him about it, but was prevented by a new contraction. Afterward she'd forgotten.

She went with her mother to visit her aunt who'd just had a baby. Her aunt was in bed next to the crib with the baby in it.

"Are you ill?" she'd asked.

"Not at all. Why?"

"Why are you lying in bed then?"

She could still see her mother's face, looking down at her.

"Because the stork has pecked Auntie's leg."

She'd immediately pictured the event vividly. The stork flying solemnly in through the window, the baby in its beak, in a kind of sling, just like on the birth card. Her aunt carefully taking the baby out, but obviously still against the will of the stork, which suddenly attacked. Auntie fighting with the stork, flapping wings, a flurry of feathers, Auntie holding the baby behind her back, kicking at the stork, and then suddenly a well-aimed peck from the long beak in her leg. The bird took flight and Auntie, bleeding profusely, had to go to bed—but she had won: She had the baby!

"And how did things go with the twins?" asked Werker as he led Mrs. Bloch to the bedroom in bare feet.

"Badly. Turned out to be triplets."

It took him a couple of seconds to fathom that answer.

"Everyone doing well?"

"Up to now. They're skinny seven-month babies, I hope they'll make it."

On the threshold Mrs. Bloch paused for a moment and nodded in approval at the sight of the exhausted Gretta.

"That's what I like to see."

A little later she felt again, looked up diagonally to the dried flowers on the wardrobe, and said:

"Three and a quarter inches. Has to be a bit more."

Relieved that a woman had taken charge, Werker went to the kitchen, splashed a couple of handfuls of water onto his face, and put the whistling kettle on the gas. After he had put his socks and shoes back on, he took the cube-shaped coffee mill between his knees, turned the reluctant handle, and thought, when it comes down to it, it's not men but women who are the strong sex. Now it was he, a senior officer who was in the kitchen. As he let a thin stream of water pour onto the filter at the stove, the doorbell rang and a second woman appeared: a pretty girl in her early twenties, who introduced herself as Ellie, the obstetric nurse. In every way she was the antithesis of Bloch; blond, frail, dressed in a cream-colored shirtdress. He was going to show her the way to the bedroom, but she said, "I can follow the groans, but you can go on and make some rusks with aniseed comfits."

Rusks with aniseed comfits. They never ate them, but he found them in a cupboard over the worktop, obviously laid in by Gretta. He buttered four rusks and went upstairs with a tray. On the threshold he stopped and surveyed the scene.

"I need to go to the loo," groaned Gretta. She was lying back on the bed, her legs apart, her knees raised, in the form of an M. He saw that she was approaching the limit of her endurance; his big, strong wife had turned into a helpless creature, fished dripping out of the sea.

"You don't need to go to the loo at all," said Mrs. Bloch. "You must press. Come on, press."

Meanwhile, Ellie had rolled in the crib. The contraption had been standing empty in the future nursery for a couple of weeks, more like a relic of a dead person than in expectation of an unborn child; now it was decked out with pillows and sheets like a Christmas tree. Werker put down the tray and sat on the windowsill, with arms folded and legs crossed. He felt totally superfluous; it didn't occur to him that it might have been better to sit down next to Gretta with an arm around her shoulders. While the pushing contractions were now coming every few minutes, he looked at Ellie, who was laying out baby clothes on the chest of drawers. So without his knowing it, Gretta had bought them—clothes for somebody who wasn't there yet, new clothes without an emperor!

Pain, puffing, waiting, listening, pain, words of encouragement, the coffee went cold, the rusks were untouched, and after an hour Mrs. Bloch said:

"It's taking too long. It's four o'clock now. You've been pushing for an hour, it isn't going fast enough. If it goes on like this we'll be still here at eight o'clock."

"No!" screamed Gretta. "I can't take it any more! I'm trying

so hard, I can't take any more! It's hurting so much, for Christ's
sake. Not another four hours!"

Werker's eyes suddenly grew moist. He knelt down beside
her, put a hand to her cheek, and said, "Hold on, Gretta, you
must hold on."

"I can't do it any more! I want to go, for Christ's sake! I'm
going to America! You lot can get on with it yourselves!"

Mrs. Bloch sat up and cast a clinical eye at Gretta.

"Where can I telephone here?"

Werker took her to the living room.

"What's going to happen?"

"I'm going to ring for an ambulance."

When the doorbell rang ten minutes later, the two women
had provisionally dressed Gretta, interrupted by contractions in
which she let herself go completely with screaming, animal-like
thrashings. She'd given up, she scarcely heard any more what
was said to her—but when the two ambulance men appeared in
the room with a stretcher, her technical instinct told her that the
stairs were too steep to be carried down them at an angle of seventy degrees.

"Get that bloody thing out of here! I'll walk!"

A foot at a time, supported by Werker and a paramedic, they
went downstairs, preceded by the paramedic with the stretcher
followed by Mrs. Bloch and Ellie with a bag of clothes. The
moment they got outside, she began screaming so loudly and
piercingly that everyone stopped in dismay, and startled faces
appeared in the windows around about—in all the centuries
that it had existed no such cries had ever resounded in the little square. Nor had Werker ever heard a woman scream like
that, not even in Germany. Who was she? What was screaming
through her? She was quickly laid on the stretcher, strapped in,
and pushed into the ambulance; a little later they were driving
through the winding streets with the siren and flashing lights
on, chasing everything and everyone aside.

And again Gretta managed to cause panic at the right moment. She'd scarcely been wheeled into the central hall of the hospital, where recovering patients in dressing gowns and slippers were drinking coffee and nibbling biscuits with their visitors, when she began bellowing again from a realm that must lie somewhere in the Pleistocene period. Werker, in his messy uniform, without a cap, made a gesture that indicated he couldn't do anything; they went up in a lift, large enough for stretchers and coffins. In the treatment room Gretta and the two women were admitted, but when he tried to follow them he was held back by a graying sister-in-charge.

"You can have a seat in the waiting room there."

"I want to be there," said Werker determinedly.

"I'm sorry, that isn't usual."

Whereupon Werker fixed her with a look which not long ago he'd been wont to glare at recalcitrant village heads in Java. That was sufficient. She took a step aside and let him through.

"I want a cesarean," screamed Gretta. "Get rid of it! For God's sake get rid of it!"

The doctor, a tall, graying lady who looked more like a librarian, flanked by two nurses, looked at her coolly.

"How about using the energy of all that screaming to push, Mrs. Werker."

Obviously she had authority over her. Supported by Mrs. Bloch, Gretta did what she could, but it led to nothing. Werker was sitting on the other side of the bed next to her, he caught something about a "vacuum delivery," his head started spinning, he saw that a catheter was being pushed into Gretta to relieve her bladder, the doctor gave her an injection somewhere near her vulva, and suddenly the real contractions began, so that she no longer cried. To Werker's dismay, a little later a smeared sticky lump of waste without a face appeared between her legs. He stiffened. But a little later, plop, it turned out to be a baby after all; the face was on the other side, gleaming shapelessly like a bank robber with a nylon stocking over its head. When the doctor removed the caul, everyone applauded, and Ellie even began to cheer.

"It's a boy!" said Mrs. Bloch and lay the child on its tummy on Gretta's tummy. As a nurse laid a sheet over him she said: "What a giant."

Werker gave Gretta a kiss on her cheek, which she didn't respond to.

"He's doing poo-poos!" She laughed, all the misery instantly forgotten.

"It is," said the doctor, looking at her watch, "ten past five in the afternoon, August 20, 1952." She said it in a tone as if she wanted to add: ". . . A.D." She took off her gloves and shook Werker's hand.

"I presume that you're the father. Congratulations. What's his name?"

"Victor," stammered Werker. All those months he'd thought that he would have "a" child, but now he suddenly saw that he hadn't had "a" child but *this* child. He'd never wanted to have *a* child, and that hadn't happened.

When a little later the nurse had fastened the umbilical cord with a sky blue clamp, the doctor handed him a pair of scissors with short curved blades.

"Go ahead."

Werker got up and, trembling somewhat, positioned the scissors, carefully looking at what he did, because with his one eye he couldn't see any depth. He had to push down hard, it was as though he were cutting through a tough rubber hose: *crack*.

DEED B

THE SPOKESMAN

the tears of death
the maggots of crystal

Lucebert,
The Flesh Has Become Word

FIFTH DOCUMENT

FIRST COMMUNICATION

UNIVERSITY OF CALIFORNIA, BERKELEY
DEPARTMENT OF BIOLOGY

January 12, 1994

Dearest Clara,
Yes, I know, I promised I wouldn't ring you anymore,
but nothing was agreed about writing. So this mis-
sive doesn't mean I'm breaking my word. And any-
way, this communication is not addressed to you, but
to our little Aurora, who can't read it. It's a copy. Per-
haps it will clarify a few things for you.

Victor

Sunday, January 2. This morning in San Francisco I witnessed
an incident that I can't get out of my mind. Market Street is a
wide, busy thoroughfare that runs diagonally across the rectangular pattern of streets, like Broadway in New York. In front of
an old house, obviously without an elevator, a tall forklift truck

was raising a boy in a wheelchair to the second floor. Next to him stood a black nurse in a grass green uniform. The boy was about ten, one leg had been amputated and he was completely bald, his skin was bluish white, as glassy as a boiled plover's egg. What he emanated was not the air of a pathetic little cancer patient: with the look of a pharaoh he rose as if into another world—while on the wide pavement below him, two huge black lads bounced a ball around. I was rooted to the spot. The scene bored into my soul like a bullet. Was the plan to let him die at home? The feeble boy, those two muscular boys . . . who had the most strength? I can't describe what went on inside me, but at the same moment I knew I wanted to tell you about it, Aurora.

I'm writing this on the campus in Berkeley, on the other side of the bay. The paths and lawns are bathed in the California winter sunshine, in the woods squirrels are tumbling about, you should see it. The administration and lecture buildings and laboratories are white and classical, there's a campanile, a miniature copy of the one in the Piazza San Marco in Venice, and between them there are a number of cabin-like wooden structures, real echoes of the Wild West, in which the faculty clubs are housed. Everything is green and everywhere here on Lower Sproul Plaza there are students hanging around, most of them holding large cardboard containers, from which they're drinking; even when they're whizzing past on roller skates with Walkmans on their heads, they're drinking. Americans are forever drinking; in an American film when someone comes home the first thing he does is pour himself a drink. I sometimes think they're still thirsty from Prohibition; perhaps it's their way of engaging with history. I'm now sitting on a bench in the sun, with my laptop on my lap, and I'm smoking a cigarette. Here that means I'm looked at with greater abhorrence than an AIDS patient, although that illness was more or less invented here—leaving aside African monkeys. What am I saying: abhorrence? Anyone with AIDS here is almost holy, but anyone who smokes is murdering himself and other people. As it happens, I have a theory about this anti-smoking hysteria, which I sometimes put to my students, after which they're quite certain I'm not right in the head. Now they've wiped out the Native Americans, the very last memory of that people must now be erased, namely smoking, their gift to mankind. Because what did they smoke? The pipe of peace. That's why Hitler was so against smoking.

Anyway, life here has its advantages too. The climate, for example. Summer and winter, it's always pleasant weather, never too warm and never too cold. And the fact that virtually everyone in Berkeley is a bit of a genius. I think that there are ten Nobel Prize winners teaching here, but as a student too you have to meet standards that in Holland would create a wave of democratic, egalitarian indignation. There the tension of the chain is adjusted to the weakest link, here to the strongest. In some way the violence of the hinterland also is reflected in this university: the nuclear laboratories, the electronic Valhalla of Silicon Valley. So you'll understand that I'm very pleased to be Regent's Lecturer here for this semester. I'm a completely free agent, I do research in the lab, I give the occasional lecture, and if I need advice I buttonhole some superbrain in shorts.

But most of all, these months far away from Europe are giving me the opportunity to come to terms with myself, and hence with Mummy. However important the work you do may be, if the situation at home is no good, it doesn't help. I'm reminded of a remark of Kierkegaard's on the all-embracing system of Hegel: What good is a palace to you if you yourself live in a shed next door?

So this morning I took the BART to San Francisco—that's what the underground is called here—to wish your grandmother a Happy New Year; yesterday she was with one of her customers in Sausalito. She lives and works in a small apartment in the center of town, not far from Union Square, where the nice shops are and the building by Frank Lloyd Wright, which he subsequently repeated on a larger scale for the Guggenheim Museum in New York. I mention this because the first thing she did when she arrived here sixteen years ago was to walk to that round building, with the upward-spiraling gallery, which if necessary you could ascend on horseback. By the way, I suddenly remember, and I'm sure Mummy does too, because we were there together, that there's also a ramp for riders in the campanile in the Piazza San Marco. God knows, perhaps Sigmund Freud in his unfathomable wisdom so arranged things that my mother's interest in architecture led me to become infatuated with an interior designer, your mother.

You'll notice I'm writing whatever comes into my head, because that's what my mood is like at present. My scientific work is all about precision, down to the letter and the smallest symbol, so that's why I'm allowing myself this kind of nonchalance. Whatever the case, we had arranged to meet in the Saint Francis Hotel and there in that lavish, marble-columned lobby, that American delirium of power and wealth which features in scores of films, she told me something astonishing. I thought I knew more or less everything about my family by now, but I heard something that made my mouth drop open. I've got three brothers! That is, not real brothers, or blood brothers, but something like milk brothers. Since when I was born my mother had too much milk, the midwife asked if she would give the surplus portion to triplets, seven-month babies who were born the same day as me. The result was that your grandfather, a colonel in the army at the time, I think, had to milk your grandmother every day—it's called "expressing," I believe.

What do you think of that? She told me about it entirely without emotion, in fact, simply surprised at my surprise. There she sat, a gray-haired lady of sixty-six, in a wide black gown, with lots of necklaces, rings, and bracelets, as befits a sculptor, her breasts still large and round. She'd simply never thought of telling me—was it so important then? No, not for her perhaps, but for me it was. For all her breadth of interests, particularly in artistic matters, she's never understood this kind of curiosity in me; I haven't got it from my father either, so it's my own muta-tion.

"Why have you never told me before, Mama?"

"Is it something so special then?"

"Of course it is! I'm immediately going to try to trace the triplets. So, they'll be forty-one by now too."

She shrugged her shoulders.

"I would have thought that a scientist like you would have other things on his mind."

"But those children drank the same milk as I did in their first weeks of life, so there must be something in common between us. I say this as a scientist."

"Do what you have to."

"Do you remember what the family was called?"

"Of course not."

"I'll keep you posted anyway."

"It's not necessary. I prefer to think of my grandchild."

It's true, I do what I have to, that's always been my guiding prin-ciple. Today, or tomorrow at the latest I will write a letter to the Registry Office in the Netherlands, explaining the matter and requesting further information; it can't be difficult. Meanwhile, that conversation with my mother has suddenly sent me back to my childhood, about which I'm not used to thinking very much.

And do you know what suddenly strikes me? That my life runs almost exactly parallel with the development of my own research field—at least if I take as my starting point the moment when I learned to speak my first words. From a philosophical point of view there's probably also something to be said for that: Life begins with speaking, just as man distinguishes himself from animals by speaking. I was born in 1952, but my philosophical birth therefore took place in 1953: the crucial year in microbiology. It was then that Watson and Crick constructed their model of the DNA molecule, the famous double helix. Deoxyribonucleic acid, as it's called in full, is an inorganic molecule that acts as an information carrier. It's the essence of all life. At that deepest level there is not only no difference between people, Jews and anti-Semites for example, but not even between human beings and mice and geraniums and AIDS viruses. Every cell nucleus in your body, Aurora, contains the genetic information for the construction of your whole body, from the color of your eyes and the shape of your ears down to the construction of your little heart, a book with a million closely printed pages—that's the equivalent of about five hundred Bibles with three and a half million letters each. And that a hundred trillion times over. A colleague of mine, David Suzuki, once calculated that a complete set of the DNA which has been tangled into an inextricable knot in a human cell nucleus—the so-called genome—would be over seven feet long if you could pull it straight; and that all the DNA from all your cells would have a combined length of a million times the distance from the earth to the moon and back.

By the way, that same James Watson, who subsequently played a decisive role in my life, is also here in Berkeley. I talk to him now and then and each of us has amiably received the other's praises. He doesn't do much himself these days; researchers with more than one crucial discovery to their name are very rare, although there are exceptions like Frederick Sanger, also a biochemist, who received the Nobel Prize twice for chemistry. So I just cling to his example. In any case I'm doing my work on mummies now as if I've never done anything else.

In my philosophical year of birth another remarkable experiment was conducted, with which I'm also closely connected. In the 1940s, provoked by a Soviet scientist, Oparin, there was a debate about the origin of life on earth. His motive of course was—after Darwin—to eliminate God even more definitively.

Everyone agreed that a major role in the origin of life was played by twenty amino acids, the building blocks of proteins, but how had they originated? An impudent student, Stanley Miller, had the kind of brilliant thought that doesn't occur to a sensible person: let's try it out. With the kind of chemical equipment that every inquisitive adolescent has in their attic, he simulated the presumed condition of the earth's atmosphere at the time with hydrogen, methane, ammonia, lightning, et cetera, and he made the sparks fly through his mixture—and what do you think? After just a week he was able to demonstrate the formation of all kinds of essential amino acids. I myself can't complain with my eobiont (after all, even the pope has warned mankind against me), but that blind simplicity of Miller's strikes me with awe.

So that's what my scientific birth horoscope looks like. I *am* modern microbiology, so to speak. And to follow this line through for a moment: In the year 1956, when my mother taught me to read and write—the next step after speaking— Mummy was born.

Thursday, January 4. It's evening. I'm sitting on the balcony of my room, a little way outside the campus. On the other side of the street there's a kind of pizzeria, Panini, which is run by Jeffrey Moussaief Masson. He's a Sanskritist, a good-looking, charming man, who is at loggerheads with the international psychoanalytic movement. He was nominated to become a very senior member of that club; but after he had crawled under Anna Freud's bed in London, so they say, looking for secret letters from her father and what's more had written a rather disillusioning book about him, all psychoanalytic hell let loose. "Panini," by the way, doesn't means rolls, as everyone thinks, but, he told me, is the name of a famous Indian grammarian from the fifth century B.C. It's busy, in the street too the terraces are full, students and professors all mixed up. It is more or less the intellectual navel of the world, which is emphasized even more by the innumerable down-and-out lunatics wandering around, bawling freaks, catatonic zombies on the street corners: it is as if the geniuses have sucked their extra-intellectual powers out of them. The cacophony of the buskers makes the sultry evening even fuller. I could have had a quiet house in a suburb, or the beautiful large room in the Men's Faculty Club, but I prefer to be in the center of things. Outside the door is my own convertible white Cadillac, which I took over from Noam Chomsky, the linguist.

I'll go on for a bit, I like this kind of casual writing. Come to that, I may be a writer manqué. When I was about thirteen I wanted to be a novelist but there was something wrong with that from the very beginning. I wasn't so much interested in literature, because I virtually never read novels or poems, but in writing. Or, more precisely: in deciphering. I could spend hours making and solving rebuses with Granddad, drawing a house and writing next to it: $h = m$. I found a book about the discovery of the Dead Sea Scrolls more exciting than a boys' adventure story. Once I picked up a book on Egyptian hieroglyphics cheap somewhere and for a few months I tried to master them, while other boys were making a revolution at school and in the street. That effort wasn't totally in vain, the study of hieroglyphics, I mean, because if I'm now confronted with an Egyptian text, I know vaguely what to do with it; I know a few hundred of those signs, and that stands me in good stead now. What fascinated me about it, and in fact still does, was that they are ideograms and not abstract geometric letters: there are no spelling rules for them, only aesthetic considerations. But nowadays I'm dealing only with letters—a practically infinite number of letter combinations, and moreover always of the same letters: A, G, T, and C, which refer to the essential building blocks of DNA. But without those four letters there wouldn't, so to speak, have been any Egyptians, or you and I.

In those same years I had a laboratory where I did chemical experiments. I was fascinated by two of them particularly; I repeated them endlessly. One consisted of filling a beaker with a solution of water glass, into which I dropped a crystal of copper sulfate. What you then see is the creation of a slowly growing, advancing blue caterpillar. It's a simple osmotic phenomenon; but what you see is quite different from a simple osmotic phenomenon: a living creature. Of course it isn't, and yet in some way or other it is. It's both a living and an inanimate creature. You'd love it. For the other experiment I never tired of watching, you need sodium thiosulphate—called "hypo" in photography, where the substance is used for fixing. If you make a saturated solution of it in almost boiling water and let it cool everything remains the same. But if then after a couple of hours you drop a single crystal of sodium thiosulphate into it, it starts growing into a long branch, which breaks; each of the pieces continues to grow, break, until the whole beaker is filled with the matte white crystals. I discovered (I was probably not the first to do so), that you can also initiate that strange process by giving a sharp tap on the glass with your nail.

My model of the projection of the fourth dimension also comes to mind now. On a round sheet of paper I drew a right angle: the two dimensions of length and width, which could be regarded as the projection onto the flat surface of three dimensions, with the third dimension perpendicular to the vertex. Next I drew a third line, creating a Y-cross ("Pythagoras's letter"). Then I folded the paper in such a way that the length and width axes became adjacent and formed a single line, so that the paper stood up perpendicular at the vertex: with the third line as the third dimension that is. If, I reasoned, the third-dimension line could also be folded topologically with the two others, a fourth line would rise into the fourth dimension; but since this wasn't possible without creasing the paper, my model was therefore a projection of the fourth dimension in three-dimensional space. Well, more or less. In any case it looked beautiful; the cross section of my model formed a so-called limaçon, also called "Pascal's Snail Line"—a very interesting figure, related to

Möbius' Strip. Anyway, that's enough. I regarded it as a deep secret, which no one must know about.

So that's the kind of boy your father was. Apart from that about that time my life had changed radically for a number of years. In 1960, I was eight, and my parents had separated. I've in fact never understood what things were like between those two, and to tell the truth I don't want to. I could ask my mother now, but I don't; in any case it's doubtful whether I'd get an answer. All she ever said to me is, "The greatest mistake of my life was marrying your father; the second greatest was separating from him." In any case I stayed with my father, which isn't very customary, but we lived in a spacious flat with a view of the Amstel and he could afford to take on a housekeeper, Corry, a delightful Surinamese woman with a formidable backside and black as the night sky; the way in which she spoke Dutch changed the language from a biting Dutch wind into a tropical breeze on a Caribbean island. His military career prospered: I believe he was already a brigadier. I never really got to grips with all those ranks, although he was always writing them down for me on scraps of paper. When I mastered ancient Egyptian, I think he was a major general, and when I did my school examinations in 1969 a lieutenant general and commander of the First Army Corps—whatever that may be. In any case there was no fighting, because being deterred, the Russians backed down.

"My profession," he was fond of saying, "is to prevent my having to practice it."

My mother on the other hand, then not yet forty and herself a portrait painter, had plunged into the artistic world. As the daughter of an anarchist, your great-grandfather that is, life among all those uniforms and officer's wives with pleated skirts and pearl necklaces was obviously not her cup of tea, and she was now having an affair with a scriptwriter called Aldo Tas, who also looked more like an anarchist than a senior officer. In my opinion he was crazy, but I liked him. There was always an incomprehensible smile playing across his deeply lined face, while he constantly hummed and talked to himself. I think he had some sexual trick or other, with which my mother had become infatuated. I never saw him without a hat, a completely dishevelled black rag, greasy and full of holes; he also kept it on indoors, in my mother's studio, where they lived. It was a few streets away, on the first floor of an old warehouse, only reachable via a steep ladder and a trapdoor. I liked going there. During the day someone was usually posing; in the evenings they sat reading, with a bottle of red wine and soft classical music on, he with his hat on, my mother with her black nails. On the modeling stand the head she was working on was packed in plastic, to prevent the clay drying out. She has talent and she's productive, but she's not really creative, she doesn't create a world of her own; she can only use her talent to duplicate the existing world.

What my father did for sex at this time, I have no idea. There was nothing going on with Corry in any case, despite her splendid backside. Perhaps he had an affair with some secretary or other at the Ministry of Defense, or with another kind of lady, somewhere in The Hague, in a flat that he had rented for her; but perhaps not. Probably there was nothing. When he was brought home in the evenings in his dark blue official car I never saw a sign of any dissipation, not so much as a loosened tie.

What was I to study? Egyptology? Spending my life as the curator of the Museum of Antiquities in Leiden, where I regularly hitchhiked to? Laying snippets of papyri on a glass plate in a dusty back room with a pair of tweezers and trying to make head or tail of them? Perhaps doing excavations in Oxyrhynchus? People who don't really know what they want to study usually choose law, but things weren't that serious with me— and the solution came just at the right moment. In 1968, when the revolution had reached its height in Amsterdam and Paris, I was sixteen, and the recently published book *The Double Helix* by James Watson came into my hands, the account of the fabulous discovery he had made in collaboration with Crick.

There was suddenly everything I wanted. Talk of deciphering! Here it wasn't a case of obscure palimpsests from antiquity, but the core of all life, my own included. I'd never read such an exciting book; I didn't understand more than half of it, but that was enough. That superior detective work, the dead ends, the surprises, the tension, the euphoria—all of it in an atmosphere of friendship, but also of intrigue. Obviously you have to do this kind of work in pairs, they themselves constituted something like a double helix. Unfortunately I can't say that of myself and Brock, my collaborator in my own discovery. He wasn't my friend (in fact I have no friends), ultimately he was no more than my technical assistant; because he refused to see that, our collaboration finally degenerated into hate and enmity.

I combined my original loves: I studied chemistry. In the background, it suddenly occurs to me, there was perhaps another factor. Once, when I was about twelve, one hot summer's day, I had incinerated an ant with a magnifying glass. I focused the scorching sunlight on the creature, which curled up into a black ball, and then a thin plume of gray smoke climbed up vertically for a second, as in the sacrifice of Abel; but I felt more like Cain, I gasped for breath, I remember thinking: I can only make up for that death by one day making an ant. You must not break anything that you yourself cannot make—so that applies to your own child.

While I was studying, my father, by this time a general, became the senior soldier in the country, chief of the general staff. He was constantly in conflict with the Minister of Defense because of his political utterances, but in view of his popularity in the armed forces they didn't dare to attack him. That filled me with a certain pride when I read about it in the paper; at home we never talked shop, as he called it. He invariably called politicians "politicos"; he would have functioned very well in a military dictatorship which wasn't too bloodthirsty in nature. But when I had finished my first degree, everything was suddenly over: General One-Eye, the last war veteran, retired, given a send-off with a nice parade and with a deep sigh of relief from the politicos.

His uniforms went into the wardrobe for good, from his macho camouflage suits down to the linen dress uniform in which he always got so hot, his medals disappeared into a shoe box, Corry was dismissed, and he moved into smaller quarters, near the Basilica. After that it was as if he had taken off his identity with his uniform. By the time I'd completed my master's, he'd become a different person: grubby, scruffily dressed, badly shaved, unrecognized, and forgotten.

Wednesday, January 4. I didn't get round to continuing this epistle yesterday. In the afternoon I was busy with a couple of Egyptologists in the lab and in the evening I dined with a Dutch philosopher, a specialist in the field of Indian rituals, who lives in a superb house in Oakland, with a view over the bay. Because he had original ideas, he was driven out of the Netherlands by the academic establishment; he has been teaching for years here at Berkeley. After dinner he suggested visiting a friend of his in San Francisco. I had expected to arrive in a scholar's den crammed with books but what I found was a large, empty light room with nothing in it except two head-high stereo speakers from which *Siegfrieds Tod* thundered. The friend, a young Thai, sat listening in a Buddha position on the tatami and made a perfect equilateral triangle with the speakers. Geometrically speaking there was really no room for us in the space. He scarcely greeted us, just glanced at the vitiligo on my hands and nothing more was said. After three quarters of an hour we got up and drove back in silence across the Bay Bridge.

Anyway, I've never even told Mummy about those things from my early years. I was never very talkative, nor was she for that matter; we both had our work, in the evenings we both sat at our desks, with our backs to each other. By now it probably doesn't interest her in the slightest anymore, for her it's over, while I have the feeling that it never really began. I've got something to say about that, but first I have to get a few other things off my chest.

In 1976 Granny immigrated to America with her Aldo Tas. He had had enough of the Dutch film industry and wanted to try his luck in Hollywood. He wasn't a great success, but they were able to survive on Granny's portraits: She soon had a set of customers from high society who paid well, particularly producers who wouldn't give Tas a chance, but who did want portraits of their children. I saw them regularly; preparing my thesis I first worked for six months in Illinois, in the lab of Carl Woese (the discoverer of the archaea with which my thesis was to deal), and then for a few months at Caltech in Pasadena, near Los Angeles. But two years later, Tas, humming and mumbling all the while, was mugged by a couple of Mexican youths in the street, robbed, and murdered. That may have been provoked by his hat. My mother didn't want to go back to Europe by this time; because she now hated Los Angeles, despite her millionaires from Beverly Hills, she packed up her modeling equipment and moved to San Francisco.

The fact that she wanted to stay in California was connected with the climate—but also with the deterioration in your grandfather's condition. He still lived alone, and as if nothing had happened between 1945 and his retirement, the war obviously suddenly returned: the liquidations, the terrors, the concentration camps. I heard from his downstairs neighbors that sometimes he tramped back and forth through his rooms all night long making strange cries, as if trying to drive away intruders. When I asked him if he was okay, he acted as though he didn't even understand the question. I'd written to my mother about it, perhaps she was frightened that he would become dependent on her again if she went back to the Netherlands.

One day, I, too, became the victim of his traumas. For the first time I had a regular girlfriend, Astrid Rost van Tonningen, who was studying Dutch, a real blond Dutch girl. I mention her surname, because when my father heard it he went berserk.

"Rost Van Tonningen? That rotten traitor! In 1945 they quite rightly threw him over the railings in Scheveningen prison. Is that her father?"

"But Dad, how can that be possible? It's 1978, Astrid's twenty, and her father is a respectable urologist from the provinces."

"Then he's her grandfather, of course!"

"Who knows, I'll ask her. What difference does it make?"

"What difference does it make? It makes all the difference in the world. I don't want my son involved with a family like that. You know as well as I do that Rost van Tonningen's widow is still active with neo-Nazis."

"Yes, Dad, I read the paper too."

"So that fascist widow is her grandmother!"

"Or not. And even if she is, it still doesn't matter. Astrid is a different person from her grandmother."

"In any case, I want to have it thoroughly investigated."

What it boiled down to was that he wanted to involve a private detective agency. I told him I thought it was an idiotic idea, and pretty immoral as well, and that in any case it wouldn't make any difference, but there was no talking to him. I suddenly felt sorry for him; there was obviously more to it, perhaps he'd thrown that Rost over the railings himself, when he was with the military authorities. So he had to do it.

I should have told all this to Astrid at once, but I was embarrassed. A few weeks later I was given a copy of the report, in which it said that the infamous Nazi was indeed some great-uncle once removed by marriage, but that her direct family was entirely blameless. But instead of tearing it up, I left it lying in my room, where she found it. That was the end of our affair.

———

Friday, January 7. Tonight I had a fairly hilarious dream, which I don't want to keep from you. When I woke up I'd forgotten it, but under the shower it came back to me. Traveling through Italy I was in Milan and I needed to go somewhere, to the cathedral I think. I'd never been to Milan and in the hotel the concierge said that I had to turn right into the Via Cavour, and then left down the Corso Vittorio Emanuele, and then cross over obliquely to the Via Garibaldi, and so on. I set off with the map of the city, but it was all wrong. The Via Cavour wasn't right but left, the Corso Vittorio Emanuele was in a completely different part of town, and the Via Garibaldi didn't end in a square with a chalk white statue of Canova, as I'd been told, but at a gigantic, carved column with the statue of a Roman emperor on the top. I suddenly realized that I wasn't holding the map of Milan in my hands, but that of Rome. It was like taking a sip of tea and discovering it's coffee.

I have the feeling that in some way it was an ominous dream. Here in the U.S. for that matter that situation is even more topical, with all those streets which don't have names but numbers. San Francisco is a bit of an exception, but just try getting lost in New York. Apart from Greenwich Village there isn't even a street or avenue with a bend in it. Think of that marvelous curve in Regent's Street in London; you won't find anything like that in the whole of America. If I were a town planner, I would never draw a straight street, because only a curve embraces you like a mother. They understood that better in the Middle Ages. But in an American city you look out of the town in four directions, four points of the compass, and every intersection. Or put the other way round, at every intersection the vast dimensions of this continent rush toward you.

By the way, I'm writing this on the plane. Today I had to go back and forth to Stanford University, where I had an appointment with Cairns-Smith, whose theory I've used for my synthesis. He also asked me how the Brock affair was going. Embarrassing; this will probably pursue me for the rest of my

life. I said that he still hadn't resigned himself to his disappointment, and probably never would now, that I was glad to be rid of
him for a little while in America. I decided to say nothing about
his threats and anonymous telephone calls. Anyway, I have to be
a little careful here in Berkeley. All those fundamentalist Christian movements, which are so against abortion and the murder
of embryonic life, are not very keen either on the creation of life
by anyone else but God.

Saturday, January 8. And after Astrid came Bea. Of course there
were a number of odd ladies in between, but I'm limiting myself
here to my great loves, of whom Mummy is—or was—the
third. You can feel of course that I'll get to her in a moment. Bea
was in her early thirties, that is, a few years older than I was.
Her hair was beginning to turn gray, but that had a genetic reason; at the age of forty her mother was whiter than most people
ever get. She'd been married to a KLM pilot who had died in an
air crash. Since then she believed that she brought everyone bad
luck. Her bright blue eyes had a slight squint, which suited her,
and she warned me against herself. That kind of nonsense
amused me and I said that I would be exceptionally careful.
From her widow's pension she could afford a beautiful flat,
where she cooked almost every evening for me and apart from
that spoiled me with great talent. She had large breasts, perhaps
slightly too thin legs, and a rather rough skin.

   She met my father at my Ph.D. ceremony—I was awarded a
distinction, if I may be so bold. He sat next to her in the front
row of the university hall, looking seedy. While I defended my
thesis (*The Energy Pathway of Methane-Producing Archaea*),
myself immaculate in white tie and tails, I saw him giving me a
strange look, as if he scarcely knew anymore who that young
man was standing there talking about recently discovered uni-
cellular creatures, so-called extremophiles, which could only
live in violently boiling water, at a pressure of 300 atmospheres,

fed on carbon dioxide, nitrogen, and hydrogen, and were killed by oxygen. During the reception they stood talking to each other nonstop in a corner and afterward she said that my father was one of the most interesting people she'd ever met. Well, you get the picture. A few days later we visited him in his neglected flat and she felt that someone should tidy up the home of this lonely man tormented by his past, his suits should be sent to the cleaners, his fridge should be cleaned out, and so on, and so on. How things exactly took their course I don't know, and I don't want to know, but what it came down to was that she swapped me for him. I never talked to her or him about it afterward, but knowing her, I believe that she was responsible for a sexual renaissance in his life. She took him into her house, and that was that. I think that he told her more about himself than he'd ever told anyone else. I've never really minded being the erotic middleman to my own father.

And then he died. That was on November 15, 1982, at the age of sixty-five. Stomach cancer, like Napoleon (perhaps that was why the emperor always stuck his hand in his waistcoat at stomach level). I myself was thirty at the time—and because a child only gets to know his parents from his thirtieth year onward, I never really knew him. It was Bea who closed his eyelids. When his mouth kept dropping open, she stuck his lips together with an impact adhesive. That shut him up for good. I knew that—now that her task had been accomplished—I could get her back; but I want nothing more to do with her. Afterward I met her once in town, almost completely white by now; she was accompanied by her new boyfriend, an orchestral violinist, a fairly gloomy Jewish man. I saw immediately that he was wearing my father's new shoes. A few years later he had died too, of a brain tumor. The last I heard of her was that she lives in Athens, in a cave under the Acropolis.

———

Monday, January 10. I read on the noticeboard in Dwinelle Hall that Slavonic Languages were giving a performance of Karel Čapek's *R.U.R.* I'd vaguely heard of that play; I've always wanted to see it. R.U.R. is the abbreviation of "Rossum's Universal Robots" and it is the first occurrence of the word "robot"; in the program I read that it was dreamed up by his brother Josef, also a writer. It isn't about machine people, but about the production of artificial people of flesh and blood, who threaten mankind with the original "protoplasm." It was first performed in Prague in 1921. The auditorium in the huge labyrinthine building was half filled with pizza-eating and cola-drinking students, their Walkmans pushed scarcely half an inch from their ears. That was probably what struck me most: the contrast between those privileged children in their sunny California and the ancient, misty Prague of three quarters of a century ago. Had they any idea what it was really about? Even Japan is in all kinds of ways closer than Europe here; straight across the Pacific its influence is felt along the whole West Coast with its exotic Japantowns and innumerable sushi bars. On the other hand it's of course true that *R.U.R.* is performed here, while I've never heard of a performance in Europe.

Wednesday, January 12. Half an hour ago, at about five in the morning, there were a couple of light tremors here. I woke up because my alarm clock fell off the bedside table; in my bed I felt the swell as if I were on a ship, tried to grab on to something, but everything was moving, a fairly chilling experience. In the depths of the earth the plates of the San Andreas fault again moved a few meters across each other. After half a minute it was over, except for a couple of small aftershocks. Meanwhile, everywhere in the street there were silent people, in bathing costumes and in slippers. To be on the safe side I rang Granny but she hadn't noticed a thing. I woke her up.

"Nothing can happen to me," she said. "This house is made of wood. You go on back to sleep."

But I couldn't sleep anymore. I took a shower, made coffee, and put on a T-shirt and a pair of jeans. Now I'm sitting writing in front of the open windows; the street is empty again and the eastern sky is taking on those kitschy red colors at which nature excels, like an amateur painter. The rising sun comes from where Mummy is; where she is it's now three in the afternoon. It's as if I can see her sitting at her drawing board. She's working on the conversion of a villa for some rich man or other, who rings up every week because he'd after all like the kitchen at the back, or at the side, or upside down so that she has to keep starting again. Now and then she looks at her watch: two more hours and she can go home. Is someone waiting for her there? Has she already got a new boyfriend? Do *you* know?

Perhaps I'm not completely awake yet, but I regard the small earthquake as a hint to me that I must round off this report. I've reached Mummy, Aurora. After Astrid and Bea, she came into my life three years ago as the third of my great loves. After getting my doctorate in 1979, I'd lived for ten years the privileged researcher's existence in laboratories in Washington, Strasbourg, Cambridge, and Zurich, where the idea for my eobiont developed. Miraculously, I was enabled financially to do the real work in the Netherlands, and the three years I needed for this coincided with our "relationship," the present plastic term for it. The way in which I met her was for me always a sign that she wasn't simply the third one, after which there would be a fourth, and a fifth, but that this was it. It seems that I was wrong about that. Shall I tell you how that meeting took place?

I was returning from a weekend that I'd spent with a German colleague in Neustadt, near Hannover, to whom I'd talked not so much about biology but about the dog-breeding farm that his wife managed. Scores, perhaps hundreds of dogs. "The most beautiful death," said his wife, as she served plum dumplings,

"is to be suffocated under a mountain of a thousand young pup-
pies." Perhaps. Better in any case than under a thousand *Pflau-
menknödel*. There was a provincial station with two open
platforms; in the small waiting room there was a girl behind a
counter selling beer and sausages to the few other passengers
who were there. In order to make the narrow space seem somewhat bigger a large mirror had been fitted on the wall behind
her, and on the opposite wall against which I was sitting on a
wooden bench. My train left at five past twelve; I was too early
and started reading the paper. After about ten minutes I glanced
at the clock that was mounted in the mirror above the counter.
It was five to twelve; I had ten minutes more and went on reading, while trains occasionally arrived and departed. When I
looked up a little later, I saw that it had meanwhile become ten
to twelve. After a few seconds, in which I completely lost my
bearings, I looked more carefully. It wasn't a clock mounted in
the mirror, it was a reflection of the clock that was in fact hanging above my head. I'd missed my train. So I found myself sitting in the following train opposite a woman with an intriguing,
asymmetrical face. She was reading a book and glanced up at
me. How do brains work? Her look reminded me of a line from
Calderón:

> *Wounds and eyes*
> *are mouths that never lie.*

To that almost transcendental misunderstanding I owed not
only Mummy, and subsequently you, but also my flat. I still
have the flat.

The sun has risen and has rolled out its light over Berkeley like
someone throwing a sheet over a bed with an undulating motion. Telegraph Street is coming to life again, the stalls are being

set up, the first customers are going into Cody's Books. I suddenly feel exhausted—not only because I haven't had enough sleep.

I'm going to fax this now. I hope that Mummy reads this sentence too, because then she will have read everything.

SIXTH DOCUMENT

SECOND COMMUNICATION

HOTEL DES BAINS
LIDO DI VENEZIA

June 24, 1994

My Dear Clara,
Here is another copy.

Victor.

Tuesday, June 21. And what do you think? When I came downstairs yesterday with my case on my way to Schiphol airport, and glanced into the letterbox, there was a letter from the Registry Office. The triplets have been located, their names are Albert, Marnix, and Sjoerd Dodemont. To find out where they are now I must refer to the Municipal Archives. Which I will do today.

As you can see from the letter heading, science doesn't drag its humble servants to the worst places on earth. On the oc-

casions that Mummy and I were in Venice, in some little hotel in an alleyway, we sometimes fled the heat and went swimming in the Lido. Then we had to take a jam-packed vaporetto,
or one of the big steamers, the *Aquileia,* or the *Marco Polo,*
also crammed with tourists, and then had to go through the
busy shopping street right across the island to get to the
crowded free beach. And there we always saw this hotel lying
in the sea in its white splendor with its own beach and thought:
You ought to be able to spend a few days there. And now I'm
living there, of course for another conference: *The Origins of
Life in the Universe.* That title is a variation on the book by
Stanley Miller (who is also here) and Leslie Orgel: *The Origins
of Life on the Earth.* By expanding the earth to the universe
we avoid having to listen to fantastic stories according to which
life on earth originates somewhere else in the universe, as was
already maintained in the last century by Svante Arrhenius
and today again by Francis Crick. (That is *his* way of getting
back to work after a great achievement.) That of course simply transfers the problem, because how did it originate *there?*
I myself am convinced for a number of reasons that signifi-
cant life only exists on earth: it wasn't brought here from
somewhere else, but will probably be taken somewhere else
from here.

I'm in a suite over the main entrance, with a huge balcony,
where I'm now writing this. I've lugged the reading lamp outside and next to my computer is a bottle of Pinot Grigio. The
screen is as blue as the sea during the day. Now the sea is dark,
and an illuminated white cruise ship is sailing across it with a
fairy-tale destination, Egypt perhaps. Above the sea, the waxing
moon is standing above a couple of transparent wisps of cloud,
which would have pleased Tiepolo, flanked by a radiant Jupiter.
How can I be so sure of that? Mercury is visible only just after
sunset, Venus, the evening star, a little later, the light is too
bright for Mars, and Saturn is virtually invisible to the naked
eye. So it's Jupiter.

Below, on the terrace, people are having a lot of fun. A rich American is celebrating his dog's birthday, a well-behaved, appallingly ugly cur. I've been told by the concierge that each year he invites as many friends as his dog is old, with tickets from America and rooms in the hotel. I think that the runt is ten today, so he will have to be constantly making new friends. There's obviously a story to it, but I don't know it (if I were a writer, I'd be able to make it up). Yes, Aurora, today I'm in the big world. I heard from the hotel manager that Thomas Mann used to stay in this suite, and here he not only spied on the handsome waiters, who are now already ninety or long since dead (what is the point of it all?), but also wrote *Death in Venice*. It was made into a film, by Visconti, which was shot here. The conference is taking place in the Visconti Room, a high, indescribably magnificent room with Venetian candelabra and Corinthian columns and mirrors and paneling from top to bottom. Apart from that there's an official function every evening: yesterday, the first day, a reception with a buffet by the Mayor of Venice, in the huge Sala del Maggior Consiglio in the Doge's Palace; this evening in the divine Teatro la Fenice two short operas by Menotti, *The Medium* and *The Telephone*. The last trifle particularly was very amusing.

The fact that I've been allotted this elegant suite shows the place that I occupy at present in the international hierarchy. The opening paper was given this afternoon by Manfred Eigen, a German authority from Göttingen, and tomorrow I am the keynote speaker. I have to get used to this myself, because for yourself you always remain that boy in an attic dreaming of great discoveries, although in the meantime he's actually made them. Perhaps you won't believe me, and you'll undoubtedly think your father arrogant, like almost everyone, but I don't have any illusions. What is taken for arrogance in my case is nothing more than an armor against intrusiveness. After all it's no *merit* of mine that I have ideas that no one else has! My merit is at most that I'm not too lazy to take the time and trouble to work them out—and really not even that, because probably that's the legacy of the military discipline of my father, who in turn got it from someone else. I'm inclined to say that no one can ever pride himself on anything—but then I get into difficulties: in that case no one would ever have anything to blame himself with. Perhaps only *other people* can ever praise or acclaim or reproach or punish anyone. Yes, talking of praising, no one here talks about the Nobel Prize. My position, on the threshold of the ultra-elite, of course leads to some envious looks here too, because in science things are no different from in literature or anywhere else— apart from the unfailingly good-humored Eigen that is, because he is already in the Swedish state of grace. Nothing more can touch him.

It's grown quiet downstairs on the terrace, the American dog whose birthday it is has probably crawled under his master's blankets, Jupiter has sunk a long way to the right, it's become a little cooler and I'm alone with the soft lapping of the sea and the irrepressible starry sky, which is no longer paled by the moon. I'd like to give myself over to it completely, but I'm tormented by thoughts of that monster, that Brock. When I think of him, I immediately feel sick; be happy that you've never known him. Once his hair was probably ginger, but it's gone gray in the pepper-and-salt-colored way that ginger hair normally does. There's nothing against that in itself, and no blame attaches to it, but in his case it fills me with revulsion. His pale blue eyes, the freckled skin which is inclined to flake off his expressionless face, it's all equally disgusting. I'm sorry, the bottle of wine is almost empty and I'm letting myself go on a bit. And then that wife of his! That epitome of a professor's wife with her bun and her stiff ankles under her long skirts.

All right, I'll restrain myself. He's of course an exceptionally competent chemist, a professor at a generally well-regarded university—the problem is that he's crazy and capable of anything. In some ways that is the reverse of his aestheticism. He is a follower of Stefan George, a highfalutin German poet and prophet with all kinds of strange views about a new nobility that will liberate mankind. Brock called his son Maximin, after the favorite of George who died young and was supposed to represent the glowing future with his divine beauty and nobility of soul. Even on the few occasions that they had dinner with us, he tried to palm that strange philosophy off on me, and of course he sees himself as a representative of that exalted elite—but if you ask me, in reality he'd most like to murder me. Those anonymous telephone calls, even in the middle of the night, that silence on the other end of the line, who else can that be but him? Who else have I hurt so deeply?

He thinks that my work is really his. According to him I stole it from him and am basking in reflected glory. But that isn't the case. He was my assistant, a very good one, I'm the last person to deny that, but both the original idea and the design of the procedure and the decisive synthesis is down to me and not to him. Initially he scarcely agreed to my project, it seemed to him a figment of the imagination, he was frightened of losing his reputation and I had a great difficulty convincing him. Subsequently he did only what I told him to do: I put him to work, as he in turn put his assistants, who don't lay any claim to any great honor either. On a few occasions he himself didn't realize the significance of his own experiments. The scientific grapevine of course ensured that everyone knew what we were working on, and that met everywhere with the greatest skepticism; as I heard, that even led him to qualify his own work to colleagues. At the end of my article in *Science* I thanked him, but when a day later the matter assumed enormous proportions and the whole world was in an uproar, with reports on all the front pages and all TV news programs, he suddenly wanted to see himself included as co-author. He came and made terrible scenes in the laboratory, one day he even attacked me, so that he had to be pulled off me by students. The fact that he didn't come up with the idea until then proves that he wasn't at all aware of the implications of our work. And the moment my results were repeated and confirmed by others and my face appeared on the cover of magazines like *Time* and *Der Spiegel*, followed by murmurings about the Nobel Prize, he obviously blew a fuse. He was no longer susceptible to reason, and talking to him became rather like reading a newspaper on a windy beach. The sight of the scientific Olympus was obviously more powerful than the Georgean vision of the future kingdom of love. It was replaced by fathomless hatred.

Well, what am I supposed to do about it? It was two years ago, and meanwhile I'm working on completely different things, but it's certain that at this moment he's sitting gnawing at himself, supported by that dreadful wife of his. That I can understand. For a moment he brushed the supreme heights and suddenly it was gone. He's ten years older than I am, such an opportunity will never occur again in his lifetime.

Good night, my child, I'm going to bed. If only you were here. Just now I looked up and saw a satellite coming past above the sea: a star, moving majestically among the other stars in the silence of a dream. Just imagine that it had been five hundred or a thousand years ago, the whole world would have stood on its head!

Wednesday, June 22. This evening we had a glittering buffet with music on the large lawn next to the swimming pool, surrounded by blooming oleanders and bougainvillea. Round, festively decked tables, waiters running back and forth, behind the long tables of food, chefs in tall caps. An illuminated fountain spurted out of the deep blue water, casting a miraculous light on the white bellies of the swallows gliding low overhead, which as they passed by occasionally drank a drop, like old ladies sipping a liqueur. When dusk fell they gave way to small bats, which fluttered through the air like black snippets of burned paper, as if they came from a great fire in the distance. The sky was overcast and later in the evening it started raining gently, but by that time we'd already got to the tiramisu. The scientists fled with glasses and bottles of wine into the hotel, the musicians hastily packed their instruments, and the staff tried to rescue what they could of the food. But I took my laptop from my room, and I'm now sitting in the covered bar of the swimming pool writing, occasionally glancing at the ruin of what's left of the dinner. At this moment the fountain suddenly collapses like the soul of a dying person—it's as if I can still see its afterimage where it no longer is.

My paper was well received this morning, but the discussion centered mainly on the eobiont. I will probably have to resign myself to the fact that this will be the case for the rest of my life. I'm the man of the eobiont, just as Fleming is the man of penicillin and Watson of the DNA molecule. It's better than the fate of Brock, who for the rest of his life will *not* be the man of the eobiont, but the awareness that my future is behind me since my fortieth birthday, and that apart from that I will probably only do laps of honor, is not very cheerful. Let's make the best of it.

Apart from that, when you look at it closely Watson is not just the man of the double helix, for which he was given the Nobel Prize, but also of the unique book that he wrote about that discovery. Not that he would have deserved the Nobel Prize for literature for it—such a double honor *was* the lot of his great rival, Linus Pauling, who not only won the Nobel Prize for chemistry, but also for peace. Although . . . if Watson and Crick had not unveiled the structure of DNA, someone else would have done that within two or three years—Pauling again probably—

but that other person would not have gone on to write that book. The same applies to my eobiont; but if Kafka had not written *The Trial* that novel would have remained unwritten for all eternity. In brief, modesty becomes us.

I'm reminded of that because two months ago Cambridge University Press asked me to write a comprehensible book of about a hundred pages on the eobiont. My original article in *Science* ("Creation of Life from Inorganic Building Blocks") no more than five A4 sides, was very technical; and every publisher knows that with one formula in a book you scare off half your potential readership, with two another quarter, and with three another eighth—in short, work it out for yourself. I agreed. Because it's a good opportunity—reluctantly—to give Brock the recognition that's due to him, perhaps even a little more: It will be a plaster on his wound, so that hopefully he will keep his aggression in check a little. It's just that I couldn't get a clear picture of the form the book should take and to whom I should really address myself. With a novelist, at least a good one, that problem probably doesn't occur; I'm not very well-informed, but I think that he writes his book the way that *book* wants to be written. It's a machine that builds itself and the reader has to make the best of it. Now the odd fact is that my eobiont is actually also a machine that builds itself, it's an organism, but I can't write in the same way about it, because with nonfiction that doesn't work. I had two examples in front of me, the book of my inspirer Cairns-Smith, *Seven Clues to the Origin of Life*, and *Stufen zum Leben* by Eigen, who wrote it in the 1980s—after the publication of their primary articles in specialist journals and their technical scientific works. Apart from that, of course, Jim Watson's *Double Helix*, which over twenty-five years ago determined the course of my scientific life. But the first two, although written for a wider public, are fairly austere, particularly Eigen's book, while the third is mainly a thrilling autobiography, for which I don't have the talent. Apart from that Watson has already done it. I was looking for an intermediate form but I couldn't find it.

But now I know how I must tackle it. My previous letter, when I told you something about DNA, put me on the track: I'm going to address you. I'm going to give you the age of Alice in Wonderland (for that matter, we'll already be in the twenty-first century by then) and it's got to be a series of conversations, for example during a holiday at the Lido di Venezia, by the side of the swimming pool, on the beach, in the town. In Amsterdam I'll show you the large line of humming robots in the laboratory, which, as part of the international Human Genome Project, are mapping the complete human DNA day and night; there I'll introduce you to my three assistants with their flaming eyes, and of course to my colleague, Dr. Barend Brock, an extremely likable man with a delightful wife, without whose scientific help and friendly support I would never have achieved my results. Not that I'm going to start on that book now, under this dripping awning, but perhaps I can get as far as a first, rough draft.

I think that it'll have to consist of two parts. In the first we'll talk about the genetic mechanism, as it is nowadays. We'll talk about the five hundred bibles of your DNA, by which you are completely determined. And that originated when a sperm of mine penetrated an ovum of Mummy's, after which my DNA merged with that of Mummy. Now the Bible is written in a language with twenty-two letters, while the Dutch translation uses twenty-six letters—but if you remember my letter from Berkeley, you know that DNA is written in a language with an alphabet of no more than four letters: A, G, T, C. Those are the initial letters of the names of certain chemical substances. In the two complementary spirals the molecule A is always connected with

T, and G with C. So at an arbitrary position a string looks something like this:

... ACTAATTGGAAAGTTTACGGTGCAGCCAATCTGGGTCAA-
CAAATTTCTTCAATTATGTTGACAGGTGTAGGTCCTACTAAT-
ACTGTACCTATAGCTTTCTGTCCACATATTTCTATGGGTATTTG-
ATCATACTGTCTTACTTTGATAAAACCTCCAATTCCCCCTGA ...

"How can you read that?" I have you ask.

"Well, now it gets a bit complicated. That is, in reality of course it's terribly complicated, as complicated as you yourself are, and it's almost a miracle that the mechanism has been unveiled. But I'll try and tell you simply, like at school when the teacher tells the story of the *Elective Affinities*, a complicated, chemically inspired novel by Goethe."

"Who's Goethe, Daddy?"

"Perhaps we'll have to deal with Goethe another time."

That DNA text is a minute fragment of the information for the structure of one of the countless proteins of which your body is made up, let's say the one for the lenses in your eyes. Between the information and the protein itself there is another stage—or in fact two, but we were going to keep it simple. That step is that the double helix splits open lengthways and the information for one protein is transcribed in a slightly different language, of a slightly different nucleic acid, in which T is replaced by U: U, C, A, G. That leads to the RNA molecule— and only then does the translation into a protein begin. That is done by ribosomes, very tiny creatures that look a little like ladybugs.

"Ladybugs?"

"Yes, I'm a little in love with them. There are tens of thousands in every cell in your body."

"I can feel them tickling."

"In the great DNA book the ribosome now reads one sentence, a gene. But for a sentence you require words, and in this core language they consist solely of three letters. With the replacement of T by U the beginning of the DNA text would look like this:

...ACU AAU UGG AAA GUU UAC GGU GCA CCC AAU CUG GGU...

"Now you should know that proteins consist of linked amino acids. Every word corresponds to a certain amino acid. What the ribosome does is to taste the word with its little head, whereupon it secretes the relevant amino acid with its much larger hind part, jumps rapidly to the next word, and attaches the following amino acid to it—until the protein is ready.

"But how do you know what amino acid is indicated by a particular word? Pay attention. In a language of four letters you can make sixty-four three-letter words—try it."

"That's a lot of puzzling."

"You can also skip it. It is four to the third, that is four times four times four."

At the same time we know that only twenty amino acids are involved. If you convert the four-word language into a twenty-word language that means that there's more than one word for a particular amino acid. What the distribution looks like you can see from the so-called genetic code. Perhaps my publisher will say that that marvelous diagram is too off-putting for a large readership, but I don't think I'm going to allow myself to be persuaded. Of course by now I know that dictionary by heart.

"Phe," "Leu," et cetera, are abbreviations of the names of the amino acids. The three padding words form the punctuation, the full stop at the end of the sentence. Because the correspondence is not one-to-one, the code is called "degenerate." That has two advantages. The first is that every mistake by the ribosome is

Second Letter

		U	C	A	G	
First Letter	U	UUU }Phe UUC UUA }Ileu UUG	UUC UCC }Ser UCA UCG	UAU }Tyr UAC UAA *stop* UAG *stop*	UGU }Cys UGC UGA *stop* UGG Try	U C A G
	C	CUU CUC }Leu CUA CUG	CCU CCC }Pro CCA CCG	CAU }His CAC CAA }Glu CAG	CGU CGC }Arg CGA CGG	U C A G
	A	AAU AUC }Ileu AUA AUG Met	ACU ACC }Thr ACA ACG	AAU }Asn AAC AAA }Lys AAG	AGU }Ser AGC AGA }Aga AGG	U C A G
	G	GUU GUC }Val GUA GUG	GCU GCC }Ala GCA GCG	GAU }Asp GAC GAA }Clu GAG	GGU GGC }Gly GGA GGG	U C A G

Third Letter

not immediately fatal: if it reads UUU instead of UUC, the result is still phenylalanine. The second advantage is that in this way small mutations become possible, which leads to evolution. But a small mistake can also be fatal. The series . . . ACU AAU . . . , which I just showed you, must according to the dictionary result in the protein:

. . . Thr—Asn—Try—Lys—Val—Tyr—Gly—Ala—Ala—Asn— Val—Gly . . .

But if the ribosome omits the A at the beginning then it leads to the words:

. . . CUA AUU GGA AAG UUU ACG GUG CAG CCA AUC UGG U . . .

That corresponds to a completely different protein:

. . . Leu—Ileu—Gly—Lys—Phe—Thr—Val—Glu—Pro—Ileu—Try . . .

That can result in your being born with a cleft palate, or later getting stomach cancer, like your grandfather. You'll now understand that by cutting and pasting those letters we are capable of the craziest things. For example, shortly we'll be able to ensure that someone will be able to smell as keenly as a bloodhound or see as sharply as a buzzard. Or that a child, instead of having ears, will have two chicken wings on its head. If we feel like it we can produce a waxworks of created fabulous creatures, which were previously reserved for fantasy: chimeras, basilisks, unicorns, dragons, griffins, centaurs, sphinxes, everything mankind has ever dreamed of.

"Or a woman with snakes instead of hair!"

"We'll do that."

"Or a mouse with a human ear on its back!"

"I'll make you one tomorrow."

Right, the first part of my book will be about all these things, which you can read about elsewhere too. In the second half I myself will come into focus. The unspeakably complicated genetic mechanism, as it functions today, was not always there: it became what it is through evolution, and even earlier it didn't exist at all. The very first beginning must have been something simple, which originated about five billion years ago from inorganic material—but how? All kinds of routes have been thought up for this, for example, by Eigen and Cairns-Smith and the other guests in the Hotel des Bains, but I don't belong at all in that group. Using the most modern means I have manufactured a primitive organism out of inorganic material, and that's of course something else. (It has nothing to do with cloning either, because that always starts from something that's alive.) Perhaps it happened back then more or less as I did it, perhaps not; in any case I wasn't there to do it. It might be that the first life was created by God on that first Tuesday, but I've demonstrated that basically it can be done without God. The faithful were of course obliged not to believe that and to classify my perverse work under the heading of "hubris."

To tell the truth it's still a mystery to me how I am to explain such a technical undertaking in nontechnical terms. In the first place it was about synthesizing a primitive information carrier, from which DNA may derive—or rather RNA, because that's older. I was put on the track by Alexander Cairns. According to him, life originated from clay. Clay consists of tiny crystals, although you wouldn't say so. With crystals you think of that purple amethyst in Mummy's ring, which I once gave her on her birthday, or of sugar crystals of which I pour a couple of hundred at a time into my cup of tea; but even crystals of a thousandth of a millimeter in diameter—as small as a microbe—are still crystals. His central idea is that crystals can grow in a supersaturated solution; when they break and the pieces go on growing, they in this way reproduce their specific irregularities. (Not even two grains of sand are identical.) He also mentions my favorite experiment with hypo, about which I wrote to you in January—and perhaps that example led to the crystallizing of the supersaturated solution of my own ideas. Perhaps the fact is that the roots of every important achievement reach back to the groundwater. Whatever the case, this extremely primitive, inorganic mechanism, which as we know passes on information, is the very first beginning of DNA. That is, that you and I and Mummy originated from microscopic clay crystals. Quite consistently therefore he called his son Adam.

"Then you really ought to have called me Eve."

"No, Eve didn't originate from clay but from a rib of Adam's. Adam was her mother, you might say. No, Lilith would have been the right name, but I thought that was too creepy. I thought up something else. The name 'eobiont' is derived from the Greek word *heoos*, 'dawn,' from which the Greek goddess Eos also derives. Among the Romans that goddess was called Aurora."

How Alex precisely pictures the process—and that is very precise—you'll have to read for yourself; moving from a beginning in constantly supersaturated cavities in porous sandstone to the development of a primitive protein synthesis, with which real organic life begins. The whole process is a case of *generatio spontanea*, as it's called. Once upon a time people thought that flies and mice originated from fermenting rubbish and frogs from rotting pools; that's not the case, but the idea that something living can only originate from something living isn't right either. According to him, it isn't true either that the origin of life was a unique event that took place those four billion years ago—it's probably still happening constantly in myriad places everywhere on earth, but it doesn't get a chance anymore: the result is now immediately devoured by bacteria, or if it's a little bigger, by insects.

Whatever the case, I'd got it into my head to make a living, reproducing creature from inanimate material. Everyone pronounced me crazy of course, but I didn't pay any attention to that. My model was Friedrich Wöhler, a German chemist and mineralogist, who in 1828 was the first to synthesize an organic compound from inorganic substances: ureum, which is found in your wee-wee. Up to that moment everyone had been convinced that organic substances can only originate by means of a special "life force." He once wrote about this; "I can prepare urea without a kidney. I'm a witness of the great tragedy of science: the murder of a beautiful theory by an ugly fact." Up to the last moment Brock didn't really see anything in my program, but I won't mention that; I will emphasize only his competence and angelic patience.

The eobiont, which I was aiming for, had to be the simplest independent life form possible. The smallest creatures that we know at the moment, belong to the class of extremophile Archaea—I know something about them, because as I told you I did my thesis on those idiots. Their DNA still consists of about six hundred letters, distributed over about five hundred genes, which code for proteins. That's still a three-hundred-page novel, but I was thinking more of a novella, something the size of a virus—but viruses are parasites, which need other cells to reproduce, so that they are creatures of a later date.

Let me try to give you an idea of our procedure with an example from typography. Let's say that **ABC** is inanimate clay and ABC is animate. How can you make ABC from **ABC**? Take a magnifying glass and look closely at the difference between **ABC** and ABC:

$$\textsf{A B C}$$

$$\mathrm{A\ B\ C}$$

ABC consists of bare, sanserif letters with the same undifferentiated thickness everywhere, which is suitable for timetables, telephone books, and street signs, but not for literature. In the years after the First World War, when everything ornamental was condemned as criminal, modernist novels and poems were also set in that type, but it was unpleasant to read. Sanserif letters are like the inelegant mountain-climbing boots with which you slog your way up the slopes, they are static, dead, suitable for consultation, not for reading a living, dynamic story. You need serifs for that. Those little twirls on the letters, but also the varying thickness of the upward and downward strokes, none of that is decoration, like the curlicues on Gothic letters; it is indispensable for a pleasant progress of the eye along the line; they are the skis and the ski poles, with which the reader glides smoothly over the snow of the paper.

What we had to do was, therefore, by means of chemical cutting and pasting, to mix and stir that inorganic **ABC**, and by creating infernal conditions change it into the organic ABC. We had to solve insanely complicated semantic problems, create paradoxical circles in which not only a beginning was necessary for the end, but also the end before the beginning. To be brief (there's nothing else I can do), after an unmentionable quantity of work, a lot of luck, and the availability of the most modern apparatus, after an endless search for the correct type of clay (mullite), taking the wrong turn and finding the way again, one day the champagne corks popped in the laboratory. My little eobiont had seen the light of day: an extremely complex, chemically highly equipped organic clay crystal, with the character of proto-RNA, a sort of primeval ribosome, which produced a couple of short proteins so that my creature, provided with energy by sunlight, reproduced and had a metabolism. "We are the champions!" we sang. The assistants, the laboratory workers—only Brock didn't join in. He still couldn't believe that we'd succeeded in something like the squaring of the circle, but there was no getting away from it. We had borne a living creature from death.

"So actually a kind of Lazarus."

"But without it having lived before."

"But still a miracle!"

No, my dear Aurora, precisely *not* a miracle. On the contrary, I've destroyed miracles with my "ugly fact," to use Wöhler's expression. Just as he, by erasing the boundary between inorganic and organic chemistry, put an end to the beautiful theory of the life force, so I, by erasing the boundary between chemistry and biology, erased a metaphysical boundary. And subsequently of course it has to be denied or played down in all kinds of ways. If my demonic pretension was true, wrote the *Osservatore Romano*, the pope's newspaper, then the basis for the sacred respect for life had been removed, even more definitively than with the sacrilegious practices of abortion and euthanasia; we had entered the tunnel of madness. Even straight murder would have lost its absolute contemptibility. But it wasn't true. My microscopic entity, the so-called eobiont, was in no way a proof of *generatio spontanea;* in essence my handiwork meant not much more than a well-known adolescent experiment with water, glass, and copper sulfate. Those priests in the Vatican didn't know what joy they gave me with that comparison. In another age I would have wound up irrevocably at the stake, but now too there were more dangerous reactions. A religious fanatic tried to set fire to the laboratory where the eobiont is constantly busy reproducing in its incubator. I myself still receive threatening letters. If there is no difference between life and death, I must experience that personally! Weird silent telephone calls in the middle of the night. From all sides, whether or not in the name of God or Allah (God is a god called God), people are spying on me.

"Aren't there any miracles anymore then, Daddy?"

"Yes there is: one. The fact that you and I are here. That something is there. The creation of space and time from nothing. I can't see how that can ever be simulated in a laboratory, because the laboratory is already there at a particular moment."

It's the middle of the night, I'm going to bed. A security man from the hotel has already appeared twice to see if I'm still sitting here. I have let myself be shown the light switch and said that I will cover my own tracks.

If this book comes off, which I am far from certain about, I shall call it *Aurora's Key to Life.*

Thursday, July 23. Last day. Tomorrow we're all going home and returning the hotel to the internal medicine specialist from Turin and the solicitor from Munich and their families. They are out of luck, because in a truly Venetian way the weather has broken totally. Constant thunderclouds come scudding in from the Dolomites in an uninterrupted stream, as though the mountains have risen up in order to unload spectacularly on the border of land and water. I even woke up because of the din, it was like the Battle of Verdun; it was raining lightning flashes, the crashing thunderclaps pounded the Lido and the Venetian flag with the winged lion with its paw on the book, which is on the corner of my balcony, had flapped itself to shreds. The sea, mostly a fairly placid blue pond, had been transformed into a gray, foaming monster; on the deserted pier, otherwise populated by scores of sunbathers, there was now only a red flag waving. There are people who are frightened of storms, but with me it always ignites a kind of anarchistic joy, at each thunderclap I have the urge to cry out "Right!" "Bravo!" Perhaps I got that from your great-grandfather. I decided to play truant and go into town, where I wanted to look up something in the library. At the reception desk I was given a large green umbrella with the name of the hotel on it and a small pack containing a transparent plastic raincoat. I looked like a monstrous jellyfish.

In general the taxi boat from the hotel is filled with lightly and tastefully dressed vacationers of the civilized kind, now there was only an English pop group on board whom I recognized from the breakfast room, five morose lads, dressed from head to toe in black, their tattooed arms bared to the shoulder, their long hair in ponytails. Even now they weren't wearing jackets, so that in my wimpish getup I felt like an old man at forty-one. After the trip through the narrow cross canal we were received into the lagoon. The immense plate of matte glass, on which Venice is wont to float in the distance like a mirage, had been transformed into a pan of gray soup that was boiling over; because of the driving rain the city was not visible. I had to grab hold of something in the forecastle so as not to be thrown off the bench; the two boatswains in their macho white rainproofs under the raised hood that is actually intended to keep the sun off, were finally enjoying their work. For a moment it was as though the storm would pass over but when I went ashore near the Bridge of Sighs it exploded again.

The moored gondolas near the Piazzetta reared like horses, the water streamed across the quay, and under the arcades of the

Doge's Palace hundreds of tourists sheltered in their dreadful clothes, which were designed in hell because the beauty of the city is an eyesore to the Devil; the traders in pigeon-feed, postcards, and tasteless hats had wheeled their barrows under the arcades. I went to Sansovino's imposing Libreria Maciana, sometimes called Petrarch's Library, on the other side, where they also have a computer with Internet access. It had to do with my book, which I was writing to you about yesterday. Both Cairns-Smith and Manfred Eigen gave the chapters of their books literary mottoes, as if literature precedes science. For all we know, that might even be the case; historically it's correct at least: the pre-Socratic philosophers, like Parmenides and Heracleitus, who were more men of letters than men of science. Cairns used the Sherlock Holmes stories by Conan Doyle, Eigen *The Magic Mountain* by Thomas Mann. Even before I knew how to start on my book I toyed with the idea of using the novel *Frankenstein* by Mary Shelley in a similar way. She herself put a quotation from Milton's *Paradise Lost* on the title page:

> *Did I request thee, Maker, from my clay*
> *To mould me man? Did I solicit thee*
> *From darkness to promote me?*

I brought her horror novel with me from home; now and then I read bits of it, also when a paper got a little too dull in the Visconti room, and I marked a couple of appropriate passages. And naturally I was also curious as to *how* Frankenstein had made his creature. This is what the sinister count writes about it in his fictionalized autobiography (it's easier to understand than the Milton):

"I see by your eagerness and the wonder and hope which your eyes express, my friend, that you expect to be informed of the secret with which I am acquainted—that cannot be—listen patiently until the end of my story, and you will easily perceive why I am reserved upon that subject. I will not lead you on, unguarded and ardent as I then was, to your destruction and infallible misery."

I doubt whether the editors of *Science* would have stood for that. And on reconsideration I abandoned the plan. A scientist who makes a murderous monster from the spare parts of corpses . . . quoting from such a horror story might evoke the wrong associations. But because one thing always leads to another, I'd meanwhile become interested in Mary Wollstonecraft Shelley. She was nineteen in 1816 when she wrote her novel, the title of which has become a household word and which over a century and a half later spawns an unending succession of new novels, films, and plays: it created a whole new genre. Nineteen! What kind of girl was she? I wanted to know more about her, and that's why I was sitting in the dusty and venerable reading room making notes, while outside the storm had obviously decided never to stop again. Fortunately no one knew that this was the ideal place to shelter.

A couple of days after her birth, her mother died. In 1814 when she was seventeen, she met Percy Bysshe Shelley, the poet, who at the time was twenty-two and married. A year later she gave birth to a daughter, who died after eleven days. In 1816 she bore a son and married Shelley after his wife had committed suicide. In 1817 she gave birth to another daughter, who died a year afterward, when they were on their way to Venice. And in 1819 her son also died, aged three, but she gave birth to a second son. In 1822 she had a miscarriage and Shelley was drowned at sea. Doom, doom. But meanwhile she managed to write her novel *Frankenstein, or The Modern Prometheus* in 1816. In the company of Lord Byron, she and Shelley were on holiday in Switzerland. It was a wet summer, and they read German ghost stories to one another, whereupon Byron suggested: "Let's each of us write a ghost story." Only hers was finished, the idea came to her in a dream. It's as though I can see them in front of me, the three brilliant people there on their Swiss Magic Mountain.

Why am I writing all this down here on my balcony (because

just as in Beethoven's *Pastoral Symphony* the storm has given way in the course of the evening to a cool, clear night full of stars)? Because on the Internet I made an additional discovery. In that same year of 1816, the same Lord Byron divorced his wife, shortly after their daughter Ada was born. Because of an incestuous scandal he could not return to England and eight years later he died in Greece during the War of Independence against the Turks, and never saw Ada again. But like Mary Wollstonecraft Shelley that girl grew up to be a most extraordinary creature: she became the first programmer in history. The computer language of the American Defense Department, *Ada*, was named after her. At the age of fourteen she became paralyzed, and as a result she couldn't walk for three years; in that period she studied mathematics. She was eighteen when she met Charles Babbage, who had invented a forerunner of the computer; her theoretical contributions to the machine were visionary and pioneering, they even anticipated the theory of artificial intelligence. But at the age of twenty-nine, having by now become Lady Lovelace, she collapsed physically and mentally, and for years was treated with brandy, opium, and morphine, believed that she was God's prophetess on earth, who could fathom all the secrets of the universe, gambled away her possessions, and died of cancer at the age of thirty-six—a year after Mary Shelley, whom she undoubtedly knew, because in every establishment everyone knows everyone else.

I disconnected from the Internet, folded my arms, and thought. What a fantastic cobweb! Here everything came together: Count Frankenstein, Alan Turing, computers, robots— and I myself; I was also caught in that fatal web. Who or what was the spider in the middle? Perhaps the god of Ada, the prophetess, after all? I remembered that as a boy I'd once seen a huge spider's web in a wood, within the middle of the silvery, mathematical pentagon a great dark brown spider. When I approached to look at it, it suddenly began shaking up and down in its web so rapidly that it became invisible. That was of course to escape birds hungry for prey—but just as everything is always also something else, looking back on it, it may also throw light on the invisibility of the procreative god.

With my fists clenched I raised my arms above my head and stretched. It was getting on for midday, I was hungry. I put the notes and printouts in my pocket, took the books back and went outside. I struggled through the crowd under the arcades toward Florian's, while the rain crashed down on the marble paving of the deserted piazza; in the sky it was still cracking and rumbling without respite. It was packed in the small booths of the café, leaning against a pillar I drank a Bellini, while I looked at the thick campanile which had scaffolding on it, the way that everything is always covered in scaffolding in Venice. In 1902 the thousand-year-old tower had collapsed, and after comparison with the depictions of the slim structure in paintings by Canaletto, Turner, and others, I was convinced that for safety reasons it had been rebuilt at least four and a half feet wider, although it's always said to be an exact replica—but my carpenter's eye never deceives me. Protected by the raincoat and umbrella I then went to Harry's Bar, around the corner on the Canal Grande. Byron had lived for years in a palazzo a few hundred yards farther on, in a chaotic household where he threw his wild parties and meanwhile found time to write masterpieces.

The beings of the mind are not of clay . . .

That line, from *Childe Harold*, might have been written with me in mind and by now you'll understand why it's stayed with me.

At the back of the small room there was still a table free. As always it was full of prosperous Americans and Japanese basking in the reflected glory of former regulars like Hemingway and other celebrities. I ordered a *risotto di pesce* and half a bottle of Orvieto, leaned back, folded my arms—and then something strange came over me. It was very brief, but it was as if I were suddenly being lifted above my own life and set down in a different space, where everything that I'd ever done and every-thing that had ever happened to me, which might have been dif-ferent, fell away from me and where all that was left was what could not have been otherwise: the fact that I am who I am. My pure I, without a past, without a future. A mysterious moment. My private life was a ruin, and yet it suddenly seemed as if in some way or other it didn't touch my core.

The door, which I was sitting directly opposite, opened and a distinguished gentleman appeared, as soaking wet as if he'd walked along the bottom of the Grand Canal from the lagoon. He was tall and thin, with wavy, thick, almost white hair; the jacket of his sodden white suit he carried over his arm; his white shirt and bright red tie were also soaking wet. The pomaded waiters welcomed him like an old friend. Dripping, he sat down at the table next to mine, on which there was a notice that said *Riservato;* I had the impression that he lunched there every af-ternoon, because without his having ordered anything a glass of *prosecco* was set in front of him.

He looked at me with a smile.

"Actually," he said in English, drying his tanned face with his napkin, "I'd prefer a hot grog, but it's better not to depart from your habits. Anybody who at my age departs from his habits soon dies, and to be honest I don't feel a bit like doing that. I tend to leave that kind of thing to other people."

I realized that this was not just any stranger. He had an accent that I couldn't pin down, but in any case he wasn't an En-glishman or an American.

"It seems," I said, also smiling, "as if you are immortal."

He surveyed me searchingly for a few seconds with his cool gray-blue eyes.

"The best thing," he said, "is to draw the extreme conclusion from everything at once. That applies everywhere, in art just as well as in politics and science. From Picasso to Lenin and Ein-stein, they all flipped. The radicals control the world."

Who was he telling this to? He nodded at me paternally, as though he were trying to boost my morale. I thought it was not impossible that he was ten years older than he seemed, perhaps he was already approaching seventy but at the same time he had the gaze of a seventeen-year-old. Apart from that, my father would have been seventy-seven now; probably he was the same age as my mother.

"Same again?" the waiter asked him, while for reasons that were not clear he put a hand on the salt and pepper pots and moved them four inches.

"I'll wait for a moment."

Since your mother left me I now eat a couple of times a week in restaurants at home too; usually I'm the only person sitting alone at a table. It doesn't escape me that I'm suddenly looked at rather pityingly, but that's of course typically Dutch: you only eat out when something special's happening, otherwise it's a waste of money. Even in Belgium it's quite different, to say nothing of France. To be honest, I think it's one of the few pleasant aspects of being alone: in a world of white linen and hotel silver you are silently mothered and you can think in peace. No, "thinking" is not the word, that denotes something active—you allow yourself to be swept along by the stream of your thoughts, like a raft on a river, and sometimes you come across something unexpected, like a long island covered with fabulous vegetation, such as you find in the Rhine and the Rhône. I've never had my best ideas at my desk or in the laboratory, but getting on a tram or waking up or in a restaurant at coffee. I had the idea for the eobiont under the shower. I conceived the plan of joining the mummy research I had heard about when I was trying to call Mummy from a hotel in Sydney, but got an incomprehensible man on the line. "You got Egypt now," said the operator. I think that's why I don't like it when someone takes pity on me and strikes up a conversation. I always cut it short as quickly as possible by taking a newspaper I've brought with me or my notebook out of my inside pocket. But now, in Harry's Bar, I hoped that my sopping-wet neighbor wouldn't turn away from me. So I did something that I had never done before: I addressed myself to him.

"The fact that you are without a coat or an umbrella on a day like this, means, I think, that you left home yesterday."

"You're a born detective, but it could also mean something else, namely that my umbrella was stolen. I was in the Palazzo Grassi, then I drank an espresso at Paulin, and there someone thought they had better use for it than I did. God knows, perhaps he was right. Perhaps it was someone made of sugar. And before you, as a true detective, ask why I didn't have something to eat in the Campo San Stefano: I've arranged to meet someone here."

He looked straight at me, as though it were me he'd arranged to meet. He talked about the city like someone who lived there, obviously assuming that I knew it as well as he did. I inquired what exhibition he'd seen.

"There's nothing to see yet, but it's coming. The problem you struggle with as in an exhibition organizer in Venice is that it's always more beautiful in the street than in the museum. This year I'm trying to solve that problem dialectically in the Palazzo Grassi."

"Dialectically? That doesn't sound very modern."

He drummed with his fingers on the tablecloth rather impatiently for a moment.

"Be careful you don't throw away the dialectical baby with the Communist bathwater."

I had had my knuckles rapped. That amused me and I asked:

"How are you going about it?"

"By exhibiting only ugly things. In that way the Palazzo Grassi itself will become all the more beautiful, and when you come outside that will extend to the whole city. My real exhibition is, therefore, Venice. All I can hope for is that someone will understand that his sigh of relief when he leaves the museum was actually the intention."

It seemed to me a risky conception, and for the first time in my life I had the feeling that I understood what dialectics was.

"Perhaps," I said, "the real intention of dialecticians like Lenin and Stalin was that the people should breathe a sigh of relief and release at the collapse of the Soviet system."

He nodded.

"Without a doubt. But only you and I know that."

I wondered whether I should now introduce myself, so that I could find out his name; but for some reason that seemed inappropriate. In any case he must be an international celebrity if he organized exhibitions in the Palazzo Grassi. Suddenly he seemed to collapse a little.

"Ultimately everything is pointless of course," he said, more to himself than to me. "Even if life has a point, you can still maintain that it's pointless, because what point is there in its having a point?" He put his hand around the base of his glass. "But within a senseless existence the point of this glass is drinking, the point of the speaking I'm now doing is to be heard by you. At this moment you are the point of my life," he said, and looked at me, "and I am of yours. Everything has a point except 'everything.'"

You may be beginning to wonder why I am telling you all this—the reason is that you also came into the conversation. After we had been silent for a while following his attack of melancholy, the door opened again and on the threshold there appeared a woman with in one hand a girl of about four, in the other the lead of a young black dachshund. Then something amazing happened. The bitch tore herself loose and in my memory she *flew* over the heads of the customers to my neighbor, with her ears flapping, dragging the red lead behind her, landed on his chest, and began to lick his face, with her two front paws with claws spread wide against his cheeks, her ears in her neck, and the white above her eyes visible. My neighbor made no move to withdraw from the embrace; with his hands on the gleaming black hips he let her have her way, so that his face a little while later was as wet as it had just been. The Americans around looked at the scene with revulsion, while a couple from some Oriental country or other gave the impression that they would most like to stone the animal to death.

After about two minutes it suddenly stopped. The dog nestled on my neighbor's lap and with his napkin he again wiped his face, as he said to me, "This is Catharina, my wife is her mother, my daughter her sister, but I am her son. Yes, that exists, total, pure, perfect love. The world is not lost yet. I don't just love this animal as you see it here, but everything that you can't see, her lungs, her liver, her kidneys, her brain, and her little heart. That's why I curse hunters. How can someone shoot at an animal that has nothing but the small space that it takes up in the world? Do we know how large the universe is? But no, even the small sacred space that a duck or a deer possesses is begrudged them. It has to be taken from them at all costs, and that's fun to do. The fact that I still eat meat I regard as the greatest defeat of my life."

A man after my own heart. The woman, who'd meanwhile sat down, had only given him a kiss when his face was dry. She was tall and slim, with the profile of a Greek Amazon, at least thirty years younger than he was—about the same age as Mummy, that is. The girl asked her something in a language that I couldn't pin down, perhaps it was Latvian or Estonian or something else from Ultima Thule. Both started laughing, whereupon my neighbor said:

"And this is our Elsa. Do you have children too?"

That question fell onto my table like a stone. You understand, of course, Aurora, that it has been put to me quite often and my answer has always been "No," after which I have immediately changed the subject. But now, with this man, this sympathetic devil's advocate, I had the feeling that I couldn't leave it at that. He gave me a strange look, as though he knew what I was going to answer.

"I should have had a daughter," I said, putting down my fork and looking at him, "but she died."

I immediately knew that I must now leave. My plate wasn't yet empty, but I wiped my mouth and tried to attract the attention of the waiter. When my neighbor saw me, he said:

"No, no, you are my guest."

"But . . ."

"I insist. You pay next time. I'll see you around. It's a small world."

His hand was as cold as a dead man's.

I feel rather stiff, the night has got imperceptibly cooler. I'm still confused by that meeting. What kind of man was it, who said that our lives were each other's point. Why did I suddenly speak to that dialectical Latvian or Estonian, a total stranger, about you?

THIRD COMMUNICATION

MENA HOUSE

CAIRO

September 27, 1994

My Dear Clara,
Still no word from you. Crying in the wilderness,
which begins a few yards from here.

Victor

Tuesday, September 6. You will probably deduce from this laid letter paper, that I am again staying in a luxury four-star hotel, but that isn't the case. I am accommodated in a kind of boardinghouse in the center of Cairo, close to the museum and the university. For the past few days I have been working here with an international team on the DNA research on mummies. It's not completely impossible that their resurrection is imminent: their afterlife, for which they've been prepared, perhaps lies in the not-too-distant future. But anyway, that is not our object. I will spare you the details of our work, but it's connected with AIDS. We are trying to find out if HIV-type viruses, which are at present fatal to human beings, occurred five thousand years ago in apes—that's an idea of Jaap's, the leader of our team. We take bone marrow from mummified baboons and macaques, but the DNA is seriously degraded; the intention is that I should repair it, like a sort of molecular-biological plumber, so that the sequence of the letters can be read again. I may have found a solution. In fact, I am overqualified for this kind of work, but I wanted to get away, out of the country, into the desert. There is an abundance of ape mummies here, in Saqqara we are excavating them ourselves, all very exciting and adventurous. Those creatures were sacred here, because they were dedicated to the writer-god Thoth, who awakened Osiris from death. Just imagine that in this way we find something to counter the modern plague, we will have to say after all that it's due to the ancient Egyptian religion. And that *despite* the Christian religion, as Catholic missionaries did their utmost to destroy those pagan animal necropolises, which thank God they didn't entirely succeed in doing.

The din and the heat and the stink of exhaust fumes and roasting meat in Cairo are indescribable, at least by me. There are about fifteen million people walking about the streets, as many as there are Dutch people, and this afternoon I needed some peace and quiet. I took the advice of an Egyptian colleague, put on a tie, and came in the smoking, crowded, creaking, incessantly hooting bus to this super deluxe hotel. In a suburb the supernatural moment arrived, when the pyramids of Giza rose above the roofs of the houses like a mirage, like refineries or blast furnaces elsewhere. You might say that the city should be kept at a considerable distance from those miraculous works, but that's not how they do things here. It's not inconceivable that one day they'll be in the middle of Cairo, like medieval ramparts with us, although hopefully the minister of tourism will be able to prevent that.

This is the kind of palatial hotel where I can just about afford a cup of coffee: sweet, wonderful sediment from a little brass-handled pot, with a sickly sweet Arab pastry. Everything here is high, luxuriant, all Oriental luxury with wood carving, mirrors, and wall tapestries, Arabian Nights, *Alf laila wa laila.* In a corner of the air-conditioned lounge a striking but rather weary company is slumped in the armchairs, about twenty or thirty people. Although she has a silk scarf knotted tightly around her head, leaving only her face free, I recognize one of the ladies: Jacqueline Kennedy Onassis. She looks bad. I asked the waiter what kind of group that is. Doubtless against his own instructions he told me that they are the guests of some industrial tycoon or other, who has invited them on the occasion of his birthday to a private performance of *Aida* in the Amen Temple of Karnak; they arrived this morning in a fleet of helicopters. Yes, Aurora, you can tell, from a distance I'm allowed a glimpse of the proprietors of the earth.

But when I look out of the window with its Moorish horse-shoe arch, I see a much greater property: the pyramid of Cheops. You won't believe it, but it really exists. I was too busy to go and look before, but now I see it anyway, that wonder of the world. An asphalted road runs past the hotel in a curve toward it. On this side of the road is the green hotel garden with lawns, fountains, palms, and all kinds of exotic trees, where a couple of gardeners are spraying—on the other side the desert begins. Nothing else grows there. Bedouins have pitched their tents, like the cocoons of gigantic insects, a few camels are hanging about. The road is no more than two hundred yards long and runs up to the plateau on which there are three pyramids, those of Cheops, Chephren, and Mycerinus. They say that it's never rained there. And what am *I* to say of this shattering scene, which somehow knocks me completely off my feet? How can I say anything about it that no one has already said? When Herodotus described them for the first time, in the fifth century B.C., they were already more than two thousand years old. But perhaps I know something after all. They are the logo of our planet. There is the Star of David, the swastika, the Soviet star, the star of Mercedes Benz, but those regular polygons are the registered trademark of the earth as a whole. If someone in outer space were to ask, "How do I recognize planet number three in the solar system?", the answer would be, "Look and see if you can find pyramids anywhere in the Milky Way."

Saturday, September 10. In the bus you get to know the people, but this time I took a taxi anyway. I've decided simply to continue these notes. The unfathomable silence that emanates from those three tombs, there on the coast of the desert, reminds me of yours, my child.

In my boardinghouse the air-conditioning has broken down, which hasn't prevented me from thinking a lot for the past few days—not just about ancient retroviruses, but also about Mummy. Time heals all wounds, they say, but obviously something in me has become resistant to time. I haven't seen her for almost a year, and there isn't the slightest improvement. It's not that I go around unhappy all day long and pound the pillows with my fists as I cry at night, it wasn't like that even in the beginning, but I can feel it as a kind of knot somewhere around my midriff. I'm tied up in knots as they say. You might find it strange (not if you'd known me), but when that image of a knot occurred to me, I looked up the entry "Navigation on the Nile" in an encyclopedia, in which there was a section on knots. If that's what it feels like and if it also exists in language usage, the science of knots might perhaps give me a solution. Apart from the Windsor knot and the slipknot I only really knew two knots, the granny knot (left over right and then left over right again) and the reef knot (left over right, right over left); but there are scores of others such as the bowline, the clove hitch, the cow hitch, the cat's-paw, and the sheepshank. All very interesting, but it didn't get me much further. Finally, there are all kinds of ingenious conjuror's knots, which undo with a simple tug. It would be nice if my knot were that kind, but unfortunately it's not. But they do put me on the track of their opposite, the knot of knots, the Gordian knot.

I looked it up in the encyclopedia. Whoever could undo the knot with which the shaft was attached to the yoke of King Gordias's chariot would, said the oracle, become ruler of the world. There are two versions recorded of the way in which Alexander the Great did this. Of course the usual one: that he cut it through with his sword—but I don't like that one, it's too crude for me. According to the other, he pulled the rod which went through the yoke and the shaft out of the knot. That's the elegant solution, worthy of a ruler of the world; that's why not far from here the port city has been called after him. He had uncoupled the shaft and the yoke without touching the knot: subsequently it fell apart by itself. This has something of the character of a conjuring trick. Could I learn something from the Great Houdini? I only knew vaguely what a shaft and a yoke were, so first of all I had to look them up. A shaft is the post between the horses hitched to a wagon; a yoke is a wooden block with pieces cut out of it, fitting around the neck of a couple of animals hitched to a wagon.

Damn, when I read this I had the absurd feeling that I can do something with it. The comparison creaks in all kind of ways, of course, but it isn't necessary to make it congruent at all costs. The yoke that links me to the shaft and the wagon is a paradoxical yoke, because it also binds me to Mummy but no longer binds Mummy to me. What must I do to get her back in the yoke or to release myself from it? Is that perhaps connected with that rod in the Gordian knot? I must pull it out and leave the knot for what it is, because then it will fall apart of its own accord. And what, in our case, is that rod? What must I pull out?

Of course, I've got it: I'll let myself float along on my brainwaves and intuition, like a windsurfer on the waves and the wind, but it hasn't stood me in bad stead. You must dare to take that side of yourself seriously too—if you have it, at least. For don-key's years I've been concerned with matters of microprecision, but the imagination always precedes that too. So I'll go on for a bit, because it really is as if I can see a vision of something in front of me that I can really get something out of. For the whole time the word "lie" has been hanging around in my head. I—

Friday, September 16. Last week I was interrupted by a tele-phone call from my Egyptian colleague from the laboratory. He said only one thing: "GGT ACC CAG CTT CCC CAA AGG TTC AAG." That was such good news—I had repaired a hole in the DNA!—that I went straight back to the city.

Today is the Islamic day of rest and I'm back in my regular place in Mena House, with my mobile telephone on the table. My colleagues already start coughing behind their hands when I say where I can be reached; if you ask me, they suspect me of having joined the international company of pyramid freaks, for whom the pyramid of Cheops is the materialization of the deepest esoteric secrets, built by mathematical-astronomical-religious superbrains. That's nonsense of course, but their sus-picion is not *completely* gratuitous. On the top shelves of my bookcases, Mummy knows, because she occasionally banged them together in front of the open window, there are a couple of dozen disintegrating books from my childhood that I never wanted to get rid of. The oldest originates from the time when I was thirteen; even then I had a built-in archivist, who dated each new book. Even chemistry, biology, and geology books, biogra-phies of great researchers on whom I modeled myself, my old book about Egyptian hieroglyphics, and God knows what else. Also a number of works by those feverish pyramidologists. What fascinated me in this, and in fact still does, is again a ma-nia for deciphering taken to extremes. Their fantastic discover-ies, their minuscule measurements, their inspired diagrams and complicated calculations, their manipulation of the facts, their

ingenious interpretations of discrepancies as confirmations—
are all serious science in a distorting mirror. Very entertaining.
I read those kinds of books for relaxation, as someone else reads
detective novels.

As I now sit looking out of the window, I can empathize with
that obsession. The most grizzly book of its kind, that of
Davidson, is called *The Stones Speak,* and the title expresses it
perfectly: that massive silence which has continued for thousands of years must be forced to speak, with no means outlawed:
third-degree interrogations, lies, threats, torture, everything's
permitted provided it leads to a meaning. The reason is that it is
death made by human hands which is standing there. No one
will write a book about "the mystery of the Rock of Gibraltar,"
although that is much larger and considerably older. Measure
it, determine the position of its slopes in relation to the pole-
star Sirius, measure the length of its shadow on June 21 at twelve
o'clock, observe that it points precisely toward Stonehenge, et
cetera. The Rock of Gibraltar is not mysterious because it is not
the work of human beings—but is that really an essential difference? My very own eobiont actually bridges that difference.
In that capacity my living crystal is in fact itself the essence.

Do you know who to my taste gave the best characterization
of the pyramids? The much decried Hegel. "Colossal crystals,"
he called them: they are the top halves of octahedrons, regular
eight-sided figures, the bottom half of which you can imagine in
the desert sand, where it points down to the middle of the earth.
Something stopped me from going toward it and looking at it
from close up until now, but just now I was actually *in* the colossal crystal.

I had myself set down by the taxi in the heat on the plateau,
where there was already a line of coaches. There was a great
throng of tourists, walking around behind umbrellas that had
been put up; everywhere Bedouins on brightly adorned camels,
who tried to sell people rides. One of them groped in his bur-
noose and offered for sale an ancient Egyptian statue from the

fourth dynasty, doubtlessly made by himself yesterday. When I waved him away he said:

"Go to hell!"

The closer I got to the pyramid of Cheops, the more its diagonal smooth side sections changed into a wild pile of blocks with only vertical and horizontal sides but even that, I thought, was in agreement with its form: It's true of an octahedron that its corners and the centers are the side panels of a cube. All the stones are weathered and battered. Man fears time, goes an Arabic saying, but time fears the pyramids, you can see how time has bitten its nails to pieces about that sole remaining wonder of the world. As I looked at it, I really had the feeling that I was looking with my naked eye at the atoms of a crystal. With a deep sigh—as if I'd finally achieved something very important in my life—I put both my hands on one of those cubic-yard blocks, warm from the sun which had been shining day after day for thousands of years, and looked up. The awesome mass of stone stood out golden brown against the blue sky; it emanated such weight that it surprised me that the pyramid hadn't long since sunk beneath the surface of the earth and plunged into the magma.

It's mostly pleasant to tell the story of something unpleasant after the event. It may of course not have been all that pleasant, but anyone who's fallen through the ice will talk about it with a smile later. That ice is in the more or less illegal glass of Scotch that is in front of me, in this marvelously cooled space and I look back with pleasure at the infernal journey to the royal chamber, a couple of hours ago. Heart patients are advised against that visit. You enter the pyramid through a hole, hacked in it a thousand years ago by a Caliph greedy for gold, the son of Haroun al-Rashid, the hero of *The Arabian Nights*. But you don't enter alone. You go in with crowds of Japanese, Americans, English, Germans, French, Italians, and whatever else Ra may have put into the world, you struggle in the semidarkness among all those sweating bodies through curves and a narrow rising passage, where you can only walk bent over, while other crowds are coming down and then through the high rising gallery with its supernatural dimensions, which was to form a timescale of the creation of heaven and earth down to the year 1953 (when Watson and Crick presented their double helix of DNA). Meanwhile, it's getting hotter and hotter and stuffier and stuffier in the oven which has been heated for forty-six centuries, you feel the pressure of those millions of blocks of stone around you; the throng, the constant barrage of flashbulbs, the lack of oxygen, the sense of the place where you are, all that affects your consciousness and turns it into an Arabian Nightmare. Finally, after having crawled for a few more yards, you're in the royal chamber. A bare, quite small room with an empty sarcophagus of black granite, one corner of which has been knocked off. It's as crowded as a crammed lift and by this time you have no idea where you are: deep in the earth, high in the sky, in another world? It is most like the latter. But I have to admit that I didn't have any mystical revelations; my thoughts were with Mummy.

Her client, that megalomaniac giant with his Jaguar, would certainly have had a vision of the way in which the pyramids could have been converted into a hotel–cum–apartment block, World Trade Center, and international multicultural center under the auspices of UNESCO. There are people who don't shy away from anything and he is one. But don't let me complain about him, because it's to him that I owe my own home in the former house of God.

Tuesday, September 20. News! Today I received the post forwarded by the caretaker: the triplets have been traced. The Municipal Archives told me that because of the shortage of staff I would have to consult a genealogist, and she has now replied. Albert Dodemont lives in Haarlem, I have his address, fax, and telephone number. He seems to be a well-known typographer.

His two brothers, Marnix and Sjoerd, immigrated long ago to Australia and Canada; whether they're still alive the lady couldn't say. I will shortly send your Haarlem milk uncle a fax to arrange a meeting. What I'm really after—I've no idea.

Friday, September 23. The air-conditioning in my room had meanwhile been repaired, but has broken down again. The best thing then is to open the window wide to the heat and the din; I've taken off all my clothes including my underpants and in this naked state I'm going to tell you about the three days in my life that I shall never be able to get out of my mind. It's a day of rest again today so I've plenty of time.

When Mummy told me that her firm had been given the job of converting the Basilica, I thought that the merciless project developer had finally gone crazy. But as the man in Harry's Bar had already said, the most radical wins. On her recommendation I was able to rent a wonderful flat, where we spent a few happy months, where you were conceived and died without having been born and where subsequently everything else fell apart.

You're in heaven now, Aurora, and you've the right to know how it all happened. I once read that medieval theologians wrestled with the problem of how things were to be conducted in heaven. After all, one person had died senile at the age of ninety, the other as an infant in childbed—do they find themselves in heaven like that? The one as a worn-out wreck the other as a screaming baby? That was of course impossible, because how were they to behold God? Someone cut the Gordian knot, I don't know who, perhaps St. Thomas Aquinas, and he postulated that in heaven all souls are thirty-three years old. Brilliant! I'm now speaking to you as a woman the same age as Christ—although you never became any older than minus three weeks.

Mummy and I knew that you were a girl from the echo that the gynecologists had made of you when you were minus a few months old; that was done just to be on the safe side, as Mummy was already approaching forty. That was why we could already give you a name. That photo is the only one we have of you; as a kind of inverted pyramid, like the Nile Delta, with the picture of an extragalactic solar system in it. Everything was ready for your birth, crib, clothes, diapers, and then one evening it went completely quiet in Mummy's tummy. That had already happened a week before, then they'd made a CTG, a cardiotomogram, and everything turned out to be all right. Still, she got worried and the following morning she went back to the hospital. She asked me if I would go with her but that wasn't very convenient: I had Woese from Illinois visiting, he was on his way to Strasbourg and was only going to stay one day. Moreover, I was convinced that it was a false alarm this time too.

You were dead. You had hanged yourself on your umbilical cord. A loop had been created which had placed itself like a noose around your neck; as a result you hadn't choked, because you weren't breathing yet, but the already twisted cord was completely constricted and the supply of blood was blocked. I heard later from the doctor that Mummy started screaming when she heard and cried, "I knew it! I knew it." And, "I'm going to go crazy!" Then she suddenly became abnormally calm.

At that moment I was eating smoked salmon with Woese, flanked by a bottle of Sancerre in a cooler; she didn't ring me afterward either. When I got home at the end of the afternoon, she was sitting on the floor with her hands folded on her fat tummy next to the sofa looking outside. I saw immediately that the situation was fatal. She didn't turn her head when I came in; only when I squatted down by her did she look at me. I'd never seen the look in her eyes in anyone before. It was as if I were looking into a dark well, a deep well like those you find in Venetian squares, into which you drop a stone which only seconds later causes a chilly splash in the black underworld. When I asked what had happened, she just shook her head, she couldn't say. But she didn't have to say. I realized that she had turned into a grave.

I sat down next to her, put an arm around her broad shoulders and also laid a hand on her belly. It was as if I could hear the silence within. How am I to describe what went on inside me? It wasn't something like "grief," least of all for you, because you existed and yet you didn't exist and I didn't know who you were or would have become; it was rather the absence of emotion, a kind of petrifaction which was only connected with Mummy. For her you were something different from who you were for me, you were part of herself, not only of her body but also of her soul, of her identity as a woman. Of course you were my child too, I didn't doubt that, but you were not that with the same absolute certainty as the fact that you were her child. That a child also has a father is a quite late discovery. When Mummy turned out to be expecting you, we considered getting married, but she felt as little need for that as I did, perhaps even less. Somewhat as a joke I said, "So let's get married when the baby's born. Seeing is believing."

After we'd sat next to each other in silence for a quarter of an hour, the sun began to set in a grandiose creation of orange and purple—nature, which in general is bored to death, is always ready to act as the illustrator of the human condition. When the tumult later died down into a gray twilight, I said,

"Shall we get married, Clara?"

There was no reaction. Only half a minute later did she slowly shake her head.

I was alarmed. It was then that I experienced the first pang of fear that our relationship might also be dying. I felt guilty for not having gone with her to the hospital, but was that the only reason? She should have nodded, and, if necessary, changed her mind later: We should have been able to come closer together, there in that situation on the floor next to the sofa, but instead a rift seemed to open up between us. I took my arm off her shoulders and sat opposite her, so that I could look at her.

"What did they say has to be done now?"

"Nothing. I wanted an immediate cesarean, but the midwife persuaded me against it. A fantastic woman. It must happen naturally. She said that it's better for me in all respects, not only physically."

"And how long will that take?"

"If it doesn't come within three days, they'll induce me."

During the three days that followed your mother was a living sarcophagus. It's already a year ago, but every time I think back to it, it's as though I open a door and on the other side of the threshold a fathomless ravine opens up, such as you find in the Rocky Mountains. My stomach turns, I have to grab hold of something. I had planted death in her—and looking back on it, it's a mystery how we got through those days. There was of course no question of my leaving her alone and going to work. She went through the rooms with her big belly, sat opposite me at the table, lay next to me in bed. We didn't talk much. There were three of us and yet two of us; but instead of that awareness uniting us, it divided us. I didn't dare ask her how she was feeling. As I looked at her out of the corner of my eye, I tried to imagine what it was like but how can a man imagine something like that? Never before had I felt the distance between man and woman so acutely. I could more or less imagine what it would be like to have a huge tumor in my abdomen, except that that's almost the opposite—a growth like that is death itself in embryonic form, out to destroy someone's life, which itself then dies, like a kamikaze pilot; but you were predestined to live, you weren't out to kill your mother. And now you're dead, while Mummy is alive, although I don't know in what circumstances.

"Shall we get out of town?" she asked on the second day.

With that she expressed exactly what I also needed without realizing it.

"Where do you want to go? To the sea? To the woods?" Under other circumstances I would have added that it's the difference between the horizontal and the vertical, that she would naturally choose the sea, but now was not the moment for that kind of intellectual acrobatics.

It was one of those mild Northern European autumn days that I recall nostalgically in this clammy heat. There was a very light mist over the dunes, like when you've breathed on the windowpane; there was a thin sun shining on the June grass and the white sand that formed the transition from the green land to the gray sea. I had expected to find myself in silence, just a couple of people with running dogs along the high-water mark, perhaps an occasional horseman, but the promenade was full of parked cars and it was very busy on the beach too. There was a kite competition going on; from loudspeakers came a harsh voice, trying to express the feelings of the crowd. I asked Mummy if she would prefer to go to a quieter section, but she said she thought it was fine. I offered her my arm and we went down the steps to the beach, those wide sandy steps closed in by wooden beams, weathered, bleached by the sea and sun. We sat down by a dismantled beach pavilion.

In my time kites had only the shape of ultrasound images, if I can put it like that, or of a kind of extended cube. Now there were huge monsters floating in the sky, colored Chinese dragons, long silvery sea snakes which suddenly dived down spectacularly, grazing the beach, and a moment later came to a regal halt at a great height. The ones I liked best were a pair of black kites, which curled against the pale blue sky like leeches or spermatozoa, as if trying to find their way somewhere.

"So she'll never get to see anything like this," said Clara, resting her chin on her hands.

"But nor will she *not*," I was going to say, but I restrained myself. There we sat on the boundary of land and water, Mummy with a corpse in her abdomen. That word "corpse" I write down very harshly, but it was only that for me; for Mummy it was you, her child. To reach the next coast, in an easterly direction, you had to go to Vladivostok, over six thousand miles away. What kind of weird thought was that at a moment like this? Perhaps out of self-preservation I wanted to put our disaster into a framework of space and time, so that it became small, a minimal incident which would one day be forgotten, when Mummy and I were no longer there. That will undoubtedly happen, but does that mean it will also have disappeared? Of course not. Sorrow can't be undone. Just as you have all kinds of other laws of conservation, I now postulate the law of the conservation of sorrow. I've never understood how theologians can maintain that in heaven souls rejoice in the blessed vision of God. How in heaven's name can you be blissful after everything that's happened in the course of time? Heaven is only conceivable as the Realm of Amnesia, that is as a psychiatric institution. Yes, Aurora, that even applies to you. If anyone is without sin and hence entitled to behold God, it's you. But has he told you, thirty-three heavenly years old, what is going on on earth, that you've never known? Or has his mother glued his lips together with impact adhesive?

I don't know. Perhaps the heat is starting to go to my head. Evening has suddenly fallen, but it's not getting any cooler. Exhaust fumes, the smoke of burning meat, hooting, shouting, that all comes floating in through my room like a steaming Oriental dish from the oven of the city. Fortunately I'm writing on my little computer; with a fountain pen and paper the manuscript would have long ago changed into the sweaty scribbles of a toddler.

From the loudspeakers on the beach there now came a sort of loud pounding music that you hear in a certain type of car waiting at the traffic lights with the windows open.

"What are you thinking of?" I asked.

"Of tomorrow."

"Can you feel anything yet?"

"I can't feel a thing. You're coming with me to the hospital, aren't you?"

"Of course."

"You haven't got any important appointments then?"

"Even if I had."

"Have you got a cigarette for me?"

For all those months she hadn't smoked, had not had as much as one glass of wine, had kept to a low-salt diet, and had faithfully done her prenatal exercises. I offered her a cigarette, which she inhaled deeply. Immediately afterward she began sobbing.

"What on earth are we going to do now, Victor?"

Her misery hit me like a dart in the bull's-eye—partly perhaps because she used my name, which she seldom did. When she laid her head on my shoulder, I had a liberating feeling of happiness. Had I been wrong about her? Was it in fact that the catastrophe wasn't dividing us but joining us together, just as a living child would have done? Or had I not understood who your mother really was until this moment?

"We're going to solve this together," I said, with my cheek against her crown. "When it's over, we'll go somewhere where it's beautiful for a few days. You just say where you want to go."

I felt her nodding. From the south three jets came roaring over the second sandbank, as if to show the paper crowd who is the boss in the sky. A chilly fog began drifting inland from the sea.

I've never felt as naked as now. Good night, my child. I'm going to try to get some sleep too.

Saturday, September 24. Wasted the whole day in a meeting at the offices of the Supreme Council of Antiquities. On the front page of *Al Ahram,* the biggest paper here, there seems to be a report from the correspondent in the Benelux, who maintains that we're trying to demonstrate from mummies that AIDS comes from Egypt. Scandalous! According to us even some pharaohs are supposed to have died of it. We were besmirching the heroic past of the nation, while everyone knew that AIDS hadn't occurred in Egypt up to now. What's more, the paper had discovered that I was involved in the research, I, the man who was trying to compete with Allah with his blasphemous eobiont. We were not so much a team of researchers as a gang of criminals, in the service of Satan. So, panic. Our residents' permits were in danger, and unless something happened we would have to interrupt our work and perhaps be deported. Endless conferences, telephoning back and forth, waiting for the officials who were going to come in an hour and still didn't come, misunderstandings, suspicion. Fortunately Egypt, like elsewhere, is not yet totally populated by fools and Jaap was able to avert the danger for the time being. But the main question is, of course: where did that journalist get that idiotic story from? From Brock? I consider him capable of anything.

The others are still sitting together discussing the matter, but I've gone to my little room in the Institute, where I am now sitting writing. I found myself during that whole fuss preoccupied with Mummy and you. That was of course because of my notes of yesterday, and I want to tell you the sequel now. For a long time I couldn't even think about it without going completely to pieces, but obviously the moment's come to talk about it. I'm doing it not just for you, but also for myself.

The very next day labor began and at ten o'clock we were in the hospital. It was as if the waves of pain came rolling in from a sea of pain in the distance and broke in Mummy. For eight hours no two labor pains were identical, but what the difference was I can't say. Just try describing the surf on the beach; you can't, you can only show it, in a film. Andy Warhol did things like that. For billions of years no two waves have been identical. I tried to support Mummy as best I could, but it was as if the morbid process was gnawing at me from inside too. Now and then I fled the room and left her to the care of the midwife, of whom she was so fond, an Indonesian lady who in some kind of way radiated the message that she was still in contact with a different kind of gynecology, like that of Indonesian women who brought their children into the world squatting, holding on to the low branch of a tree with both hands. The reception area of the supermodern academic hospital was a huge, towering white space with flower stalls, kiosks, restaurants, everything very cozy, no trace of death anywhere, don't worry, nothing's wrong, it'll all be all right. But when I'd drunk an espresso with trembling hands and had eaten a lukewarm sausage roll, I still had to go back to Mummy's room, where more and more experts in white jackets were assembled, since death was in the process of being born there.

How horrible. It's been so appointed that human beings, unlike animals, must give birth in pain; when the child is born, the pain is immediately transformed into happiness. But that neutralization was not to be Mummy's lot. The concentrated salic acid would be followed not by a base like sodium sulfate, but by concentrated saltpeter: the alchemists call that mixture royal water, *aqua regia*, because even gold dissolves in it. My head was spinning. I was sitting next to her on the bed wiping the sweat from her forehead, when I heard the midwife say:

"I can see the head."

Mummy had also heard and called:

"I've still got it! I've still got it!"

At that moment something incomprehensible came over me. Suddenly I began sweating and shaking all over my body as had happened to me only a couple of times before in my life. Was it the fear that I would shortly see a monster—created by all kinds of errors in the transcription and translation at DNA level? Mummy and I had discussed that possibility with her doctor. When I said that perhaps we should hope that you had something wrong with you, so that it was just as well that you were no longer alive, he had said, "No, Mr. Werker, you mustn't hope that." But if something monstrous were wrong with you after all, apart from your being dead, all those trained staff would certainly be able to hide it from Mummy by wrapping you quickly in a cloth and whisking you away, but I would see it. And it would pursue me for the rest of my life. Whatever the case, I was no longer in control of myself, and I rushed out of the room.

I stopped in the corridor, panting, of course I must go straight back, but I couldn't. A little farther along I saw a door with the sign SMOKING ROOM on it. Although I am still a confirmed smoker, it was like going into the anteroom of hell. The little room was filled with scores of patients and visitors who were sitting, silently inhaling, shrouded in a thick fog as if in an opium den. To light up a cigarette myself would be the best defense against this abomination, but I was reluctant to join those suckers crowded together in this cancerous den, which with devilish dialectic was allowed in the sterile confines of the hospital. The only place left was a window ledge. I don't know how long I sat there before going back, perhaps a quarter of an hour, or half an hour.

As I opened the door, heads turned toward me. I'd never been so ashamed in my life. Of course the doctors knew who I was: the manufacturer of the eobiont, the world-famous maker of life, who, when death is concerned, runs away. Only Mummy and the midwife did not look at me. Mummy was sitting upright in bed, again under the sheets and the midwife handed you to her with the kind of gesture with which queens are crowned. Your gallows had been removed, the blood and slime washed off, and what I saw was not a monster but a serene vision from another world. With you in her arms Mummy looked down at you like in a pietà. You were as white and still as the marble of Michelangelo in St. Peter's. You were limp, long, extended, your eyes were closed. Mummy too seemed to have turned into a statue, she didn't speak, she didn't cry, she didn't even seem to breathe. I went over to her, knelt down next to the bed, and put a hand on your narrow chest. You were warm! You were dead and yet warm! But it wasn't your warmth, it was Mummy's. From now on you would cool down minute by minute, until you had reached the room temperature of your death. You had just brushed past the world, your hereafter; afterward you would rot in the ground, which you had never seen. The silence which emanated from you was more silent than silence: it was the eternal silence that hangs between the stars. I looked at Mummy, but she didn't return my look. Then I saw the damp patch of a drop of milk appear on her nightdress, at nipple height.

That drop, I sometimes think, destroyed me. Although you couldn't catch cold, the midwife dressed you and put you under a blanket in a cot. Only at that moment did I realize that Mummy had brought clothes for you. The doctors disappeared one after the other, Mummy took a shower, gave you a final kiss on your forehead, and the two of us went home in silence.

Only when I'd put the key in the lock did I say: "I'm sorry . . . I couldn't handle it."

She shook her head, still without looking at me.

"I understand."

Is it conceivable that from then on in the most literal sense she never looked at me again? I'm not so sure but that feeling suddenly comes over me. Because I felt the need for a requiem, I put on Mahler's Fourth; before I sat down to listen, I turned the key in the lock of the nursery. Mummy doesn't know, but since then the door has never been opened again. For some reason or other I didn't dare. Now and then I work with fossil DNA and one night I dreamed that there was a monster in your room—not a dinosaur but a gigantic, felt-like moth, which was living on your clothes and your dolls.

Three days later we buried you in your little coffin in a part of the cemetery called the Garden. Here and there there were flowers on the tombstones, teddy bears and other toys; on most of them nothing more. We buried you like a human being who has never breathed its last because it's never taken its first breath. You had died without being born. That's impossible, and hence according to all the rules of logic the whole world became impossible. You achieved that impossibility, Aurora.

Sunday, September 25. Instead of spending my free time on *Aurora's Key to Life,* I now write to you every day. Today—I'm sitting at my familiar table in the Mena House—I'm going to tell you about two letters I received.

A few days after your funeral we flew to Marseille, where we took the train to Arles. Because Mummy couldn't come to a decision about our destination, I had chosen that fairy-tale little city on the Rhône; I'd been there once in my student days. I had the illusion that beauty could help us fight against our unhappiness, but now I think differently about it. Beauty rules not only art, but also science, technology, sport, almost everything you can conceive of; according to some people even war. But for individual grief there is no aesthetic medicine, just as a cancerous tumor will not disappear if one looks at a van Gogh self-portrait or listens to Mahler's Fourth. Only faith seems able—if not to take it away—at least to give amorphous grief some kind of form. Quite possibly, but Mummy and I lack religious talent.

In Arles you don't have to look for churches, those grief-processing machines, for very long. The most beautiful is of course the medieval cathedral of Saint Trophime, which we visited on the Place de la République with the obelisk. Except that it wasn't intended to be beautiful, but more a kind of emotional transhipment company, where the suffering of the individual issues like a small river into the vast ocean of Christ's suffering and death. Those who admire it just for its beauty, like virtually everyone who is inside, except for a few old ladies, thereby indicate that they have lost God.

I would have liked to say these kinds of things to Mummy at the time, but she was so focused on herself that it wasn't possible. On that first day we walked silently through the churches and monastery courtyards and the colossal Roman remains, the Arena, the Amphitheater, in the evening we sat opposite each other in silence in the restaurant—and my thoughts went back to that afternoon on the beach when she had laid her head on my shoulder. It was as if nothing remained of that moment, but even there I couldn't speak about it. The following day at break-fast she said that she'd like to spend the morning alone, I must just do what I felt like doing, we would see each other in the ho-tel at lunchtime. I didn't like it, but of course I respected it. I wandered through the town in the mild autumn weather, visited a museum, drank an espresso on a terrace, and on a bench on the quay I looked for a long time at the Rhône, that river between its overgrown, overhanging, enchanted banks, with its glittering currents and countercurrents. Now and then large dead branches floated past, like the antlers of deer running along the bed of the river. So was it after all beauty, the timeless beauty not created by human hands, that could console?

When I got back to the hotel Mummy had left. Her part of the wardrobe was empty, her suitcase had gone, her passport and ticket had gone. On the small desk by the window that looked out onto the intimate, rectangular Place du Forum, lay her letter. I haven't got it here, but I know it by heart.

Dear Victor,
I'm sorry, I can't help it. I've tried, but I can't. I'm leav-ing you and I'm not coming back. The reason is that you weren't there at Aurora's birth, that you left me alone. I said I understood, and I do, but I can't get over it. I couldn't run away. If you'd stayed, we could have solved it together, as you said, but we can't do that anymore. Something's broken beyond repair. I'm sorry, I can't express what I feel very well. We've had a lovely time together, but it's over for good. Swear to me that you'll never ring me up to try to talk me around, because there's no point. I'll ask my brother to contact you to move my things. Look after yourself.

Clara

It was as if I'd had a slap full in the face. I realized there, in that room in Arles with the letter in my hands, that I'd made the cardinal mistake of my life. She'd gone. First you, now her. I was overcome by an unstoppable fit of weeping. I dropped forward onto the bed and for ten minutes wretchedness raged through me like a storm through the treetops. Looking back on it, I wonder whether it was connected with the departure of my mother when I was eight. At the time I wasn't very concerned, as far as I can remember; perhaps the sorrow only found an outlet on this occasion. But anyway, I must be careful of those kinds of psychoanalytic considerations, because then nothing is what it is any longer.

What now? Should I leave at once too? What was left for me in France? To drive the blood from my brain into my stomach, I had a copious lunch in the restaurant opposite the hotel, all kinds of wonderful dishes à la Provençale, with a bottle of Gigondas and two Armagnacs with the coffee. I remember that at another table there was a blond American woman with a face-lift: she looked fifty and still you could see she was eighty. Then, fairly tipsy, I went into town and out again. How I got there I can't remember, but at a certain moment I saw that I was in Les Alycamps. On my previous visit to Arles, twenty years before, I'd been there too; but I had resolved not to go there with Mummy because it might have too great an effect on her. It's one of the mythical places in the earth, like one of those where I'm now sitting writing. A stately, straight avenue, lined on both sides by sarcophaguses, which followed each other like ships queuing at a lock, here and there interrupted by monuments and memorial chapels, all shadowed by filigree foliage. The necropolis dates from the Roman period, when it was called the Elysii Campi, the Elysian fields, where the blessed rest; gradually the name became corrupted into Alycamps. Dante writes about it in canto 9 of his *Inferno*, in which the graves are hellishly hot from the fires burning among them, and in *Orlando Furioso* Ariosto has

Raging Roland hack the Saracens to pieces in these Champs Elysées, which in the future will hopefully happen again, because nothing is ever over. (According to their own calendar those same Saracens are now living at the beginning of the fifteenth century, and that's just about right.) The place is so sacred that in the Middle Ages poor people in the north let the corpses of their loved ones float down the Rhône in pine coffins, so that they would find their way to Les Alycamps.

You notice that I'm writing about it in a very relaxed way, it's a year ago and my comments would not be out of place in a guidebook—but at the time I was completely beside myself. Not far from a memorial to van Gogh, who often came to paint here, I leaned against a sarcophagus without a lid, in which there were cigarette ends and cola cans, with a buzzing fly around my head, attracted by the fury raging in it. What on earth was I to do? It wasn't just helplessness that I'd been abandoned by my partner, but mostly because you'd been erased more finally than you already had been—and all through my own fault. Whom could I speak to about it now? How could I make up for what I'd done to her? Something was broken beyond repair, she'd written, I must swear not to ring her anymore. So I shan't—but what then? There had to be a way out, a way around, a back door!

When I got back home the following day her brother, your uncle Karel, turned out not to have leaped into action yet. Her things were still there, but different from usual, as if they'd all also died. Her beautiful Empire desk with the square columns on either side of the lid, crowned on the top with bronze women's heads, and finished at the bottom with bronze feet, the trestle with drawings on it, which she often worked at in the evenings; and all those other objects spread through the rooms. With my jacket still on, and on my lap the pile of mail that I'd taken out of the letterbox, I sat on the sofa and looked at them. My eye fell on the door of your room, with the key turned in the lock. So I would have to live alone with that forbidden place too. Should I perhaps immediately clear it out? Eliminate every trace?

After throwing all the colorful nonsense on glossy paper into the wastepaper basket, I sorted the newspapers, the magazines, and the letters. One envelope I took a dislike to at first sight, a specimen of the cheapest kind of envelope without a sender's name, addressed in spindly writing to *Professor V. Werker*. I haven't got this second letter either, but I know it by heart too. On ruled paper which had been torn off carelessly it said in large letters:

> *Congratulations! Have you got what you wanted now? You paid for the eobiont with your own child. An eye for an eye, a tooth for a tooth! Soon it will be your own turn, bastard!*

That was all, but I froze when I read those few sentences. Who could be so despicable? Of course I thought immediately of Brock: Could he really have sunk that low? The handwriting wasn't his, but the awkwardness was obviously deliberate; he was left-handed, perhaps he'd written it with his right hand. Should I take it to the police? I'd been threatened, and a threat is a crime in itself, and anyone who has knowledge of crime is obliged to report it, otherwise he is an accessory. An accessory to my own death! But then I would have to say whom I suspected— and if it turned out subsequently not to be him? Then he really would have cause to murder me.

Monday, September 26. This morning I had a fax from your milk uncle Albert Dodemont. He was absolutely flabbergasted to hear the story of Granny's surplus milk; their mother had never told them. Every autumn, he, his Australian brother Marnix, and his Canadian brother Sjoerd have a reunion at one of their places. This time it's in Haarlem; he suggests we meet each other next month. I'll invite them to my place in Amsterdam. I'm really curious!

Anyway, I've been here for more than three weeks, our concessions are expiring and I've got to work very hard for these last few days, so I shan't have any more time for these notes. But by now you know more or less everything. I would like to have traveled around a bit through this country of the imagination and reported on it to you, but I won't be able to this time. Until this afternoon I hadn't even seen the Sphinx. Imagine: three weeks in Egypt without seeing the Sphinx! Like someone returning from heaven and saying he hasn't seen God. Too busy. Didn't have time. But this afternoon, before I went to the Mena House, I made time and went, a ten-minute walk.

How is a person supposed to talk about silence? Like a gigantic gold-brown dachshund with its front paws stretched out, between a hundred and fifty and a hundred and eighty feet long, eighty feet high, it lies in the sun in front of the Pyramid of Chefren. And behind it there is nothing but desert. Unlike the Greek sphinxes it's a "he," with the face of the pharaoh. The nose has disappeared, shot off by the wanton artillerymen of Napoleon if I remember, so that he looks like a boxer. I'm sorry, but again it's Hegel, who in my opinion spoke the last word on the creature: "The symbol of the symbolic." In Greece it sets riddles ("What creature walks on four legs in the morning, on two in the afternoon, and on three at night?"); here it is itself the riddle. I stood looking at it for half an hour, while a bleeding twilight fell and while around it horses and camels kicked up pink desert sand in the hot trembling light, and somewhere in the distance the electronically amplified voice of a muezzin called plaintively to evening prayer. "Man," is the traditional answer of Oedipus, but here I didn't experience anything as general as that. "Know yourself," says a Greek adage, which can be read in the temple of the Delphic oracle ("Deny yourself," they say a little farther away, on the other side of the Indus, where Alexander's advance ended). Here I was overcome by a more disturbing riddle still. Suppose that you finally know yourself, you're such and such—then the final question arises: Why? Why are you such and such? Because your DNA looks like such and such? But why does it look like such and such? That's the question that the Sphinx itself is, and there is no answer. Then you're in the desert for good. Then you can die of thirst.

KING DAVID HOTEL

JERUSALEM

Saturday, October 1, 1994

A quick postscript about the pharaoh's revenge! I've just arrived here, my suitcase is still unpacked on the bed. Tomorrow I have an appointment with a colleague from Hebrew University, to-day it's Sabbath and I'm looking out over the Old City: a sandy yellow mirage of domes and churches spread out over the hills, motionless in the golden evening light.

This morning, at Cairo airport, I was grilled for ten minutes by an Israeli security man. I had a flight on an El Al plane, that is to say an object in which certain Palestinian groups have a particular interest. As we were flying in a beautiful arc to the right over the Mediterranean, a film was started; the plane was moderately full, most passengers pulled down the cover of their window, but I went on looking outside, where there was a nicer film on. On my lap lay *Alice's Adventures in Wonderland,* in which I was looking for quotes for *Aurora's Key to Life.* Sud-denly a six-foot-long flame roared out of the engine. I'm not that easily alarmed, Aurora, but now I went rigid. The orange flame kept flapping like an infernal flag in a hurricane and I was the only one who saw it! Because, of course, I mustn't cause any panic, I pressed the button for the steward. I pointed silently outside. He bent down, looked for a moment, and then quickly went forward to the cockpit. Less than a minute later he was back and, without looking at me, sat down in the empty seat in front of me, obviously to observe the fire on the orders of the pilot. For a moment something rumbled and banged in the engine and the flame disappeared, but I had no opportunity to feel relieved, because a moment later it was back, against the peaceful background of the sea. I began sweating with fear. The Palestinians! Never before had I felt death so close, any second it could appear like a globe of burning kerosene as large as the airplane. While everyone was relaxing and watching the film, I tore the last, blank page out of Carroll's book and very quickly wrote a short farewell note to Mummy in pencil, folded it, and pushed it into the breast pocket of my shirt, so that it might perhaps be found if a bit of me washed up on some coast or other.

The fire was brought under control after all, no one noticed a thing, but if I had been a film fan, I probably wouldn't have survived. The letter is still in my breast pocket and, with a feeling of embarrassment, I'll transcribe it for you:

My Dear Clara,
The engine's on fire. My last thoughts are with you.
I ask for your forgiveness.

Victor

DEED C

THE CONVERSATION

Someone must (. . .) outlive him.

Franz Kafka, *The Trial*

EVENING

CLARA LOOKS AT HIM with an unfathomable smile. In her white robe she is sitting with legs wide apart in the shadow of the boulder, in front of the cave of Oedipus, at the foot of the Acropolis, the apple in her hand. During their Greek holiday he'd been there with her for curiosity's sake to see if he could find Bea, his previous girlfriend, whom he had once passed on to his Cyclops of a father—but all the caves were deserted.

He starts at the sound of the downstairs bell. As he goes to the intercom in the hall, he dabs his eyes and looks at his watch: seven o'clock. Right on time.

"Yes?"

"Mr. Werker? Dinner service."

"Take the lift to the fifth floor, I'll meet you."

No one can ever find the way in the converted neo-Gothic Basilica in which he lives. The colossal space, rescued at the last moment from the demolition hammer, is filled in the aisles on the ground floor with shops, cafés, galleries, a cinema, a bowling alley, a children's nursery, a little theater in the former consistory, a wine bar in the sacristy, and a discotheque in the crypt; there is also an Italian restaurant, Mirafiori, where he eats a couple of times a week. The upper floors, with imposing, brightly colored groups of columns anchored to the pillars and columns, are divided into scores of flats, occupied by affluent tenants, but also by the offices of small publishers and advertising agencies, idealistic lawyers' collectives, advice bureaus, the editorial offices of fringe magazines, and by nontransparent enterprises with names like "Interhabitus and Co.," popularly known as "the villains"; they have congregated particularly in the massive tower above the intersection of the nave and the transepts, where a silver floor has been suspended.

He turns off Mahler, picks up the telephone, and walks across the reflecting floor of the hallway, onto which the bright red doors give, flanked by crossed aluminium beams, via adventurously confusing staircases, indoor squares, and bridges, all constructed of metal, erector set-like elements, to the lifts. Like harsh blue beetles they creep up and down one wall of the great shaft, which stretches like the soul of the building from the apse to the open-work glass-covered vaults, of which the cross ribs are painted a shocking shade of yellow, which betrays the hand of Clara. Here and there slender trees grow out of the semicircular bulges between the stained-glass windows, which give the constructed indoor world a paradoxical air of an outdoor world.

The tall, delicate-looking servant is in evening dress, with a black bow tie, as befits a waiter. In each hand he carries a pile of gleaming pans, makes a polite bow and introduces himself as "Frank." Victor has gradually got used to the fact that people often no longer give their surname, although it cost him some effort; that used to be the custom only in the underworld. Obviously the whole world was turning into the underworld. He is struck by the gleaming, feverish look in Frank's eyes: eyes like black puddles in a park, left after a cloudburst; through the middle of his thick dark hair there is a straight parting, revealing a white scalp—as if, thinks Victor, a careful executioner has made room there for the ax which is to cleave the skull. He is accompanied by a woman with a coarse, empty face, which wears its emptiness openly. Baguettes protrude from a wicker basket. "Felia," she says, proffering a limp, moist hand.

"I'll show you where the kitchen is."

After they have put their burden down on the worktop, he shows them around his flat, which is on the nicest side of the transept. Since Clara's brother has removed her things, the living room still has a dismantled look about it. The white bookshelves are still only half full and the pattern of discoloration on the wall shows where things used to hang. Only Clara's writing desk is left. Virtually all he does here is watch television, late in the evening, with a glass of wine.

"Will you be eating in here?" asks Frank, pointing to the round dining table.

"No, that's more for a family meal. Tonight it's a dinner for four gentlemen."

He sees Frank pause for a moment on the threshold of his large study, in which he now spends virtually all his time. As a contract waiter with a catering company he of course visits all kinds of accommodations, but obviously he's never seen anything like this before, and at the same time he is sensitive enough to notice. The layout and furnishings have scarcely anything in common with those of the previous room, in which Clara had a hand. The floor is covered from wall to wall with a dark red carpet, on which a pool of blood would not be noticed; a couple of Persian rugs interrupt the red flood, the walls are paneled in dark wood. The tall bookshelves, which take up a whole wall, are filled exclusively with books relating to his work; the dust jackets have been removed, so that the beautiful dark blue and green bindings of Oxford and Harvard and other university presses are visible. On some shelves and on a couple of long tables there are manuscripts, notebooks, and photocopies in neatly ordered piles. Here a hand had been at work that either had no notion of chaos, or had fought a successful battle against it. "I have extended my life by years," he is wont to say, "by never having to look for anything." The walls are covered only in etchings and prints in black and white as if the tiniest glimmer of frivolity must be excluded from this serene environment. On his desk with the small black computer, where order, though not an exaggerated one, prevails, there is a small marble bust of Hermes; on its left shoulder is a tiny hand of the vanished child of Dionysus, whom he must have been carrying in his arms, which had broken off. Next to it was an antique *yat* in ivory and chased silver, ending in a tiny hand with an extended index finger, for pointing at the words in the Torah, which must not be touched by human hand—and which has returned in the world of technology as the cursor on his liquid crystal display screen. On the edge of the desk is a grubby, oblong package of grayish brown linen that must once have been sparkling white: the mummy of a baby monkey, as an X-ray photo has shown.

It is the room that he wanted even when he was only about sixteen and still in high school—the same age at which he was firmly convinced that he would one day win the Nobel Prize for literature. Back then he had drawn on ruled notepad sheets the plan of the writer's room that he later wanted for himself. When fitting out the study he had had in mind the atmosphere which now prevails, without the room having originated from the memory of those plans, because he'd forgotten them. But when a few years ago, thanks to Clara, he moved in here and designed the room, he suddenly saw that it had become that old ideal room: everything was in its place, and in the meantime he turned out to have acquired precisely those things that were necessary to make the room into something like the depiction of his soul.

He points to an oblong table with folders and a fax machine on it.

"We're eating there. We'll fetch upright chairs from the living room."

After he has cleared the table, he goes over and stands with his hands in his pockets in front of the magnificent window that is formed by the top of a huge pointed arch, which disappears into the floor and also supplies light to the lower floors. The light is gray, a chilly autumn mist hangs over the roofs; it is raining. The Dodemont brothers are arriving at seven-thirty, as he has arranged from Egypt with Albert in Haarlem; in hindsight, it doesn't really suit him, but today was the only possibility. He thinks that a certain telephone call from Stockholm is not impossible, after which his mind will be on other things. The day after tomorrow is the day on which the Nobel Prizes will be announced; all over the world physicists, chemists, biologists, and writers will be sitting at home today and tomorrow looking out of the corner of their eye at the silent telephone, doing their best to relax and read the paper. Television crews are probably already on the doorstep of the writers tipped for the prize so as to be able to pounce immediately when it emerges that it's their turn—or else to pack up their things with a sigh and disappear when the radio announces that someone else has won the jackpot, abandoning the poor candidate as someone who has *not* won the Nobel Prize for the umpteenth time. He can console himself with the thought that he is still in a very select company, from Tolstoy and Proust and Valéry to Joyce and Borges. Just imagine that this year he is the chosen one—what will Brock do then?

While Felia lays the table behind him, in a white apron, he wonders what he's actually going to talk about with the three men. Suddenly he has a brainwave. He decides to use them as a kind of tribunal that must judge his situation with Clara, from whom he's heard nothing even after his three letters. Of course he knows a few people to whom he could talk about it, but he knows them so well that he is certain in advance what they would say. Perhaps he'll get further with a full court of independent judges.

When the bell rings just after half past seven and a funereal voice says "Dodemont" in his ear, he goes back to the lift with his telephone. He waits with his arms folded until the lift arrives. As the doors slide open he has to control himself in order not to burst out laughing. What appears is impossible! Three men, who can be fully described by describing one of them. Stocky, almost a head shorter than he is, coarsely featured, rather proletarian faces, blue eyes; their thin, lank, pale blond hair brushed upward from the temples to cover their bald pates. They're wearing dark gray suits with brown shoes, only their club ties have a slightly different pattern. To make it easy for the rest of mankind each of them wears a silver badge on his lapel, one with an *A*, the second with an *M*, the third with an *S*.

"Brothers!" says Victor, opening his arms wide. "Welcome! I am Victor Werker."

"Albert."

"Marnix."

"Sjoerd."

They shake hands and look at each other with curiosity. Their voices too have the same dark timbre, as if the meaning of their surname, "dead mouth," needs emphasizing. The Australian Marnix and Canadian Sjoerd have English accents, but very slight; so they're not posers. It had already struck Victor that people who have lived in America for five years sometimes come back with a heavy American accent, while people who've been in Germany for five years never come back with a German accent. For example, there's no trace of American audible in the Dutch of his mother, who's lived in America for donkey's years. Besides pretension it's probably also connected with musicality.

Each of them hands him a carton of milk as a gift, which he accepts with a grin of assent. Once they're sitting in his study on the sofa and in the armchairs, and are having a glass of champagne poured for them by Frank, Victor feels obliged to make a declaration. He has no idea what it will sound like, but experience has taught him that you must simply start talking, and the content will then follow of its own accord. He raises his glass and says:

"Well, gentlemen, here we are then. I don't think any of us

know which of us is the eldest, but I propose that we use Christian names. We've known each other long enough, if I can put it like that. When my mother told me about you at the beginning of this year, my mouth dropped open in astonishment."

"Just like ours," says Albert, "when we heard about it from you. Our mother never said anything about it. And she only died a few months ago."

"And your father?"

"We never really knew him. Our mother took us away with her when we were about six. A few years later he seems to have met a violent end, but we've never managed to find out the details."

"So your mother is still alive."

Victor sees from the badge that it is Marnix talking.

"Of course. She's sixty-seven now."

"Is she coming this evening too? Then we'll be able to thank her at last for her good offices."

"That'll be difficult, she lives in San Francisco."

"Have you got a photo of her, Victor?"

"Of course." Victor gets up and from the bookshelf takes a photo album, which belonged to his father. He opens it at a photo with the three of them in it. *At the Zoo, 1956*, his father wrote under it. The year of Clara's birth. Perhaps, he thinks, her umbilical cord was cut at exactly the same moment that this photo was taken by some helpful passerby or other. In the background a panther is prowling past the bars.

"Good-looking woman." Marnix nods. "Is your father still alive too?"

"He's been dead for twelve years." He looks at the stern figure with the black patch over his eye. When you look at the photo of someone who's now dead, he wonders, do you see the living or the dead person?

"What was his job?"

"Soldier. And what was your father's?"

"Contractor."

Victor is about to ask whether they have a photo of their parents with them, but something stops him from doing so. The sight of the three spitting images makes him a little dizzy, as in a hall of mirrors. It doesn't matter much who says what, it could also have been said by one of the others. In the not-too-distant future, he thinks, it'll be possible to make a thousand clones in the laboratory, or a hundred thousand, or a million. He tries to imagine that he himself has two monozygotic brothers who are exactly like him, but he can't even imagine there actually *being* someone with the same parents as he has.

"We are familiar with that look you're giving us at the moment," says Marnix.

"I don't doubt it," says Victor with a laugh. "I'm sorry, but it's unbelievable. I'm more or less in the business myself, and I've done my homework for this occasion. Statistically there is one set of twins in every eighty-five births, a set of triplets for each eighty-five squared, a set of quadruplets for each eighty-five to the third power, and so on. Apart from the fact that that figure eighty-five is a mystery, that means that there is a set of triplets for roughly every seven thousand or so births, but they usually originate from two or three fertilized eggs. But when I look at you, I have the impression that you are monozygotic triplets."

"That's right," says Sjoerd.

"And that almost never occurs."

"We know. But that was no reason for us not to be born."

They're amusing chaps. Victor has a feeling of affinity with them, which he quite simply ascribes to their shared mother's milk.

"So what is your subject then?" asks Albert. "I got your fax from Cairo on exceptionally interesting headed notepaper."

Obviously they don't follow the scientific news in the media. After he's told them in broad outline the kind of work that he does, without mentioning the eobiont, Sjoerd, or Marnix, or Albert says that they are all in the book trade. Albert is a typographer in Haarlem as he knows, Marnix is a printer in Sydney, Sjoerd is a designer with a publishing house in Toronto.

"Books are obviously in the genes too." Victor nods. "And that surprises me, because genes were there before books. Although," he says, making a vague gesture, "genes are actually also a kind of book." As Frank refills the glasses, he takes a photocopy off the table and says, "By the way, what I also found in the literature, and it might interest you, is the case of a man who had eighty-seven children from three marriages. With his first wife four sets of quadruplets, seven sets of triplets, and six pairs of twins; and with his second wife two sets of triplets and sixteen sets of twins. Just imagine," he says looking up. "Eighty-seven children! Having to think up eighty-seven names!"

"Do you have children?" asks Sjoerd.

Victor puts down the photocopy, folds his arms, and looks at the large brandy glass in the middle of the low circular table, filled to the brim with obsolete keys. That was an idea of Clara's; if he were to put the key of the nursery in it, it would be difficult for him to find it again.

"No," he says. And a few seconds later: "I'm not a success in an evolutionary sense."

The Dodemont brothers sense that they have touched a nerve and are silent. In order to break this silence, Victor asks:

"What did you three weigh at birth?"

"About three pounds."

"Then I was as heavy as the three of you put together. So that means that now in fact . . . what do you weigh?"

"A hundred and sixty pounds."

"Then now I should really weigh five hundred pounds."

"And what do you actually weigh?"

"A hundred and thirty-five. That's about four-fifths of one of you."

"But you can add up faster than the three of us together anyway."

Victor smiles.

"It's quite possible that there is no such thing as a fat mathematician. In any case I can't come up with an example offhand."

Keeping an appropriate distance, Frank makes a small bow and says:

"Dinner is served."

Victor gets up, and with a gesture of his hand utters the sentence which he has previously prepared:

"Gentlemen, dinner is served, and bear in mind that without me you would have already starved."

As he closes the curtains before they eat, the telephone rings. Immediately his heart starts pounding.

"Yes, hello?" Total silence at the other end of the line. "Hello?" he says again, at which point he is cut off. He puts the telephone down and shrugs his shoulders. "A fault at the exchange, or a lunatic." Or Brock, he thinks. "Sit down."

During the crab soup he inquires about their domestic circumstances. All three of them are married and all three have three children, two boys and a girl, in the same order and virtually the same ages.

"Everything's the same with you three," says Victor. "It's only your ties that are a little different."

"But not very much," says Marnix. "I bought this one last week in Sydney, before I left for Europe." Without saying anything he looks at Sjoerd.

"In Toronto. Last week too."

"And so yours was last week in Haarlem," says Victor to Albert, shaking his head.

"That's right."

"It'll be a long time before science can explain your ties. Black holes are a trifle by comparison."

After the difficult moment just now, obviously none of them dares to ask about his own situation. So he must bring it up himself. After a mouthful of bread he tastes the red Bordeaux, while Frank shows him the label and waits for a reaction, his left arm behind his back. He nods and says:

"Everything about me is different, although we imbibed the same mother's milk. Not only have I not got any children, I haven't a wife either. I'm a sad bachelor. Shall I tell you about myself? I can imagine that it doesn't interest you."

"Of course we're interested," says Sjoerd. "But you must only tell us if it isn't compromising for you."

"'Compromising, compromising . . .'" repeats Victor. "The facts are compromising, telling you them isn't. All right then. Cheers!"

And after they have clinked glasses, and while they enjoy the rolled joint of meat, he tells them the story of Clara and Aurora; he also mentions the letters that he has written to Clara via Aurora. When he has finished, nothing is said. He realizes that the three of them are looking into an unfamiliar world; they had a big problem at their birth and in the months following, subsequently their lives were channeled into respectable, bourgeois channels, without real calamities. Apart from that they always have one another. In some mysterious way they are never alone, although they live thousands of miles apart; in some way or other they remain enclosed by a common egg as large as the world. The fact that they buy ties in the same week has nothing to do with telepathy, but the mechanism works via their common origin, in the way that some plants are linked by a subterranean root stock. For that matter, he thinks, wiping his mouth, if all life really did originate from one living primeval cell, the archaeoeobiont, everything that lives and lived in space and time, from the most primitive archaeon to Albert Einstein, from this beef to the salad—is linked in a similar way to the triplets. All living creatures together would then form something like an infinitiplet, with one exception, his own eobiont. Perhaps he must talk about this in *Aurora's Key to Life*.

"Tell me what I am to do," he says.

While Frank clears the table and brushes the bread crumbs off the tablecloth with a small narrow curved brush into his hand, the three men look at one another rather dismayed.

"What exactly do you want?" asks Marnix. "Do you want her to come back to you?"

"What I really want is to undo what I did—or rather didn't do."

"Then you'll have to invent a time machine and go back into the delivery room."

Victor nods.

"I made the wrong discovery in my life."

"Has she got a boyfriend?" asks Albert.

"A Viennese baritone."

"What kind of man is he?"

"No idea, never met him. About our age, I think. He seems to be famous."

"And how serious is that relationship?"

"I don't know. Perhaps it's serious but I can also imagine that she's only taken up with him to get rid of me. Of course I always remind her of the time when she was carrying death around inside her."

"But if she really doesn't want anything more to do with you," says Sjoerd, "that's the end of it."

"Of course. It's just that I'm not absolutely certain."

"Why not?"

"A week after our trip to Arles she removed all her things, except for one. In the room next door there is still her Empire writing desk, a very precious piece of furniture, the most beautiful thing she possesses, with all kinds of personal things in it. What is the message? She can't have forgotten it."

"So there's hope." Albert nods. "Do the obvious thing then."

"Which is?"

"Ring her up."

Victor shakes his head.

"I promised her I wouldn't."

"Isn't that a bit formal?" Marnix looks at him skeptically. "Surely you can do it anyway even if you promised not to do it?"

"You'd think so. But then I'd find myself in the same situation that destroyed everything."

"In what way?"

"That I'd promised to be there for the delivery, and wasn't. Anyway, it's less formal than you think, because in that farewell letter that she wrote in Arles she says that I must promise not to ring her. I could take the view that I haven't promised, but that's too subtle for me."

"And to my mind the fact that you're keeping a promise that you haven't made," says Albert, "is not less formal but much more formal."

"There's something in that."

"It's all very subtle."

"That's obviously my nature."

"But you've got her number at least?" asks Marnix with a rather shrewd smile, which shows that in his view life sometimes runs a little less formally.

"I've got it. Her brother once gave it to me in his innocence."

"Can't you accidentally bump into her?" suggests Sjoerd. "You know where she lives, don't you?"

"At the moment in Vienna."

"Or did you agree anything about accidentally bumping into each other?"

The irony isn't lost on Victor. While Felia serves the strawberry bavarois and Frank pours the Sauternes, they are silent. Victor stares at the polished silver bell on the table, with which the staff can be summoned. He is reminded of a dreadful sentence he once read, but can't remember where: "Love is the fact that you are the knife which I burrow in myself." He's never talked to anyone about his problem, and now the fact that he has done so seems to have changed things. An alarming thought has occurred to him: how much does he really want Clara to come back to him? He's already been living for a year without her, and he can't say that he was so terribly unhappy all that time. He's enjoyed his work, and as far as sex is concerned something always turns up. In Berkeley he had a thing with a small, shapely Egyptologist, who after she'd come would sit astride the toilet with the door open, and puff as if she had climbed the pyramid of Cheops; in Venice a nameless Dane showed up, who jerked him off at the speed with which one whips cream; in Cairo an indolent Scottish globetrotter was interested in him, and at home it's no problem at all. So what's it about? Perhaps it's really about something completely different. Perhaps things are the complete opposite of what he's always thought. Can it be, he thinks, thrown into confusion, that it's not so much about love as about guilt? What was really the deepest reason for his fleeing when she was giving birth? After all, with monkeys he's not so sensitive. "The monkeys are for it," is the standard expression in the lab when the poor creatures are about to be injected with something dreadful, which is going to kill them, and no one knows better than he does that chimpanzees at least—as near as, dammit—are people. The genetic difference is 1.6 percent: smaller than that between a chimpanzee and an orangutan. That tiny fraction may account for the fact that the chimpanzee cannot talk—but it may also be connected to the construction of its tongue, because it's been shown that it can acquire a deaf and dumb vocabulary of thousands of words. If vivisection of human beings is not allowed, it shouldn't be for chimpanzees. So although he doesn't shrink from something like murder, why does he from the birth of a dead child? Was it really from fear of seeing a monster emerge? Anyway . . . murder? If a person who kills a chimpanzee is something like a murderer, the same applies to a chimpanzee that kills a human being, and it must also be sentenced in a trial. In earlier centuries such animal trials did take place, followed by public executions, and that in fact showed more respect for animals than can be found nowadays. But then that genetic near-as-dammit suddenly manifests itself, because the guilty chimpanzee cannot understand the charge or the sentence. So perhaps after all it's innocent and not capable of murder, only of killing, and in that case it is perhaps admissible to experiment on it. Anyway, that's how he salves his conscience—although he's aware that in that case it would be permissible to carry out vivisection on the deaf and dumb. But in what convoluted way is he to salve his conscience over his fatal flight from Clara's delivery room?

He'd most like to pursue his train of thought, but he sees that his guests don't know what to make of the silence that has fallen.

"It was reasonably tasty," he said, "although it was nothing compared with the breast, because that's something like a thousand-star restaurant. Shall we leave the table," he suggests, forcing a smile.

Once they've returned to their previous places Frank provides them with coffee and liqueur and offers cigars. They light up from a burning taper of wood, while Victor lights a cigarette. He'd prefer them to leave now, and probably they would have preferred to do that themselves, but for half an hour they go on talking about their work and circumstances in Haarlem, Toronto, and Sydney.

"Are your wives along too?" asks Victor.

"The three of them have gone for a meal in town," says Sjoerd, looking at his watch. "Come on, I think it's time for us to go."

Victor gets up without a protest.

"Give my regards to the Mrs. Dodemonts. Are they also triplets?"

"In a certain sense, yes, but not biological."

"Well . . ." says Victor, about to wish them farewell, but Marnix suggests:

"Couldn't we give your mother a ring? I'd like to hear her voice."

Victor hesitates, he'd rather not use the telephone now. He looks at his watch.

"There's no point," he says with a bad conscience. "It's three in the afternoon in San Francisco now and she's never home then."

"But of course you'll give her our regards," says Albert.

"Of course I will."

NINTH DOCUMENT

NIGHT

AFTER THE DEPARTURE of Frank and Felia it is quiet in the flat again. He puts the telephone on the table, takes off his jacket and pours himself a double scotch. Putting his hands with their white patches together for a moment, he notices that one is warm and the other cold, but it's impossible to say which is warm and which cold; he only knows that when he puts them against his cheeks for a moment. With his hands in his trouser pockets he lies down on the sofa. Ultimately, he thinks, you're always left alone. What do you suppose the three men were saying to one another now, and what would they be saying in a little while to their three wives? That they'd met a sad recluse who didn't know what to do with his life? Of course they remained strangers, but nevertheless their presence opened up something in him. A moment ago he wanted to reflect as quickly as possible on that opening, but now for some reason he wants to put it off, just as a cook suddenly thinks that a dish may perhaps do better to stay in the oven for a while. He knows that phenomenon from his scientific work too: when he has a fruitful brainwave, which he could develop immediately, he first makes a cup of coffee and stares out the window for a while. For that matter, he remembers it from a completely different sort of work, that he pursued as a boy—at night, keeping an ear open to make sure he didn't hear his father or mother approaching. He didn't know how other boys masturbated; probably they jerked off quickly, turned over, and went to sleep. But he was sometimes at it for more than an hour, not because he couldn't come, but because he didn't want to come yet. One fantasy succeeded another and whenever he almost got to the point, he stopped and let things subside. Each time he had the feeling that it could be even more intense. He would scour his memory of the past day for a link and let his imagination loose on it. That woman who'd been sitting next to him in the cinema that evening; he cautiously put his hand on her knee, whereupon she slowly spread her legs, so that he could reach the ultra-erotic zone between the top of her stocking and that of her panties; next her hand appeared on his thigh, crept inch by inch toward his crotch and slowly began kneading him. The large, dark blond woman who that morning on the way to school had stood up against him in the chockful tram . . . her arse fitted so exactly into his groin that she couldn't help wiggling it for a moment, which for him was the sign to winkle out his penis with one hand and lift up her dress with the other. She wasn't wearing panties for the occasion and pushed her buttocks a little farther back, so that he could climb into the neck of her hollow tropical tree, while she went on talking to her husband as though nothing were going on . . . that girl that he'd seen in the afternoon in the bookshop . . . she had lost her purse, and it also had her train ticket to Maastricht in it, she didn't know where to spend the night; after he had sworn to behave himself, Scout's honor, she came with him; in bed they kept their tops and bottoms on and lay as far apart as possible, but in the middle of the night he woke up, they were both naked, arms, legs, prick, cunt, punt, crick, everything compressed into a clammy lump, like two soft clay puppets. . . . What it finally resulted in was usually not the ultra-orgasm he was looking for, but a fairly low-level satisfaction, though by now his penis was black-and-blue with masturbating, the skin shiny with pink fluid from the wound, with a pointed hat of white foam on the head. The organ looked like a ridiculous little man—a little man who occurred to him years later, when out of curiosity he immersed himself in the alchemical writings of Paracelsus, in which he describes the production of a homunculus, an artificial human being. With him, too, the major role is played by "Phantasey," while the sperm is divided from the "living water," like "scum on soup." Was his homunculus perhaps the product of self-abuse?

He loosens his tie and lights up a cigarette. Can you want something, he wonders, when you actually want the opposite? Of course. Someone can light up a cigarette when he really wants to stop smoking—with decent people that conflict occurs with all vices. But what is it like in his case then? The smoker is aware both of one thing and the other, while he himself is only aware of one thing: that he wants Clara to come back to him. At least that was what it was like up to an hour ago. Is it really possible that "unconsciously" he doesn't want that at all? Unconsciously! He hates that term, you can explain everything with it, hence nothing, it's like the I Ching. And yet . . . Is it conceivable that he has to dig even deeper to understand himself? He feels as if he's lying on Freud's sofa, with himself at the same time in the role of the Viennese code breaker. In earlier years he had browsed through Freud's work for a while, like that of Paracelsus, and he tries to imagine what Freud might have said. Perhaps this: "When you were eight your mother left you and you were obviously never able to come to terms with this properly. When subsequently your daughter also left you, that was too much for you and you behaved in such a way that in the third instance your wife also left you. And why did you do that? So that out of self-preservation you could cherish the illusion that you could also handle being deserted by your mother. You could imagine you were master of the whole situation."

Brilliant! A loud laugh escapes his mouth. None of those

Freud vilifiers of recent times could think up something like that. Perhaps it's even true. And if it's not true, then it's usable. He sits up, takes off his shoes, and rests his elbows on his knees. So how do things stand? Through his doing Clara left and in that way he has settled the account with his mother. That means everything is as he really wants it. But meanwhile he's written her three indirect letters with the intention of getting her to come back to him, which he ultimately doesn't want. In that case isn't she bound to know? In the living room her writing desk stands as a signal that for her the situation has still not been dealt with, while for him that is obviously the case. Perhaps she's waiting for a word from him to say that everything's going to change, whereupon she will say "*Grüss Gott*" to her baritone in Vienna and take the next plane. But that word really ought to have been in his letters, to which he has had no reply. What can he add to them? The fact that his inner Sigmund has told him that it's his mother's fault that he couldn't bear the appearance of their dead Aurora? Anyway, even if this is all true, despite that, can't he take a *salto mortale* over all interpretations and analyses, an unhesitating death leap, which results in her coming back to him after all?

His head is spinning, he wants what he doesn't want and he doesn't want what he wants; with each step he becomes more and more lost in the maze of his broodings. Experience has taught him that he can't get through this by thinking but only by doing something. "Ring her up," said Albert, or Marnix, or Sjoerd. Isn't that a solution after all? Didn't A or M or S have the right end of the stick when he inquired whether he at least had her number? He pours himself another scotch and looks at the telephone. It's almost twelve, it's improbable that his number will be dialed this late in Stockholm. She herself never goes to bed before one, so that's no problem.

While he sits looking at the telephone, he imagines how the conversation might run . . .

"Hello?"

"Clara? It's Victor."

There is a moment's silence.

"Yes, Victor?"

"I can understand that you're surprised about this call, we had a tacit agreement that I wouldn't ring, but I couldn't help myself."

"Just say what you have to say. There's nothing seriously wrong with you, is there?"

"It depends how you look at it. Did you get the copies of my letters to Aurora?"

"Yes . . ."

"And have you read them?"

"Of course."

"Well?"

"What do you want me to say?"

"Well, that's for you to say. I'd like you to say that you understand everything better now."

"That's true."

"But?"

"But that doesn't change anything."

"Why not?"

"I wrote that in my letter in Arles. You abandoned me once and for all in the hospital on that dreadful afternoon, and nothing can ever change that."

"Not even if I tell you who the monster really was that I daren't look at?"

"What do you mean? Aurora, of course."

"No. My mother."

Again there is a short silence.

"Victor, are you quite right in the head? Your mother! How can you say a thing like that? You should be ashamed! Have you been drinking by any chance?"

"I have, but it's quite separate from that. Tonight I had dinner with the triplets who drank my mother's milk as babies, you remember, I wrote to you about that. *Trink, trink, Brüderlein, trink!* I'm sure your new fiancé has that song in his repertoire."

"Listen, if your plan is to insult me, I'll hang up straightaway."

"Is he in the room too?"

"Yes."

"And when you heard my voice just now, you looked at him and you mouthed the word 'Victor' with your lips, didn't you?"

"What are you getting at?"

"If only I knew."

"In your last letter you wrote about that Gordian knot that untied by itself, but if you ask me you're tying it ever tighter."

"No, no! I'm glad you've come back to that, I'm trying to find precisely the rod that Alexander pulled out of it."

"If you ask me, there isn't any rod. Listen carefully, Victor. It's pointless. I'm surprised you don't understand that. You're such an intelligent man, the whole world is amazed at your work, but when it comes to your personal circumstances you're suddenly like a child who wants the impossible."

"Exactly! And that's what I've done with my work."

"So that turned out not to be impossible."

"No, in hindsight not."

"Are you by any chance trying to say that nothing's impossible?"

"I'm inclined to say that. If someone said a century ago that within a hundred years there would be a machine that could calculate in a few seconds what takes a thousand mathematicians a thousand years, everyone would have said that that's impossible."

"When you were in a talkative mood in the past, you sometimes said that one thing's certain in the world, namely that a greater speed than the speed of light is impossible."

"I'm not even so sure about that nowadays. . . . What's left of Freud? And of Lenin? The same fate might also befall Einstein."

"Freud, Einstein, Lenin . . . what are we really talking about?"

"That the impossible could also happen between us, Clara."

"But that's precisely the difference. Our relationship is not a theory."

The twelve strokes of the cathedral bring him back to reality. He takes a deep breath and closes his eyes for a moment. Would the conversation go like that? No, of course not. It wasn't a conversation between him and her, but between him and himself, in the form of Clara. He gets up and opens a new bottle of scotch. Outside it's grown quieter, the murmur of the traffic is softer, as if it's been snowing. Back on the sofa he looks at the telephone again. After all he knows her well enough to know what she would say! After all, a writer does nothing else: he even knows what people say who don't even exist.

He looks up Clara's number in his diary, takes the telephone off the table, and taps twelve figures with his index finger, but without pushing in the keys . . .

"*Ja, wer spricht?*"

An unpleasantly loud man's voice. Conversation, laughter, music in the background.

"*Mein Name ist Victor Werker.*"

"Oh, Herr Werker! Good evening. Jäger-Jena. Nice to hear your voice at last."

"I'm sure your voice is more important. Please forgive my disturbing you so late."

"No trouble, no trouble."

"Could you perhaps call Mrs. Veith to the phone?"

"But of course, Herr Werker. Just a moment."

He dislikes the smooth courtesy of the singer too. Through the hubbub, six hundred miles away, he hears an ambulance or a police car passing.

"Victor?"

"Hello, Clara."

"Wait a moment, I'll take the telephone into the music room."

Suddenly it becomes quiet. "It's me again. What's got into you, Victor?"

"Well, that's the sixty-four-thousand-dollar question right away. The *Gretchenfrage,* isn't that what you call it over there?"

"Quite possibly. Why are you suddenly calling at this ridiculous hour? Has something happened?"

"A lot."

"Are you drunk?"

"Not completely yet, but I will be. Do you remember those triplets I wrote to you about?"

"Wrote to me about? Oh yes, what was it again?"

"Don't worry. I'm pleased just by the fact that you've obviously read my letters."

"Surely you're not ringing me to hear that I've read your letters?"

"Of course not."

"Why then? But do try and keep it short, we've got guests."

"Listen, Clara. Can't we use force?"

"Force? What do you mean for heaven's sake?"

"I'm using force now too, because I'm ringing you, although I wasn't supposed to. Can't we break right through everything that's happened and been said, and start all over again? So the sword stroke through the Gordian knot after all?"

"What are you thinking of? Do you really realize what you're doing? After a year you ring me in the middle of the night and suggest just forgetting everything. I'm really beginning to doubt your sanity. Anyway, how did you get hold of our number?"

"From Karel. I wormed it out of him."

"It's all very annoying. Do you know what this reminds me of? Of the kind of guy who after a night out on the town rings a girlfriend who's already in bed at four-thirty in the morning, because he still fancies a little something in his drunken stupor."

"Thanks for the compliment."

"It's not a compliment."

"I understand that too."

"So let me tell you once and for all what the situation is, and I hope it'll finally sink in. There's nothing left of what there was between us, nothing at all, so nothing can be put right. You made sure of that. Since I've been with Dietrich, our whole episode has turned into a stillborn child. I never think about it anymore."

"I don't believe you."

"Don't believe me then. You never understood a thing about me."

"Perhaps even less about myself."

"Exactly."

"So I've got that much understanding at least."

"Don't start on with your eternal subtleties again. That attitude may be good for cutting and pasting molecules for your microprecision, as you always call it, but when it comes to people you're a complete dunce."

"That must be because of those molecules. One day I'll be able to point them out exactly to you."

"Yes, yes, and so shall we just put an end to this now? I'm really fed up with this conversation. And in future please spare me your letters too."

"Why are you getting so worked up? Is he standing in the doorway looking at you by any chance?"

"Who? Dietrich? Do you imagine perhaps that he's frightened of my leaving him? Forget it, there's no chance of that; I've never been so happy with anyone. We had a couple of nice years together, I won't deny that, but it was really more friendship than love."

"You know what Nietzsche said, don't you?"

"He said all kinds of things."

" 'Most marriages collapse not out of a lack of love, but out of a lack of friendship.' "

"Quite possible, but without love it's impossible too. Behind your great love the main underlying question is probably:

Who's going to iron my shirts? Where on earth do you get the idea that I could come back to you?"

"From your writing desk."

"My writing desk? What do you mean by that?"

"The fact that it's still here."

There is a moment's silence—then she rings off . . .

He puts down the telephone and rubs his face with both hands. He remembers the conversation that has taken place in his head as if it has really happened. Is it something to do with Clara? Not entirely unconnected in any case, since if he'd had it with Astrid or Bea, it would have gone differently. Though he knows he must stop drinking, he pours himself another drink. Isn't it time he rang her up? Every minute is a minute later, the world is rotating on its axis and Vienna is farther into the night anyway—is it perhaps already an hour later than here? Improbable, Austria is still part of western Europe; the time zone probably lies somewhere around Bucharest. He could look it up, but he lacks the energy to get to his feet. His eyelids are drooping. This silence in the Basilica and outside in the town surrounds him like the blanket that his mother used to pull up to his chin and tuck in from the side before planting a kiss on his forehead and turning off the light.

He picks up the telephone again. After a glance at his diary he keys in eleven figures of her number, zero-zero-four-three-one-two-nine-seven-one-nine-two, but not the twelfth one . . .

"Clara Veith."

"It's Victor."

"Victor? It can't be! Is it you?"

"Certainly is."

"I can't believe my ears. I was just thinking of you!"

"Then that's telepathy. The only question is, who influenced whom."

"How on earth is it possible! I was reading Stefan Zweig's *The World of Yesterday,* and suddenly it was as if your face appeared from the pages and came toward me. It's so quiet here; I felt as if I were the only person in the city."

"Just the same as here. Isn't Dietrich at home?"

"No, he's giving a recital. In Salzburg, I think, or in Graz, no idea."

"*Leise flehen meine Lieder durch die Nacht zu dir.*"

"Something like that, yes. Victor! How fantastic of you to call. Why didn't you call before?"

"Because you forbade me to."

"Yes, that was then, but the situation doesn't always stay the same."

"If the situation has changed, why didn't you call me?"

"Because I was ashamed. I was very hard on you, but I didn't realize until later that there was obviously much more going on when you abandoned me at the birth of our poor little Aurora."

"And what might that be?"

"Well, you may find it strange, but it may have been connected with the fact that you yourself were once abandoned by your mother, which you were always so cool about."

"Well, well. That sounds a bit Freudian, but for all I know you may be right. After all, he only lived a few doors down from you."

"In any case I'm sorry now. After reading your letters I've come to think of you quite differently."

"I'm sorry, Clara, I have to take this in for a moment. I rang you in a last desperate attempt to hear from you whether there was perhaps a glimmer of hope, but suddenly everything looks completely different. Are you saying that you're not happy with Dietrich?"

"Dietrich? Me happy with Dietrich? If you only knew what a bastard he is. He's acclaimed all over the world for his mellifluous voice, but at home he's a merciless dictator for whom only one thing exists: himself. Everything has to take second place to that. Perhaps that attitude is the reverse side of his talent, that's quite possible, but I've nothing to do with the front, only with the reverse. You're not a saint either, and neither am I, but he beats everything. I think it's connected with his humble origins from a petty bourgeois milieu in Linz. In the meantime he has got every decoration that Austria and Germany have to offer, and if he could he'd wear them on his pajamas, but for himself he always remains that unappreciated lad from the provinces. It's never enough for him. He's as egocentric as a baby."

"And that's saying something."

"Apart from that he hits me."

"He hits you?"

"And he kicks as well. When there's anything he doesn't like, he immediately has a tantrum. If a colleague of his scores a success, there's a good chance I'll get bruises."

"What a shit! Why do you stay with him for God's sake?"

"I don't know. Because despite everything I'm crazy about him."

"But, Clara, that's masochistic! You've got to get out of there, and the sooner the better!"

"And what then? Come back to you? That's not possible either, after what's happened."

"Everything's always possible. The only thing you've got to be able to do is to jump over your own shadow."

"I can't do that."

"Then I'll teach you."

"No, Victor, he's a bastard, but I love him."

"You know what Nietzsche said, don't you?"

"No?"

" 'Most relationships don't collapse because of a lack of love, but because of a lack of friendship.' "

"Yes, that's terribly true."

"Terribly true. . . ."

"Why do you repeat that?"

"I'm just taken aback by the expression."

"Yes, you obviously find that strange, as a man of science. No one will ever say that about two times two is four."

"That's what you think. Then you don't know Dostoyevsky, his *Notes from Underground*. Somewhere in that it says something like: 'Two times two is four, that's the most unbearable thing of all. Two times two is four is in my view just an outrage. Two times two is four looks at you like a dandy, puts his hands on his hips right across your path and spits.' Dostoyevsky and Nietzsche belong together."

"You haven't changed a bit, do you know that? We're talking about something that affects our lives, but at the same time your thoughts are going in all directions."

"I'm sorry, you're right, I can't help the way my brain works. I read that when I was about eighteen and it hit me like a punch in the eye. I forget a lot, but some things I never forget. Can't we talk sometime about what we've got to do? If you like, I'll come to Vienna tomorrow."

"On what basis? You know there's no point, Victor."

"Because of your writing desk. Tell me, why is it still here?"

"Because," she says after a short silence, "I wanted there to be something of mine remaining near Aurora's room. To keep watch."

While his eyes grow moist, he takes a sip of his scotch.

"If," he says hoarsely, "we had kept a couple of arbitrary body cells of hers, perhaps it might be possible one day to awaken her from the dead."

"I've got some."

"What's that?"

"Before she was put in her coffin, I cut some hairs from her head and put them in a medallion. I wear it around my neck."

"Clara! Bring it! Bring it right away! In a few years' time I'll make a clone of her, before the century's out, a monozygotic twin sister, and everything will be all right again between us! If only you'd *pulled* it out of her head, so that the root was still on it, then I would have known for certain that it's possible."

With the telephone in his hand he sinks back on the sofa. A little later he leans forward again, and with the feeling of someone letting off an explosive charge, he presses the twelfth digit of her number: seven. After the telephone has rung three times, a soft, friendly voice which is nothing like the sonorous sound that he'd just imagined announces:

"Dietrich Jäger-Jena and Clara Veith are unable to take your call at the moment. Please leave your name and number and any message. We'll get back to you as soon as possible."

When the beep sounds, he actually wants to ring off, but he says:

"This is Victor Werker from Amsterdam. A message for Frau Clara Veith. Clara, could you ring me back tomorrow? I've something important to say to you."

As soon as he disconnects he is sorry. What he would have most liked to do is erase his words, but they are irrevocably on the tape in the Berggasse. Where is she now, in the middle of the night? Is she waltzing with her lover at this moment in a rustling gown across a parquet floor at some *Opernball* or other? He must go to bed now; tomorrow morning at eleven o'clock he has an appointment at the Institute with an American who is not only a great art connoisseur but more important in Rockville, near Washington, D.C., is also in charge of the human genome project, involving billions of dollars from the pharmaceutical industry. Probably he wants to make him an offer. When he gets up, he wobbles for a moment. With a rapid movement he manages to retain his balance, so that it looks as if he's executing an elegant dance step. He is about to turn the lights off, but instead he takes Mahler out of the CD player, and with his cheek on his shoulder searches along the row of cassettes. The end of his last fictional conversation with Clara has given him an idea, but he can't find what he is looking for. *Orfeo ed Euridice* by Gluck. Then he remembers that he only has the opera on LPs now. The large box is on the bottom shelf of a wall cabinet; it's a German version: *Orpheus und Eurydike*. He pours himself another glass and lays the first record on the turntable, which he hasn't used for years. He carefully lowers the needle onto the dark ring after the cheerful overture, which he has never liked. He lies on the sofa with the libretto.

An homophonous four-part choir of shepherds and nymphs has gathered at Eurydice's grave and sings a lament:

> *Oh when in these dark groves,*
> *Eurydike, your shadow still*
> *Floats round your bleak tomb . . .*

And then right through the measured song, Orpheus's cry of lament:

> *Eurydike!*

His eyes fill with tears. Unbearable! Music is unbearable! Music has been planted in the world to bring human beings down a peg or two, to make it clear to them that there is another story going on besides theirs. Twice more Orpheus's desperate cry rings out, sung by a phenomenal voice, and then the emotion becomes too much for him. He switches the record off and slides it into the sleeve. The cover of the box catches his eye: *Orpheus—Dietrich Jäger-Jena*. He takes a deep breath and lies down again.

Orpheus—Dietrich Jäger-Jena. He had been in his flat for all those years, without his knowing. Probably without Clara knowing either: he met her when the CD era had already begun. CD. The initials of the two of them. She met Dietrich when her firm had a commission in Vienna, at a reception at the Dutch embassy. She too ended up in the artistic world, like his mother with her Aldo Tas. . . . He drops off to sleep and dreams that an open book is pursuing him, like a bird with its wings flapping . . . *Dietrich*—in German it's not just a proper name, but also a word for a passkey, a forgery. He turns his head to the side and looks at the key turned in the lock of the nursery. Should he go in there now? Is this the moment?

His eyes fall shut again. . . . In the Egyptian darkness the Sphinx of Giza suddenly turns its head to the left, then to the right, as though it hears something, a question perhaps, rises up after four and a half thousand years, shakes itself and breaks into a run. Smashing everything in nighttime Cairo, people, animals, houses, the stone creature runs northward, in search of the questioner, swims across the Mediterranean to Europe, where it disappears thunderously into the Rhône Valley. . . . Once more, in the middle of the night—he didn't see the flash of lightning through the chink in the curtains—he starts awake for a few seconds because of an autumn thunderclap which reverberates across the city, as if the Sphinx has finally pounced on its prey with a dreadful leap . . .

MORNING

VICTOR SURFACES from his dreams like a deep-sea diver. His brain is immediately working again. Self-consciousness, he thinks, keeping his eyes closed, is like a flash of lightning after a sultry night—waking up is not interrupted by sleep, but sleep by waking: unconsciousness is man's natural condition, only the sleeping and the dead are really at home. "It's only been thundering for a hundred thousand years," he says aloud. He reaches out to look at the alarm clock by his bed and gropes in the void. When he opens his eyes, he sees that he's still lying on the sofa. He has his clothes on, all the lights are on, the curtains are no longer shutting out the darkness but the light. It's nine o'clock. He gets up with a groan and pulls the curtains open. Fog is hanging over the old town center, cut in two by the elegant S of the river with its bridges. He feels clammy and grubby in his clothes from the previous day, like someone who has to eat from the same unwashed plate as yesterday. He soon perks up under the hot shower, washes his hair, shaves, perfumes his cheeks, and dresses carefully, as though there were a special day in prospect. Back in his study he stops and looks pensively at the floor. In a while he will have his appointment with the American genome tycoon, who will probably make him some attractive proposition or other, several hundred thousand dollars a year, which he will not accept. Of course he can earn lots of money these days if he wants to, but he doesn't want to. What good is money to him? He wants to do DNA research on mummies and fossils, because that interests him, and that's what his life has been like from the very beginning. Even when he was at school, it annoyed him that in chemistry they were always talking about technological applications. When his mother put a whistling kettle full of water for tea on the stove in the kitchen, that was something completely different from when he heated water above a Bunsen burner in the laboratory in an Erlenmeyer flask. The increasing instability of the liquid, the convection currents with their hexagonal Bénard convection cells on the surface, the smell of the steam . . . that was pure scientific research, that had nothing to do with anything as vulgar as "social relevance." Of course with lots of money he can buy a seagoing yacht and cruise through the Mediterranean, but he doesn't want to cruise through the Mediterranean at all, he'd be bored to death on board. Nor does he feel like moving to Washington, where it is as grand as it is parochial.

While he makes coffee, he thinks back uneasily to the message that he left on the Viennese tape yesterday. Clara may ring him any minute now, what on earth is the important thing he announced he wanted to say yesterday? That he wants her to come back to him? As if she doesn't know that. She'll realize at once that he was tipsy. No, the best thing would be to ring Vienna again immediately and admit that he's done something stupid and that it would be better if she forgot about it; meanwhile, the message that matters are still not closed for him will have got through anyway. Hopefully she's still not home, so that he doesn't have to talk to her.

He takes the coffee into his study, picks up the telephone, presses the redial button and holds the receiver to his ear. The digital tones of her number succeed each other like the whistled signature tune he once used with his girlfriends. But before all the digits have sounded, he suddenly hears two male voices. He listens with raised eyebrows. They are speaking English and one of them is explaining carefully to the other how to find the way somewhere. Now and then he pauses for a moment, presumably to give the other the opportunity to take notes; when the other man says yes, he continues. They are not English or American: one of them has the awkward accent of a Dutchman with no feeling for language, and he can't place that of the other. Fascinated, holding his breath, he goes on listening. It's none of his business, and it's not right, but he suddenly feels like someone from the police, or the secret service, who with headphones on his ears has caught unsuspecting criminals or traitors in his net, while a tape is running. It also fascinates him that he is a witness to this one conversation from all the millions of conversations which are being conducted at this moment everywhere on earth. The content is completely insignificant: The second man has to go left, right, straight ahead, left at a fork, and so on. But just as he is about to ring off, he hears the first man say:

"When you recognize him, stab immediately."

"Okay."

"You'll receive the rest of your money at the airport."

"You bet."

"Good luck."

The moment the engaged tone sounds, Victor's mouth has dropped open in astonishment. Is what he heard just then really possible? Did he really hear "stab"? Instructions to a hit man! There's a murder about to happen! He must inform the police at once! In his excitement he is about to key in the emergency number, but he realizes that he must note down as well as possible what was said, before he forgets. He sits down at his desk, pushes the notes for *Aurora's Key to Life* aside, and tries to remember what was said. He came into the middle of a conversation, and because he didn't listen with his full concentration, most of it has already gone from his mind. There was something about a fork by a restaurant, after which he had to cross a bridge, a fork by a theater, left at a disco—he gives up, he can't remember. With trembling fingers he rings the police.

"Police," says a friendly woman's voice.

"Good morning, my name is Victor Werker. I want to report a murder that's about to happen."

"I'll put you through."

A little later a deep male voice says:

"CID."

"My name is Victor Werker. I was just trying to ring my girl-friend in Vienna, but for some reason or other I found myself in the middle of a conversation between two men planning a murder."

"A murder? I don't think it can be as bad as that. What do you deduce that from?"

"One of them said to the other that he had to take such and such a route through town and when the door was opened he had to stab at once."

"Well, well, were they speaking German?"

"No, English, but I reckon one of them had a Dutch accent."

"Where do you live?"

"In the Basilica."

"Nice spot."

"What do we do next?"

"The best thing would be for you to drop by the main police station."

"But it might be urgent."

"That's why."

"I'll be right there. Who shall I ask for?"

"Inspector Sorgdrager."

He rings for a taxi and tells it to wait by the main entrance of the Basilica. Then he switches his calls through to his mobile phone, puts the phone from ring into vibrate mode, stuffs the notes in his pocket, and goes out. The car is already there. As he drives through the busy misty city, he does his best to remember more details of the conversation, but only a few incoherent snatches have stayed with him. He imagines someone now sitting behind those baroque housefronts reading the morning paper with a cup of coffee, ignorant of what's hanging over his head. Obviously everything in life can change completely from one moment to the next.

In the police station he has to wait his turn on a wooden bench. He sees that no one is at ease among all those uniforms, but for him they have something familiar about them, they remind him of his father—although the difference between the police and the army is rather like that between a fox and a lion. He is looked at suspiciously from the counter, as if he is a suspect—quite simply because he appears here, without being in the police. When he says that he's been summoned by Inspector Sorgdrager from CID, he is sent to a department on the third floor. In the neglected steel lift, which bears the marks of countless fights, a shabbily dressed woman with a shopping basket stares uninterruptedly at him, as though she can expect help from him.

He has difficulty finding his way in the old building, which has obviously been frequently renovated and modified. The CID is based in a couple of large rooms, the dividing wall of which has been knocked through to make a single room, where scores of inspectors in civilian clothes are sitting at small tables, on the other side of which someone is making a statement. Computers obviously haven't penetrated here yet; they are all sitting at high, old-fashioned typewriters. Because no one pays him any attention, he buttonholes a short, red-haired detective in shirtsleeves, who appears from a side door with a carton of milk and eating a sandwich.

"Can you tell me where I can find Inspector Sorgdrager?"

"Sorgdrager?" the man repeats, chewing, continuing on his way. He shakes his head. "Never heard of him."

"How is it possible? I was talking to him on the telephone half an hour ago."

"If you knew all the things that are possible here. Come this way; you'll have to make do with me."

"What's your name, if I may ask?"

"Lont."

"Let's hope that at least you still exist in half an hour's time, Mr. Lont."

"I expect I'll manage that."

Inspector Lont has his desk by the window. On the windowpane he has stuck a couple of children's drawings with lots of red and blue in them, on the windowsill there is a row of tiny pots with tiny cactuses in them. After he has noted down Victor's personal details, he folds his arms and leans back.

"Tell me about it."

Victor tells him what's happened to him, while Lont observes him with a look of someone who trusts nothing and no one anymore, except perhaps his child. With his legs stretched out and his head back he looks at the ceiling for a while, on which there are large dark brown damp patches.

"There are a couple of things I don't understand. On the face of it it sounds like a settling of scores in the criminal world, but it doesn't quite fit. This scumbag fetches a hit man, from Marseille, for example, he buys a stiletto somewhere and takes a taxi to an address he's been given, near the spot where he has to go. Obviously he doesn't have the taxi drop him at the door, because then that taxi driver would know too much. He walks the last bit, does his work, gets rid of the knife, and before we appear on the scene he's back on the plane. But that man of yours, who obviously doesn't know the city, has to take a very long walk before he can do his stabbing. All very strange."

"So?"

"So nothing. We might understand it all better soon."

"But then it'll be too late."

"That's how it goes. That often happens with understanding."

"And that's that as far as the police are concerned?"

"Yes. What can we do, Mr. Werker? There's nothing for us to

go on to take any action. Those notes of yours are far too vague and incomplete; it could be anywhere. Nothing concrete's been mentioned, not a single street name, not in the part of the conversation that you overheard, and perhaps they were careful enough to avoid it too. We don't even know where that conversation came from. Perhaps from Vienna or Rio de Janeiro. Nor did they say when it was to happen. Today? Tomorrow? Next week? The only thing we know is that a certain Mr. A, with an accent that's probably Dutch, gives a liquidation contract to a certain Mr. B, who also has some kind of accent."

"It may have been slightly Arab."

"I'm sure it was."

"And you've no idea what Mr. C might be on a death list?"

"At least a hundred. But on what grounds are you assuming that C is a mister and not a Mrs.?"

"You're right," says Victor with a wave of his hand. "I confess I'm not being politically correct."

Lont glances at him, but says nothing. While he takes down the statement and the rattle of his typewriter merges with that of the others, Victor looks outside. Because it's only ten-thirty, the gray cloud cover is so thick that it looks as if dusk has fallen. So he can't count on the police, but obviously he can't leave it at that. Perhaps C is really a villain, who more or less deserves to be in line to be bumped off, and who if he saves him will go on to wreck many lives, through heroin for example. But perhaps it's different. Perhaps A's wife is C and she has deceived him with X and hence has to die by B's hand. Or perhaps he simply wants to cash in her life insurance. Everything is conceivable, the detective series on television are about nothing else, but he had the feeling that he mustn't allow himself to be paralyzed by this kind of consideration, which will finally lead him to do nothing—and it's as if suddenly somewhere in the far distance he hears the voice of his father, telling him about the war.

Lont yanks the statement out of the typewriter, makes a

cross, and puts it in front of him. He signs and shakes hands with Lont.

"Tell yourself," says the policeman, "life is just one long succession of mysteries."

"But they're there to be solved."

"I wish you the best of luck."

The moment he gets outside, a taxi pulls up at the curb. He waits until the driver has helped a girl with a bandage around her head from the car and gets in.

"To the main offices of the telephone service."

If the police don't have the idea of going into things in more depth, then he'll do it himself. The offices are housed in a former hospital, where illness still seems to cling to the grubby yellow walls.

At the inquiry booth, he asks to speak to someone from technical services. After waiting for a quarter of an hour on a wooden bench, watching the bustle in the hall, he is received in a small room by a friendly man in a sports jacket, who introduces himself as "Van der Made." On the wall there is a poster of a carrier pigeon. When he has told his story and states that according to the police the conversation could just as well have taken place in Vienna or Rio de Janeiro, Van der Made says emphatically:

"Impossible. The police haven't got a clue. Where do you live?"

"In the Basilica."

"Then that conversation took place within a radius of a thousand meters around the Basilica."

"How can you be so sure of that?"

"Because mobile telephone conversations in town are regulated by base stations, which are sited every thousand meters—let's say, aerials, which transmit the conversations to the exchange. In your area the base station is on the roof of Hotel Excelsior. For a reason which I could explain, but which would not mean much to you, you found yourself on the same channel as those two villains. It's absolutely certain that we're talking about the center of town by the river."

In the street he stops indecisively. What next? Back to the police with this information? Lont will be bound to dream up another reason for doing nothing. He'll probably say that though the conversation may originate in town, it doesn't mean that the murder is also going to be committed here; it could still be Vienna or Rio de Janeiro. That is of course true, but it's not impossible that he will go to work now and tomorrow may read in the paper who's been murdered. He has to pursue this himself. From a clock on a power pole he sees that it's already nearly twelve. His appointment! He takes the telephone out of his pocket and rings his institute. While passersby on the pavement walk around him, he asks, looking down at the paving stones, whether his American visitor is still there, but he turns out to have left in a huff half an hour ago. He says that something idiotic has happened, that he won't be coming in this afternoon either, and that he'll explain later. In a hotel he asks at the reception desk if they've got a map of the center and he is given a colourful tourist brochure, next he goes to the nearby Café Arco, which he used to frequent. The old, toothless doorman in his blue footman's jacket with epaulets, the tortoiseshell glasses on the tip of his nose, is still standing at the entrance.

The Art Nouveau interior is dark, the walls are covered in black leather, printed with red and gold stripes; because all the tables are occupied, he sits down at the reading table with the green-shaded brass lamps. He orders a portion of ham with horseradish and a glass of pilsner, opens the small map, and takes out his notes of the conversation:

> Fork by restaurant.
> Over bridge.
> Fork at theater.
> Left at disco.
> Something about a tree.

That is all that remains of a dozen instructions. He's not even sure of the order. He bends over the plan; who knows, he may find something to go on. The scale of the map is 1:15000, one centimeter equals 150 meters, so one thousand meters are about seven centimeters. He locates the famous Hotel Excelsior, and it's correct that only the center, where the Basilica is, really comes into it: restaurants, theaters, discos, around the river, because there's no other water in town. The river makes almost a right angle around the town center, he counts eight bridges. Because you can go over a bridge from two sides, that means that there are in principle sixteen possibilities; but because the theater and the disco only appear after the bridge, the direction is therefore probably toward the center. So the junction with the restaurant has to be on the left bank. He goes down the bridges one by one and tries to imagine the situation, but he hasn't been near several of them for years; for that matter discos also tend to disappear as quickly as they've appeared, particularly recently. The link is obviously the theater. He estimates that there are thirty in town, not all of which he knows; but in combination with the bridge and the disco, it must be possible to reduce the possibilities quickly. As he eats his lunch, he goes on looking at the map out of the corner of his eye, meanwhile searching in his memory for theaters near the river. Suddenly he stops chewing. At the Ketting Bridge there is a constellation which may meet the conditions. There is the theater where he once saw a performance of *Fiddler on the Roof* with Clara, and there is a junction. Apart from that, it suddenly occurs to him, not far away is the bus terminal for the airport! But are there trees there?

He decides to go there. Even if it's right, that of course will still not get him any further, but perhaps he'll remember more of the conversation if he walks around a bit in that neighborhood. He tries to fold the map, which he manages to do at the third attempt, pays the bill, and sets off.

AFTERNOON

THE TRAM follows the current upstream along the muddy banks of the river, on the other side the citadel on the hill has become almost invisible in the mist. Where the tram has to turn left over the Ketting Bridge it suddenly stops. The driver gets out and with a heavy iron rod yanks a point to the right. At the stop on the other bank Victor gets out and looks around. There is a junction, he already knew that, but no restaurant anywhere. Perhaps he remembered incorrectly and was confusing two directions. He slowly walks back to the right bank. In the distance he sees the Basilica, now included in the splendid panorama of towers and domes. He feels ridiculous, but if a murder really is committed today or tomorrow, he would never forgive himself for not doing everything he could. It is lunchtime; despite the chilly wind blowing across the water, the pavements are full of office workers strolling along eating sandwiches from plastic bags. In the center of the bridge a man with a black mustache and dressed in dark clothes comes hurriedly toward him. He steps aside, and the other steps aside in the same direction, and then again and again. When Victor smiles at the situation he is given a menacing look in return, as though he were being deliberately obstructive, whereupon the man walks around him in a demonstratively wide arc. Victor turns for a moment and watches him go. Even his back seems to be radiating danger. Is he the one? Is he returning after his work is done, with the knife in his trouser pocket that he'll throw over the railing in a moment? He considers following him for a moment, but immediately puts the thought out of his mind. He must be crazy.

Nevertheless, he now starts observing the passersby more closely. Some of them seem to see immediately that something's wrong about the way he's looking at them and meet his look with a challenging expression, whereupon he looks down. With a feeling that it might be better to go to work than play the sleuth here, he reaches the musical theater and the fork. That's right at any rate—but on the corner, where he should turn left, there is not a disco but a florist's. Of course there are instructions missing again. He also now realizes that the location of the terminal doesn't correspond with his notes: the bus station is two bridges farther on, but also on this bank; there is no bridge in between if someone walks from there to the theater; apart from that he would then be going in the wrong direction. Were Lont and Van der Made perhaps both right? Had the conversation been conducted around here? But was the murder to take place somewhere completely different? In Vienna? In Buenos Aires? He notes that a strange kind of doggedness is taking hold of him. Without seeing anything he stops in front of a shopwindow containing women's underwear, again hearing in his memory the voices but he only makes out those four sentences:

"When you recognize him, stab immediately."

"Okay."

"You'll receive the rest of your money at the airport."

"You bet."

"Good luck."

All he hears of the rest are snatches and the timbre, as if from a conversation in an adjoining train compartment. Nor is there

sign of a tree anywhere. Although he realizes that what he's doing is absurd, he turns left by the florist's.

The boulevard with its prestigious blocks of flats and banks
was laid out at the end of the last century on the Paris model
on the site of the demolished ghetto. Perhaps the indications in
the telephone conversation were more fitted to that vanished
labyrinth—but if one thing is certain, he thinks, then it's that he
didn't pick it up from the Jewish quarter, because that hasn't existed for a hundred years. Feeling that he'd at least eliminated
one possibility, he continues aimlessly. Imagine great danger, he
thinks, consider that it doesn't exist, and you're a happy man.

At a junction an old, stooping tramp in rags, with long hair
and beard, rags that have come loose around his feet, is trying to
keep control of a shopping trolley from a supermarket. It's piled
much too high with his absurd possessions, rags, plastic bags full
of rubbish; the small wheels, designed to make short turns
around the shelves on smooth linoleum, can't cope with the
rough bricks; now pushing, then pulling he struggles to reach
the other side, as cars swerve around him beeping furiously.
Suddenly the trolley tips over, instantly creating a rubbish dump
at the crossroads. The tramp stands there looking at it for a moment; then he sees the hopelessness of the situation and shuffles
off, without paying attention to the traffic, leaving the rubbish
behind like a dying man leaves his memories. Victor feels a vi-
bration in the region of his heart.

"Werker," he says, continuing on his way.

Silence. He stops, and as if flicking a cigarette end away he
taps the telephone receiver with the nail of his middle finger, in
the hope that the other person will now think that a machine
has been switched on with the tick.

"Stay on the line, then the exchange can check your number."

The caller immediately rings off. Perhaps the trick worked,
and he really has silenced the silent caller. He curses Graham
Bell and looks around. What is he doing here? Is he still looking

for a murderer? The old Jewish cemetery, which was left largely untouched in the slum clearance, stretches away between the bare elderberry trees. Countless tombstones, covered with thin wisps of mist, are standing and lying alongside each other like the rotten teeth of an antediluvian monster. The roots of the trees are being forced down by ten layers with hundreds of thousands of skeletons; each time it filled up again, century after century, a new layer of clay from the river was spread over the site, on which the tombstones were laid in closer and closer formation. Because the shortest route to the tram stop is across the cemetery, he goes in through the gate.

There is a bitter smell from the fallen leaves. Here and there groups of tourists are walking around, mainly Japanese, who probably have no idea what Jews are, constantly photographing each other against a background of graves. He'd like to know what they're going to say when, back in Hiroshima and Nagasaki, they show the slides to their family and friends. It's been years since he was last here, with an American cellular biologist, Fleischmann, who waxed lyrical at the tomb of some legendary miracle-working rabbi from the sixteenth century. In passing he casts a glance at the large, well-maintained stone in Renaissance style, with Hebrew inscriptions, a vignette of a lion with two tails crowned by a pinecone. Only after he has looked away does he see the man who is looking at it: hands in the pockets of his black leather jacket, in jeans, trainers on his feet, on his head a baseball cap, and on his nose sunglasses, although the sun isn't shining. Victor stops, picks up a pebble, as he had seen Fleischmann do and puts it on a tombstone, looking at the man out of the corner of his eye. What is visible of his face seems in some way North African, from the look of it not Egyptian, rather Algerian or Moroccan. The hit man? Too early for his job and killing time here now?

He slowly strolls on, his eyes fixed on the inscriptions, with the Arab constantly on the edge of his field of vision, meanwhile feeling like an illiterate among all those Hebrew characters. He considers asking the man for a light, so that he may recognize his voice, but in that case he will have made himself visible too. After a few minutes the man looks at his watch, turns up his collar, and walks along the winding paths to the exit on the other side of the cemetery. As he follows him, Victor thinks: I'm suffering from reverse persecution mania—but his work has taught him to take even his most absurd intuitions seriously in the first instance. All great discoveries stem from absurd intuitions. What will the world look like if I sit on a beam of light, Einstein had wondered when he was sixteen. It's impossible to think of anything more absurd; yet that was the germ of the theory of relativity. If the brainwave really is absurd, that only becomes apparent when the wrong track has been covered in part and the swamp becomes visible.

Back in the world of the living, not yet sunk into the earth, he shadows the seedy individual through a narrow back street with tourist shops and souvenir stalls, where the subject enters a small coffee shop. When he himself passes, he stops and lights up a cigarette, and as he does so sees the suspect leaning forward and kissing a woman on the mouth, who's obviously been waiting for him. Now, murderers too are in the habit of kissing women, but in this case it seems sufficient for him to abandon his suspicion. He takes a deep breath and decides to put the matter out of his mind. He's done his duty, because of some technical combination of circumstances, which even experts can't explain adequately, he's been the witness of a murder plot, which may already have been carried out somewhere else in the world. So be it. How many murders are committed every day? A hundred thousand? Five hundred thousand? Probably enough to fill up a cemetery like the one he has just come from every day.

With the same refreshing feeling that one has when leaving a cinema, he continues on his way to the inhabited world. It's almost two o'clock, the afternoon is not yet lost, but first he wants a cup of coffee. He's now in the vicinity of Hotel Excelsior, on top of which the telephone base station is situated—a hotel in the style of the Ritz, with deep flowered armchairs in the lounge, where coffee is served in creamy white pots, on silver trays, with a round doily under the cup. Now and then he passes a small synagogue, which has remained like the fragments of memory from someone suffering from amnesia, and in a narrow street at the side of the hotel he has to step over cables leading from a window to an outside broadcasting van from the television; a little farther on there is a dish aerial, focused on a point in the sky where there is an invisible satellite hanging. The moment that he arrives at the red carpet leading to the terrace, a white stretch limousine with tinted windows and an aerial in the shape of a boomerang on its trunk stops. The porter takes a step forward, takes off his top hat, and the first person to get out, no, leap out, fly out, is—no doubt about it—Catharina from Harry's Bar.

A smile crosses his face and he stops. At the other end of the red carpet the Amazon appears, followed by her husband. He is wearing a black cape and a black hat with a wide brim over his long white hair making his narrow face look even narrower. Elsa, their little girl, is not with them. They stop and talk for a moment on the pavement, he seemingly trying to persuade her to do something, but she shakes her head; they give each other a kiss and the woman wanders off with the small black dachshund. He watches her go for a moment, but she doesn't turn round. I'm looking for a murderer, thinks Victor watching the scene, and I find an art guru. Like three months ago in Venice he hopes the other man will notice him, if only to put an end to the ridiculous situation that he has found himself in today. As the latter is about to step up onto the terrace, he recognizes Victor and approaches him, hands flapping.

"Mr. Werker! What a surprise!"

Victor looks at him in astonishment.

"You know who I am?"

"Of course I know who you are, everyone knows who you are. I never forget a face. I'd seen your photo on the cover of

L'Expresse." He puts out his hand. "Kurt Netter." His hand is still just as cold. "Are you coming out or going in?"

"I was intending to go in."

"Then we'll go in together." In Mediterranean fashion Netter puts his hand on Victor's forearm and leads him up the steps, giving the latter the vague feeling of being arrested.

"How was your exhibition in the Palazzo Grassi received?"

"Disastrously. Not a soul understood it. That is, except for Catharina, of course. I think that for the time being I am persona non grata in La Serenissima."

"Dialectics are too good for this world." Victor nods.

"You make a great statement calmly," says Netter, taking the cape off his shoulders with a joyous sweep at the cloakroom, so that the red lining becomes visible for a moment; underneath he is also dressed from head to toe in fashionable black; the cuffs of his shirt are not buttoned, which for some reason gives not a slovenly but a worldly impression. "But I don't seem to have been written off entirely yet, otherwise I wouldn't be here. Are you also on the panel?"

"The panel?" repeats Victor in amazement. "I on a panel? What do you mean?"

"But you're here."

"That's true. For a cup of coffee. I live here—in this city, I mean."

"Coffee, yes," says Netter. "Good idea. Let's do that first, although I really haven't got time. I arrived from New York an hour ago, we scarcely had time to unpack. The world is getting as small as a pea, distances are only a matter of money these days—that is, for other people. My journeys are always paid for."

Sunk in an armchair, Netter tells him what's going on this afternoon. As the year 2000 approaches, twelve European television companies have launched a co-production, taking stock of the twentieth century. In two series of six broadcasts, panels of judges, each containing twelve international authorities, will decide who has achieved most in their field in the last century. All the hoo-ha about the millennium doesn't of course have much bearing on it, because if human beings had had six fingers on each hand instead of five, there would have been nothing to celebrate shortly. But anyway. The series is called *The Verdict*, and it's being recorded in the twelve capitals of twelve member states of the European Union. The first six programs are on science and politics, the second six on the arts. In Paris Kafka recently came out as number one in the novel, after a fierce fight with Joyce—and despite the opposition of a French professor of literature, who tried to push the candidacy of Proust to the bitter end.

"For that matter, when it comes to biology, you may be in the running too."

"I have no illusions on that score. It will be Watson and Crick. I'm just a simple locksmith."

"Well, but then it's a very special lock to which you found the key." Putting his cigarette into a silver holder, he looks pensively at Victor.

"*The key*," smiles Victor, "for some reason that reminds me of the title of a novel, but I can't remember ever having read anything of the kind."

"Tanizaki wrote a novel with that title. It gives you the creeps. Anyway, today it's the turn of the visual arts." With his head Netter indicates a girl in jeans, with a notepad in one hand and a telephone in the other. "She's looking for me."

When she looks in their direction, he makes a short movement with his hand, like someone bidding at an auction. She hurries over to them.

"Mr. Netter?"

"Absolutely."

"We were worried you hadn't made it. The broadcast is starting in ten minutes, you've got to go straight to makeup."

"My own mask will be enough," says Netter, getting up. And to Victor, "Have you got anything on?"

"I don't really know. I've rather lost the plot today."

"Well, keep me company then, and later we'll eat at an Italian restaurant, at your expense."

The hotel banquet room, with its chandeliers and mirrors and marble columns, intended for the self-stylization of the bourgeoisie, has been transformed into an ambivalent domain that no one from the beginning of the century would have recognized. Technology has invaded the Victorian pomp and ceremony like a virus invading the nucleus of a cell. Series of cables and wires are running across the Persian carpets and the parquet, stuck down here and there with black tape, cameramen and -women with headphones on are looking up into their cameras, other technicians at flickering monitors at their feet. Everything is focused on a table in the shape of a π with three sets of four chairs behind it, on which the panel has already nestled. Only a chair in the top section is still empty, in front of it there is a card:

KURT NETTER

RIGA

So he's from Latvia. In any case he belongs to that international set of experts who are becoming more and more authoritative in all fields in Europe. The authorities are sitting in a relaxed way talking to one another, most of them very distinguished and contrasting with the scruffy television staff—mainly because of their characteristic faces, which themselves seem to have changed into works of art. Obviously, thinks Victor, you become what you do. Some audience members are grouped along the walls, intended to give the viewers the impression that they are also present. With the feeling that he is completely out of place here, Victor takes his seat among the human wallpaper.

Before Netter also takes his seat, he quickly greets the others, all of whom he turns out to know, whereupon the chairman takes his place between the legs of the π. Victor knows him by sight: Arthur Marcelis, a feared politician from the social-democratic quarter. He looks like a Russian general in civvies, thickset, square, but with the slim, sensitive hands of a violinist, which don't seem to go with him. The floor manager gives a few more instructions and asks for silence. With his arm raised, his face turned toward the ceiling with cherubs painted on it, he listens in turn to the instructions from his headphones. After a few seconds he lowers his arm in the direction of Marcelis, as though he is cleaving him in two with a sword.

After welcoming everyone here and at home, the chairman apologizes to the camera for having to speak English, because that's how things are these days in the world, but outside the United Kingdom that will be made up for by subtitles—anyway reading never does you any harm. With a provocative laugh he announces that he personally doesn't care at all for the modern visual arts, and that precisely for that reason he is qualified to chair the discussion. His five-year-old son could do that daubing of those painters in the twentieth century just as well, the minimalism of Mondrian reminds him of traffic signs, and as far as the kind of works of art that consist of lumps of grease in the corners of a room and a pile of coal in the middle, above which there is a pig's head dangling from a rope—if his son were to get that into his head at home, he'd smack him and send him to bed without supper.

Not everyone laughs, but the tone has been set. Against this shrewd background, which will now grip the other half of the viewers, it's been made difficult for the pictorial gurus not to appear ridiculous. But a smooth, elegant man, according to his card director of the Kunstsammlungen Nordrhein-Westfalen, immediately hits back.

"It's not impossible that your five-year-old son can actually do what Picasso can do—to mention the winner of this panel immediately—but at any rate, you can't do it anymore."

"You've got a point there," says Marcelis, after he's waited for the laughter and applause from the public gallery. "Artists are children. They play."

"But then we must talk about the word 'play,'" interjects the director of the Tate Gallery, so that the camera is forced to make a sudden turn toward the tawny-faced Englishman, who in his checked suit, checked shirt, and striped tie looks like someone playing an Englishman. He puts his middle finger on his thumb and lectures in exquisite Oxford English, "If you see your son playing, you say to your wife 'Isn't he playing sweetly.'" And then you think of the way in which you yourself play. But when you play you know that you're playing while a child's play is something totally different for a child, namely the most profound seriousness. *That* is the childlike way in which artists play, and that's almost the opposite of the sweet way in which you and I tend to play. Art is child's play. Perhaps we must interpret your refreshing view of art in that sense."

Renewed applause. But then a drop of vinegar falls into the discussion. A lady in an ample dress and with gray hair hanging loose, who looks like a fortune-teller but is the director of the Musée d'Art Moderne in Paris says in French:

"Anyway, it strikes me that in that stupid cliché people always talk about sons and never about daughters."

That remark merits the third round of applause, but Victor doesn't join in the clapping. Daughters. A little gloomily he looks at the fierce Frenchwoman, from a distance she looks a little like Clara: older and uglier but with the same aura of aloofness.

"*Mea culpa, mea culpa,*" says Marcelis and beats his heart with his right fist. "*Mea maxima culpa.* That's Latin—another language we hadn't agreed as our working language, madam."

After that reprimand a professor of art history from Madrid suddenly raises his arms.

"You may have once been Catholic, as I still am," he shouts with a pair of reading glasses on the tip of his nose, "but it still doesn't give you the right to throw your dignity to the winds! It's politically very correct to proclaim the equality of sons and daughters in art too, that wins you applause, but is it true? No, ladies and gentlemen—considerably fewer ladies than gentlemen by the way—it isn't true. I'll put it even more bluntly: it can't be true. Ladies and gentlemen are equal but not identical, because gentlemen can't bear sons and daughters. Even in prehistoric times the fact was that only the gentlemen were hunters, because the ladies were pregnant and had to look after the children at home in the cave. That's how it's always remained."

"There's that stupid division of roles again," the Parisienne interrupts him sharply, this time in English. "I thought that was in the past by now. You were just saying that because you don't feel like doing the washing up."

"Oh, how I hate that word, 'division of roles.' I'm a bachelor, madam, I do the shopping, I cook, I wash the dishes, and I like doing it, because that's when I can think best, better than in my study. About these kinds of things, for example. They're not roles. A woman giving birth isn't acting any more than is a creative artist."

"Aren't you getting a little carried away?" inquires the director of the Kunsthaus Zurich.

"Perhaps, but that's precisely my point. Can I just finish what I'm saying? Hunters could go on for the whole day, in pursuit of a bison, but women had to do first this and then that in the household, pick herbs, milk the goat. They did not have and they don't have any obsessions, instead, they have children—female obsessions would cost the children dear. The only thing that's changed, but not essentially, is the bison. Now the obsessive hunt of men is focused on such gigantic animals as fortune, power, fame, making discoveries, developing a scientific theory, creating a work of art. They all have the character of the original bison."

"So it's not impossible, Tomás," says the only other woman in the company, the president of the Museum of Modern Art in New York, "that the Paleolithic rock drawings in those caves of yours were made by women, while their menfolk were chasing bisons like madmen."

"A brand-new hypothesis!"

"Women can obviously get carried away too," observes Mar-

celis dryly. "Some women at least." He glances at the floor manager, who nods and makes a revolving gesture with his index
finger. Go on, the producer has obviously whispered in his ear.
With a satisfied grin on his face, Marcelis allows the discussion
to take its course: they'll see in the editing suite what is usable.

"Perhaps women were the first visual artists," continues the
American woman with her piercing gaze, "and perhaps that can
be proved."

"Now I'm really curious to know what you're going to say,
Agnes."

"I remember certain fascinating depictions of hands. They'd
been laid with fingers outstretched against the wall of the rock and
marked off in an aura of paint, as if a spray can had been used."

"Negative hands." The Spaniard nods. "That's what they're
called."

"Well then. Has any research been done to see whether those
negative hands are male or female hands? Surely you can tell
from skeletal remains whether they're male or female?"

The professor takes the spectacles off his nose and looks at
her in astonishment.

"As far as I know, no one has ever thought of that. But I fear
that those rock paintings were created by a metaphysical obsession of some kind, and that the first visual artists were therefore
men. Just as the most recent ones are for that matter. We are
now ten or twelve thousand years further on, but it's a hundred
percent certain that our jury will shortly come up with a man's
name."

"If that's a hundred percent certain," Marcelis intervenes,
"then our task has become fifty percent easier, and then this discussion wasn't entirely pointless. The distinction being made
here between men and women anyway reminds me of that between politicians and civil servants. Politicians as the obsessive
hunters of the bison of power, civil servants as the eternal, domestic continuity, where the goat is milked. The civil service is
obviously the female element in society."

"A poignant inequality!" shouts a cheerful male voice from the audience.

"Outrageous discrimination!" Marcelis nods, laughing. "Did you know by the way, that women make up no more than one percent of the prison population? Isn't it a disgrace."

"Can I perhaps add something?" asks the director of the Amsterdam Stedelijk Museum thoughtfully. He speaks in a soft voice that immediately puts an end to the hilarity and restlessness that's arisen in the audience. With his round face framed by golden gray locks, he looks like one of the cherubs on the ceiling who has grown up.

"Of course. And then we'll get down to business."

"Perhaps we can also look at that constellation from a different angle. Perhaps those who have too little are not women but men. Might it not also be true that men hunt bisons out of despair? Out of a deeper vulnerability, which they can't confront without losing themselves? Perhaps the problem isn't so much that women lack obsessions, but that men lack children. In prehistory the connection between copulation and having children was still unknown; that's a discovery of a much later date. To limit myself to the visual arts: perhaps all those masterpieces are ultimately nothing more than desperate leaps to compensate for the fact that their makers can't bear children. Perhaps they're trying as well as they can to emancipate themselves by creating surrogate children. That is to say, perhaps it's women who are the true lords of creation. They have no reason for despair."

Marcelis looks around questioningly. "Is this the magic word? Can we agree on this?" When no one says anything, he turns to the camera: "Then the hour of truth has come, ladies and gentlemen. The artistic Sanhedrin, assembled here in a unique composition, will now proceed to indicate the greatest surrogate child-maker in the visual arts in the twentieth century." Thereupon he invites those present to list two candidates each in a clockwise direction, accompanied by a short commentary, after which the real deliberations can begin.

The telephone vibrates against Victor's chest like an alarmed little animal. In agitation he puts his hand into his breast pocket and turns the handset off, having been thrown from the distant Stone Age into the bewildering present. He feels besieged because everything that's happening seemed to be pointing at him, as in a novel—that paranoid genre in which all events are geared toward the main character. He wants to get out of here, at once, go straight to a travel agent and book a holiday on the other side of the world, on a small Caribbean island where the sun is blazing in the sky and where there's always a wind blowing and a green iguana on a boulder looks out motionlessly across the ocean, even more motionless than the boulder. But he doesn't get up; he crosses his legs in the opposite direction and listens to the experts—no, he doesn't listen, he hears their proposals, they float past him in snatches: the elegiac Picasso of course, the devout Mondrian of course, the pioneering Duchamp of course, the saintly Beuys of course . . .

When it is Netter's turn, he remains looking at his notes for a moment.

"What strikes me in the names that I've heard up to now is that there isn't a single sculptor among them. Duchamp and Beuys are not painters in the first instance, but not sculptors either, they represent a third category, that of the makers of installations, to whom our moderator has already subtly alluded in his carefully crafted introduction. I agree that Brancusi, Giacometti, Moore, and all the others don't have the stature of Picasso or Mondrian—but why is that? Why in our century is painting so exciting and sculpture in fact fairly dull? No one knows. Even the discovery of African masks and statuary really only influenced painting and scarcely influenced sculpture. Questions, questions. Why in a country like Holland were there countless top-class painters in the seventeenth century, and why was that completely over a century later? They're obviously a bit like epidemics, which also break out suddenly, spread like wildfire, and then disappear as quickly as they came. For unfathomable reasons the twentieth century is a century of painters and not sculptors. In classical antiquity exactly the opposite was the case. There was no Greek painter who could vie with Praxiteles. His equal appeared only two thousand years later in the form of Michelangelo."

"Everyone can undoubtedly learn a lot from you, Mr. Netter," Marcelis interrupts him, "myself first of all. But perhaps you could now come to a conclusion. We don't want to know who your candidate is *not*."

"*Mea culpa*," says Netter ironically. "But I have to go one step further back than Praxiteles to make clear who it is. That takes me to the first sculptor: Pygmalion. Everyone knows the story. The misogynist carved the figure of a naked woman from ivory, with which he fell in love and which came to life. Through the intervention of Aphrodite the ivory turned to flesh and blood. Well, that's what I call creation. He has abolished the boundary between art and reality. If Pygmalion had lived in the twentieth century, he would have been my candidate."

"But he didn't live in the twentieth century. If you asked me he never lived at all."

"No, he's a mythical figure, who lives only in Ovid's *Metamorphoses*. But Ovid didn't invent Pygmalion's story by himself. He's a creation of . . . well, whom? No one knows—but the twentieth century has thrown up Pygmalion's equal in flesh and blood."

Marcelis's mouth drops open a little, and the others also look at Netter in alarm.

"And who may that be?"

Suddenly Netter gets up, and Victor sees that he is suddenly filled with a prophetic fervor. His eyes spark, his white locks seem to be starting to undulate.

"I can hear the cry reverberating in the twenty-first century!" he cries in a loud voice. "There's something sinister going on! They're preparing a dreadful *Walpurgisnacht*, a gruesome witches' Sabbath—and it's the result of the creative work of the greatest surrogate child-maker not only of the twentieth century, no, but of all time! Or maybe his super-bison will on the contrary be the greatest blessing ever to have descended upon mankind. Perhaps both, because that's how things tend to go in life. There sits my candidate," he says, extending his arm. "The second Pygmalion, who's abolished the boundary between life and death—who has brought not ivory but clay to life: Victor Werker!"

Is he dreaming? Has Netter gone mad? When Victor sees the pointing finger, the astonished faces turning in his direction, the camera that is quickly directed at him, he is overwhelmed with fear. He stands up trembling.

"I . . ." he stutters.

He wants to say that it's nonsense—that Netter hasn't understood his work, that he's perhaps confusing him with the researchers who are cloning animals and will shortly be cloning human beings, but that his own work really has only philosophical significance, that he's actually turned himself from a chemist into a biologist. Or does Netter perhaps realize that only too well? Better than anyone else, better even than the Holy Father, and at any rate better than he himself? Is it precisely the "philosophical significance" of his monocellular bison which will lead to a witches' Sabbath in the next century? Nietzsche's Zarathustra had a vision of God being dead—had he, Victor himself actually perhaps eliminated God a hundred years later by creating life? Is the soul of the commandment that thou shalt not kill perhaps the commandment that thou shalt not create life?

His head is spinning, he can't find any words, he waves his arms helplessly, and suddenly quickly leaves the room. In the lobby he hears a girl's voice calling his name, but he doesn't look around. He leaps off the terrace and runs into the street. The weather has changed, a thick fog has moved in from the river. Only on the corner by the Altneuschul, beneath the clock of the Jewish town hall whose hands move in the opposite direction, does he stop in a sweat and with his heart pounding take a deep breath.

THE APPOINTMENT

IT'S BUSY in the Basilica, the shops are open, there is music in the air everywhere. The discotheque is still closed, but there isn't a single free table on the terrace by the bowling alley, and there's a queue of people waiting at the box office of the small theater in the vestry. When he gets to the wine bar he slows down, takes the telephone out of his pocket, and retrieves his voice mail.

"There is one new message. To listen to your message, press 1."

As he listens to the other suggestions of the disembodied woman's voice, he hesitates; but then he nevertheless presses the figure 1.

"Message received today, at 4:02 P.M."

Silence.

"To save this message . . ."

He erases the message that is not a message and yet is a message. To shake off the feeling of threat, he decides first to go and have a bite to eat at Mirafiori.

In the shopping gallery, next to the escalators, flanked by an art dealer with mainly posters and a slightly seedy bureau de change, the *Ristorante Italiano* is situated like a relic of fifty years ago. Even in Italy you scarcely find restaurants like this anymore, with its creaking parquet floor, its panels crowned by washbasin mirrors, folkloristic figures cut out with a fretsaw, and nailed to them, one wall covered with signed photos of long-dead opera singers. But the waiters are in black, the napkins are linen, and there are no pizzas on the menu. It's still quiet. With a vague greeting to a couple of regular customers, a writer and a painter with their wives, and a lonely lawyer with a newspaper, he sits at the smallest table. Really he ought to have been sitting here with Netter now.

He rests his elbows on the table and rubs his face with both hands. A day in the life of a madman, he thinks. He feels like a sheet of paper torn five times in the wastepaper basket, thirty-two scraps covered with writing on both sides, which have been turned into a jigsaw puzzle. He should now dig them out and try to arrange them into a whole, but he doesn't want to think about it anymore.

"*Buona sera, professore.*"

The waiter is standing next to him, a napkin over his left forearm, the menu in his right hand.

"Just bring me a plate of spaghetti, Mauro. Aglio olio peperoncino. And half a bottle of Orvieto."

"*Va bene. Subito.*"

Mauro hurries away like someone who has been given an order that can't bear a second's delay. Victor lets his eyelids droop a little and wonders whom he was so furious with this afternoon. Himself? "I must make a leap," he articulates with his lips, but soundlessly—and thinks, a leap from this life into another life. Take a leaf out of his mother's book. Write *Aurora's Key to Life* and then immigrate to Canada and become a lumberjack. Forget all chemistry and microbiology and start an antiques shop in the Dordogne. Palm wobbly farm chairs off on expatriate Dutch people. He's still got time. He's forty-two, scientifically successful and hence written off, his laurels somewhat resembling the tattoos on the shrunken arms of an old man, branded when his imposing muscles still shone with youth and oil and made a certain kind of man jealous, although they were perhaps intended for women, though they left women indifferent. Disappear. Become invisible. When the telephone rings, don't answer, even if it's the Swedish embassy. And what if it's Clara? Don't answer.

When he is drinking his coffee he wonders how he will spend the evening. He's not going to get any work done now, and the idea of visiting the cinema goes against the grain with him. So he decides simply to slump in front of the television upstairs and watch some thriller or other, with cars, pistols, and sunglasses as the universal main characters. When he's paid the bill, he shakes hands with Mauro and strolls outside, where it is still inside. Near the crèche two security men are trying to get an emaciated junkie moving; motionless, arms outstretched, half bent forward, he's staring at the paving slabs, straight through the paving slabs, straight through the whole earth. He takes the lift, and goes up to his flat via the silent labyrinth of footbridges, stairs, and indoor courtyards. In the gallery the old caretaker is watering the plane tree; the leaves are hanging there so unnaturally still between the stained-glass windows like old banners in a medieval knight's hall. It is as though the silence has also taken possession of him, the curved jet of water from the hose in his hands has the same shape as his back, his white eyebrows, and the corners of his mouth.

"All well, Mr. Werker?"

"We're doing our best, Hendrik."

"You look tired."

"You're right. I think I'm going to have an early night tonight."

"I try that myself sometimes." The caretaker nods, turning off the tap. Werker can see that he's preparing to launch into one of his extensive lectures. "But a couple of hours later I'm suddenly wide awake. What do you do then? You get out of bed in the middle of the night and sit down in a chair and then you just start reading for hours on end, some weekly paper from last month that you forgot to throw away. Endless articles that don't interest you. Continued on page so-and-so. Just the other day. The article was about a book that's just appeared on the pyramids. That may interest you, you were in Egypt last month, weren't you? I forwarded the post to you. If I remember correctly the writer has discovered that the three pyramids of Giza are a projection of the three stars that make up Orion's Belt, and they have been laid out in such a way that the Nile corresponds with the Milky Way. He proves that by—"

"I know before you tell me," Victor interrupts him. "Everything must always be something different. What's the name of the book? I collect stuff like that."

"I can't remember. Something with 'mystery,' I think."

"Bound to be."

"The constellation of Orion was Osiris for the ancient Egyptians. He was murdered a few times, but always rose from the dead—"

"Awakened by Thoth." Victor nods.

"Yes, of course you know all that. But do you also know that Isis also had a child by his corpse on one occasion when he was dead?"

"That's a new one on me," says Victor and tries to laugh, but isn't able. "Yes, Hendrik, those were the days—and they'll soon be coming back, but for real."

The caretaker dabs his eyes with a handkerchief and Victor can see that his hand is trembling a little. Doctor James Parkinson is approaching. Doctor Alois Alzheimer too perhaps. His brain is still sound, but the instinct is declining; the words are becoming more fluid and are starting to dribble out of his mouth by themselves, as the handwriting is also becoming gradually smaller—until it has become a straight line, like the encephalogram of a dead person.

Victor looks demonstratively at his watch.

"Excuse me. I've got an appointment."

"Good night, Mr. Werker." And when Victor smiles at him: "God be with you."

In the stripped living room he takes off his jacket and slumps into an armchair, his legs outstretched and wide apart, his hands crossed behind his neck, and looks around. Everything unchanged. Clara's writing desk. The white, half-empty bookcases. Because the stillness of the things upsets him he puts the television on, which obeys his every gesture: the trailer of an interview program, on which the faces of the previous guests quickly and seamlessly merge with each other, politicians into sporting heroes, sporting heroes into delinquents, delinquents into artists ... "Morphing" is what that computer technique is called, he knows: all modern horror films make use of it. Netter might call it the "Ovid Principle." He turns off the sound and goes into his study. On his desk, next to the mummified baby monkey, lies the opened album with a photo of Clara outside the Cave of Oedipus, just as he put it down yesterday—the little Hermes looks down at it attentively. The fax machine has not yet been put back on the table at which he ate with the Dodemont brothers. Three cartons of milk. He takes *Metamorphoses* out of the bookcase, looks up the passage on Pygmalion and sits down at the Gothic window.

> As soon as he came home, straightaway did Pygmalion repair
>   Unto the Image of his wench, and leaning on the bed,
> Did kiss her. In her body straight a warmness seemed to spread.
> He put his mouth again to hers, and on her breast did lay
> His hand. The Ivory waxed soft: and putting quite away
> All hardness, yielded underneath his fingers, as we see
> A piece of wax made soft against the Sun, or drawn to be
> In diverse shapes by chafing it between one's hands, and so
> To serve to uses. He, amazed, stood wavering to and fro
> 'Tween joy and fear to be beguiled, again he burnt in love,
> Again with feeling he began his wished hope to prove.
> He felt it very flesh indeed. By laying on his thumb,
> He felt her pulses beating.

Moved, he looks out of the window. Dusk has fallen over the S-bend of the river; Hotel Excelsior has become invisible in the mist. He has wandered around down there like an idiot, looking for a murderer. When he hears the siren of an ambulance down below, he goes into the living room and presses for teletext on the local television station: nothing about a murder in the city, but that doesn't mean much, perhaps it's only just been discovered. Suddenly he sees Netter's extended forefinger pointing at him again. It was as if his misplaced praise were more like an indictment, that of an accusing prosecutor, as if *he* is a murderer—while he is rather the only human being on earth who is the exact opposite of a murderer.

Back in his study he goes on reading Ovid at the window, until he can no longer make out the words. Now there is only the faint glow from the screen on the television in the living room, the door of which he has left open. No, there's no need to go chopping down trees in Canada, he must simply do his work, although his greatest achievement is almost certainly behind him. Most people have never achieved anything great and yet they simply do their work; isn't it absurd, that having achieved something great leads to more discontent than not having achieved anything great. But perhaps the greatest achievement is always in the distance, perhaps the ultimate achievement is dying: that transition from something to nothing, as impossible as the transition from nothing to something, which has happened to everyone. Human beings, he thinks, must keep themselves in equilibrium, on a rope which is strung from nothing to nothing.

What he'd most like to do now would be to turn on all the lights, close the curtains, and put on some uncomplicated music—not Mahler that is, rather Smetana or Dvořák—but he remains sitting in the dark without moving. It's morning in San Francisco now; with her cigarette in the corner of her mouth his mother shuffles through her flat in a worn-out dressing gown and puts on a kettle of water. It's as if he can see her. Everywhere drinking students are again walking across the campus in

Berkeley. As a boy of about seventeen he was in the habit of reviewing the events of the previous day before he went to bed, even the faces of the people with whom he'd sat on the tram—perhaps it was then that he developed his visual memory. He lights a cigarette, and because you can't taste the smoke if you don't see it, he blows it into the glowing tip. Autumnal Venice has been returned to the Venetians; in the deserted Piazza San Marco, sunk back into its thousand years of existence, the pigeons have also withdrawn under the ridge beams of the Procuratie. In the soft lamplight under the arcades, past the lowered shutters of the shops, walk two well-groomed old gentlemen. Whenever one of them says anything he stops until he's finished speaking, they take a few steps, after which the other stops and replies—at their age they can obviously no longer walk and talk at the same time. He can see it as though he is there, but he isn't there. Are they really walking there at this moment? Of course not, clairvoyance doesn't exist; someone with a mobile telephone there on the Piazza would doubtless confirm that. Nor is it a memory, because he's never been to Venice in the autumn. So where do they come from? One old gentleman is wearing a hat—where does that hat come from? From his imagination? But why then did he imagine precisely that and not something else, for example a little girl with her grandmother? Or a couple of Venetian lads with slicked-back hair chasing a group of girls? The ascending path to the plateau with the pyramids on it is not lit; in the valley next door there is the shuffling of Bedouins, camels, and goats among the tents, those gigantic cocoons. An English couple, no longer that young, have just decided to go for a walk to the pyramid of Cheops, before reading for a bit in the lounge of Mena House. They are the only ones. Arm in arm, their fingers intertwined, shrouded in tough tweeds despite the sultry evening, they approach the dark mass, silhouetted against the starry sky, which seems to be screaming in its ear-splitting silence. There is no moon. When they get to the top, he sees them suddenly stiffen. Five or six yards away from them, a black creature as big as a sheep moves, but it is not a sheep, rather a gigantic salamander, or scorpion, or beetle low on the ground, scarcely distinguishable in the darkness, a repulsive ghost, a terrifying fabulous animal . . .

Now and then the faint light in the living room changes a fraction, as the text on the television screen changes. He finds himself with his eyes focused for minutes on end on a faint glow—when it dawns on him that it's the key to Aurora's room, he puts Ovid away and half sits up. Suddenly, without deciding, he has got up and looks at the key without moving. His heart begins to pound, it's as though the key is attracting him like a lighted window attracts someone who is lost on the heath. Slowly, with reluctant legs, like a robot, he starts walking toward it in the dark. He crosses the threshold and although a few yards still separate him from the key, he stretches out his right hand. When he has the metal between his fingers, he closes his eyes and lets his head hang back. He stays in that position for a few seconds, feeling like someone who's on the point of blowing up a building. The moment he turns the key, the doorbell rings.

As if woken from a dream, he comes to his senses. He's not expecting anyone, it can only be Hendrik—perhaps he wants to know something about the predictive nature of mythology. Without turning on the light, he goes to the door of his flat and opens up. From then on everything happens very quickly. In the light of the doorway he sees the outlines of two figures, one takes a step forward and puts two strangling, gloved hands around his throat, the other also comes in, closes the door, and a moment later he hears the click of a stiletto flicking open. The telephone starts vibrating in his breast pocket. Who is it? Clara? Stockholm? Not a word is spoken—and suddenly he understands. The route the murderers had to follow referred not to the city but to the Basilica. The restaurant, the theater, the disco, the trees . . . Was it Brock whose voice he'd heard during that conversation? Has he sent these two? Are monotheistic fundamentalists behind it, who can't forgive him for the eobiont? The knife is deflected by the telephone, which doesn't stop vibrating. On the second attempt the steel takes possession of his body and penetrates his heart. When it leaves him, like the rod that goes through a yoke and a shaft, he raises his blotchy white hands and spreads his fingers. After the mystery of life he has finally unveiled the mystery of death too. If man in his last moments sees his whole life going past in a flash—from the crunch with which his umbilical cord was cut up to that last moment—then in the end he reaches that flash and so he again sees his whole life passing him by in a flash, and again, and again—an infinite number of times, so that he never reaches his death . . .

Victor Werker is happy. The light of a dazzling dawn surrounds him. I am immortal, he thinks, as his eyes cloud over.

TRANSLATOR'S NOTE

The translation on page 1 is by Mary M. Innes in *The Meta-morphoses of Ovid* (Harmondsworth: Penguin Books, 1955), page 231. The translation on page 226 is by Arthur Golding (1567); I have slightly modernized Golding's spelling.